FISHBOWL

Despite his enviable view from a balcony on the twenty-seventh floor of an apartment block, Ian the Goldfish has frequent — if fleeting — desires for a more exciting life. Until one day, a series of unfortunate events gives him an opportunity to escape . . . Our story begins, however, with the human inhabitants of Ian's building. There is the handsome student, his girlfriend and his mistress; an agoraphobic sex worker; the invisible caretaker; the pregnant woman on bed rest; and the homeschooled boy, Herman, who thinks he can travel through time. As Ian tumbles perilously downwards, he will witness all their lives, loves, triumphs and disasters . . .

SPECIAL MESSAGE TO READERS

THE ULVERSCROFT FOUNDATION
(registered UK charity number 264873)
was established in 1972 to provide funds for
research, diagnosis and treatment of eye diseases.
Examples of major projects funded by
the Ulverscroft Foundation are:-

- The Children's Eye Unit at Moorfields Eye Hospital, London
- The Ulverscroft Children's Eye Unit at Great Ormond Street Hospital for Sick Children
- Funding research into eye diseases and treatment at the Department of Ophthalmology, University of Leicester
- The Ulverscroft Vision Research Group, Institute of Child Health
- Twin operating theatres at the Western Ophthalmic Hospital, London
- The Chair of Ophthalmology at the Royal Australian College of Ophthalmologists

You can help further the work of the Foundation
by making a donation or leaving a legacy.
Every contribution is gratefully received. If you
would like to help support the Foundation or
require further information, please contact:

THE ULVERSCROFT FOUNDATION
The Green, Bradgate Road, Anstey
Leicester LE7 7FU, England
Tel: (0116) 236 4325

website: www.foundation.ulverscroft.com

FISHBOWL

BRADLEY SOMER

ISIS
LARGE
PRINT

First published in Great Britain 2015
by
Ebury Press
an imprint of Ebury Publishing

First Isis Edition
published 2016
by arrangement with
Ebury Publishing
Penguin Random House

A catalogue record for this book is available
from the British Library.

ISBN 978–1–78541–176–2 (hb)
ISBN 978–1–78541–182–3 (pb)

Published by
F. A. Thorpe (Publishing)
Anstey, Leicestershire

Set by Words & Graphics Ltd.
Anstey, Leicestershire
Printed and bound in Great Britain by
T. J. International Ltd., Padstow, Cornwall

This book is printed on acid-free paper

For B. Tyler

CHAPTER
ONE

In Which the Essence of Life and Everything Else Is Illuminated

There's a box that contains life and everything else.

This is not a figurative box of lore. It's not a box of paper sheets that have been captured, bound, and filled with the inkings of faith, chronicling the foibles and contradictions of the human species. It doesn't sport the musty smell of ancient wisdom and moldering paper. It isn't a microscopic box of C, G, A, or T, residing within cell walls and containing traces of everything that ever lived, from today back through the astral dust of the Big Bang itself to whatever existed before time began. It can't be spliced or recombined or subjected to therapy. It's not the work of any god or the evolution of Darwin. It's not a thousand other ideas, however concrete or abstract they may be, that could fill the pages of this book. It's not one of these things, but it's all of them combined and more.

Now we know what it isn't, let's focus on what it is. It's a box containing the perpetual presence of life itself. Living things move within it, and at some point, it will have been around long enough to have contained absolutely everything. Not all at once, but over the

1

years, building infinite layer upon infinite layer, it will all wind up there. Time will compile these experiences, stacking them on top of each other, and while the moments themselves are fleeting, their visceral memory is everlasting. The passing of a particular moment can't erase the fact that it was once present.

In this way, the box reaches beyond the organic to the ethereal. The heartbreaking sweetness of love, the rending hatred, the slippery lust, the sorrow of losing a family member, the pain of loneliness, all thoughts that were ever thought, every word ever said and even those which were not, the joys of birth and the sorrows of death and everything else will be experienced here in this one vessel. The air is thick with the anticipation of it all. After it's all done, the air will be heavy with everything that has passed.

It's a box constructed by human hands and, yes, if your beliefs trend that way, by extension, the hands of God. Regardless of its origin, its purpose is the same and its structure reflects its purpose. The box is partitioned into little compartments in which all of these experiences of time are stored, though there's no order to their place or chronological happening.

There are compartments stacked twenty-seven high, three wide, and two deep that house this jumble of everything. Melvil Dewey, the patron saint of librarians, would cringe at the mere thought of trying to catalog the details of these one hundred and sixty-two compartments. There's no way to arrange or structure what happens here, no way to exert control over it or systematize it. It just has to be left a mess.

A pair of elevators connects all of these compartments. Themselves little boxes, each with a capacity of ten people or 4,000 lb/1,814 kg, whichever comes first. Each with a little plaque attached to the mirrored wall near the panel that says it's so. The irritating pitch of the alarm that sounds when there's too much weight inside also says it's so. The elevators trundle tirelessly up and down their dingy shafts, diligently delivering artifacts and their custodians to the different levels. Day and night, they shuttle to one floor and then to the next and then back to the lobby. There's a staircase too, in case of fire or power outage, so the custodians can grab the artifacts most dear to them and safely exit the box.

The box is a building, yes. More specifically it's an apartment building. It sits there, an actual place in an actual city. It has a street address so people who are unfamiliar with the area can find it. It also has a series of numbers so lawyers and city surveyors can find it too. It's classified in many ways. To the city it's an orange rectangle with black crosshatching on the zoning map. "Multi-Residential, High-Density High-Rise," the legend reads. To many occupants it's a "one-bedroom apartment for rent, with underground parking and coin laundry facilities." To some it was "an unbelievably affordable way to experience the convenience and excitement of downtown living. This two-bedroom, one-bathroom condo with uninterrupted city views must be seen to be believed," and is now home. For a few, it's a place to work on the weekdays. For others, it's a place to visit friends on the weekends.

The building was constructed in 1976 and has hobbled through time ever since. When it was still new, it was the tallest building on the street. Now that it's older, there are three taller ones. Soon there will be a fourth. For the time, it was an elegant and stately building. Now it seems dated, belonging to a period in architectural history that has its own name, a name that was not known at the time it was built but is applied knowingly in hindsight.

The building was renovated recently because it was in much need. The concrete was painted to hide the spalling cracks and compiled graffiti. The drafty windows and gappy doors to the balconies were replaced to keep the evening chill outside and the temperate air in. Last year, the boiler was upgraded to provide adequate hot water for washing up. The electrical was updated because building codes have changed. It was once a building entirely full of renters. Now, it is a condominium where most people own but others still choose to rent out their suites to offset other investment risks, to "diversify their portfolios."

The building fulfills an Arcensian mission of carrying everything mentioned thus far, housing the spirit and the chaos of life and those beings in which they reside, through the floods and to safety every time the water recedes. Depending on where you live, this box may be just up the street. It may even be within walking distance from where you read these words. You may drive past it on the way home from work if you work downtown but live in the suburbs. Or you may even live there.

If you see this building, pause for a second to ponder what a marvelous arcanum it is. It will sit there long after you turn the last page in this book and long after we are dead and these words have been forgotten. The beginning and end of time will happen there within those walls, between the roof and the parking garage. But for now, only a handful of decades old, it's a growing marvel in its nascent days and this book is a short chronicle of its youth.

Spelled out above the front door, bolted to the brick in weeping, rusty black metal lettering, is the name of the building: the Seville on Roxy.

CHAPTER
TWO

In Which Our Protagonist, Ian, Takes a Dreadful Fall

Our story doesn't begin with a goldfish named Ian's perilous plunge from his bowl on the twenty-seventh-floor balcony where he, for as much as he can comprehend, has been enjoying the view of the downtown skyline.

In the long shadows of the late-afternoon sun, the city is a picket fence of buildings. There are dusty-rose glass ones, reflecting a Martian sun. Others are gunmetal-blue mirrors, and still others are simple brick-and-concrete blocks. There are office tower thrones proudly wearing corporate logo crowns, and there are hotels and apartment buildings, prickly with balconies ribbing every side of their vertical space. All of them have been shoved into the ground, into a grid that brings some order to their apparent incongruity.

Ian looks out over this megalithic flower garden of skyscrapers and sees only as much wonder as his mind can muster. He's a goldfish with a bird's-eye view of the world. A goldfish held aloft on a concrete platform with a god's perspective, one that's lost on a brain that can't fathom what it is looking at, but by that fact, the view is made even more wondrous.

Ian doesn't take his plunge from the balcony until chapter 54, when a dreadful series of events culminates in an opportunity for Ian to escape his watery prison. But we start with Ian for a few reasons, the first being that he's a vital thread that ties humanity together. The second is, with a fish's brain capacity, time and place mean little because both are constantly being rediscovered. Whether he takes his fall now, fifteen minutes from now, or fifteen minutes ago doesn't matter because Ian can neither comprehend place and time nor comprehend the order that each imposes on the other.

Ian's world is a pastiche of events with no sequence, no past and no future.

For example, just now, at the beginning of his career as a Cypriniforme skydiver, Ian remembers that his watery home still sits there on a thrift-store folding table with flaking green paint. His bowl is empty now, save for a few pebbles, a little pink plastic castle, a fog of algae on the glass, and his roommate, Troy the snail. A rapidly growing length of empty air spans the distance between the bowl and its former resident. It doesn't matter to Ian that this event doesn't actually happen until chapter 54 because he already forgets how it came to be. Soon he will forget the bowl he spent months living in. He will forget the ludicrous pink castle. With time, the insufferable Troy will not just fade to a memory; he will disappear from Ian's experience all together. It will be as if he never existed at all.

While falling past a twenty-fifth-floor window, Ian catches a glimpse of a middle-aged woman of considerable size taking a step across the living room. The glimpse, a fleeting flash in the mind of a creature with no memory, has the woman wearing a beautiful gown, her movements as elegant and graceful as the drape and flow of the fine material she wears. The gown is a stunning shade of red. He would call it carmine if he knew the word for it. The woman's back is to Ian, who admires the tailored cut of the gown and how it accentuates her voluptuous form and the valley of her spine between her muscular shoulder blades. She's in the process of stepping around a coffee table. The way she moves betrays a level of shyness and a hint of terror. Her toes point slightly inward, her knees touch lightly together. Her hands are clasped on one side, one arm held apologetically across her belly and the other resting on her hip. Her fingers are knotted into a nest.

There's also a round hulk of a man in the center of the living room. The man has an arm outstretched to her, thick hair on his thick forearms, sporting a blissful look in his eyes. His face is calm, which is in contrast to the anxiety shown by the woman. A hint of a smile curves his lips. He wears the look of how a loved one's embrace feels.

All of this is a flash, an inert moment as Ian passes the twenty-fifth floor on his approach to terminal velocity. With a goldfish's sensibility, Ian cannot fathom the oddly divine nature of the existence of this constant velocity. If he could, Ian would wonder on the beautiful and quantifiable order that gravity imposes on the chaos of the world, the harmony of a marriage between a constant acceleration and an ultimate speed that all objects in free fall reach but don't breach. Is this universal number divine or simply physics, and if it's the latter, could it be the work of the former?

Having very little control over his descent, Ian tumbles freely and catches sight of the expansive pale-blue sky above and hundreds of fluttering white sheets of paper, twisting gracefully through the air, graciously flitting and swooping after him like a flock of seabirds to a trawler. Around Ian, swirling in the wind, are exactly two hundred and thirty-two pages of a dissertation in progress. One of these floating sheets is the title page, the first to fall and now teetering on a breeze below all the others, upon which is printed in a bold font "A Late Pleistocene and Holocene Phytolith Record of the Lower Salmon River Canyon, Idaho," under which is an italicized "by Connor Radley."

Their descent is much more delicate than the clumsy, corklike plummeting of a goldfish, which evolution has left ill prepared to pass a rapidly decreasing number of floors of a downtown high-rise. Indeed, evolution did not intend for goldfish to fly. Neither did God, if that's what you believe. It really doesn't matter. Ian can neither comprehend nor believe in either, and the result of this inability is the same. The cause is irrelevant at the moment because the effect is irrevocable.

As his world pitches and spins, Ian catches flashing glimpses of pavement, horizon, open sky, and the gently swirling leaves of paper. Poor Ian doesn't think how unfortunate it is that he isn't an ant, a creature known to be able to fall a thousand times its body length and still hexaped on its merry way. He doesn't lament the fact that he wasn't born a bird, something that is obviously lamentable at present. Ian has never been particularly introspective or melancholic. It's not in his nature to contemplate or to lament. The core of Ian's character is a simple amalgam of carpe diem, laissez-faire, and *Namaste*.

"Less thinking, more doing" is the goldfish's philosophy.

"Having a plan is the first step toward failure," he would say if he could speak.

Ian is a bon vivant, and given the capacity to ponder, he would have found it a statement of the language's character that English has no equivalent descriptor and had to steal it from French. He's always been happy as a goldfish. It doesn't dawn on him that, with the passing of another twenty-five floors, unless something drastically unpredictable and miraculous happens, he'll meet the pavement at considerable speed.

In some ways, Ian is blessed with the underanalyzing mind of a goldfish. The troubles associated with deeper thought are replaced with basic instinct and a memory that spans a fraction of a second. He's more reactionary than plotting or planning. He doesn't dwell or ponder at length about anything. Just as he realizes his predicament, it blissfully slips from his mind in time to be rediscovered. He sleeps well because of this; there are no worries, and there is no racing mind.

10

Alternately, physiologically, the repeated realization of the terror of falling is quite draining on a body. It's the rapid-fire release of adrenaline, the repetitive pokes in his flight response, that stresses this gold-encased nugget of fishy flesh.

"Now, what was I doing? Oh my, I can't breathe. Oh shit, I'm falling off a high-rise! Now . . . what was I doing? Oh my . . ."

Blessed indeed are the thoughtless.

But, as was pointed out earlier, when he was tumbling from the twenty-seventh-floor balcony, before he got here to the twenty-fifth, our story doesn't begin with Ian.

CHAPTER
THREE

In Which Katie Approaches the Seville on Roxy on a Vital Mission

Our story begins about half an hour before Ian takes the plunge. It starts with Katie, Connor Radley's girlfriend. That's her standing at a pharmacy door two blocks up the street from the Seville on Roxy, looking out at the late-afternoon sun. She rests one hand on the handle, but instead of opening the door and leaving the store, she looks up Roxy. The sidewalk bustles with shoulder-to-shoulder pedestrians, and the road is clogged, bumper to bumper, with the mounting rush hour traffic.

There's a construction site next to the pharmacy, in front of which a billboard reads, "The Future Home of the Baineston on Roxy, 180 luxury suites now selling." A clean line drawing shows a boxy glass high-rise building bracketed by green trees, with people walking by the front. The trees and people are abstract sketches compared with the clarity with which the building is depicted. A sticker splashes across one corner of the billboard. It reads, "40% Sold." It peels and curls a bit at the edge, which makes Katie wonder how long it has been up there. Her eyes are drawn to the people in the sketch, anonymous and blurred with movement, bodies filling space more than people living lives.

The construction site had been busy with gawking workers wearing hard hats when she entered the pharmacy ten minutes ago. The air smelled like burning diesel and concrete dust. She ignored their gazes. She could hear them talking but only caught enough lewd snippets of their conversation to inform her that she was their topic. It was enough to make her feel uncomfortable but not enough to inspire her to confront the pack of them about their impropriety, had she been able to muster the courage.

The site is now deserted, and the machines are all quiet. A solitary figure stands at the chain-link gate. He wears a blue uniform that has a "Griffin Security" patch on one shoulder and the name "Ahmed" stitched on the chest. There's a chair beside him with prolapsed orange sponge billowing through a rip in the covering.

Katie is a beautiful young woman with short brown hair, kohl-encircled pale-blue eyes, and a sharp chin. She hasn't been contemplating the street as much as waiting for the workers to grab their lunch boxes and leave. She pushes the pharmacy door open and steps into the street, her petite frame encountering the soft, round one of a mountain named Garth.

Garth is a scruffy, unshaven man who wears concrete-smeared work pants and a hard hat. He smells of physical labor, of sweat and work and dust. Garth has a backpack strapped to his shoulders, and he carries a bulging black plastic bag in one hand. With the other hand he reaches out to steady Katie as she takes an uncertain step back, ricocheting off his bulk.

"Sorry," Katie mumbles. She's slightly embarrassed, but her mind is elsewhere. She's distracted by her task at hand to the exclusion of the world around her.

Garth smiles. He's ever conscious of his size and how intimidating he seems to those who don't know him. His default reaction is to try to defuse any ideas that he's a threat.

"It's okay," he says and stands in an awkward silence for a moment, seeing if Katie will say anything else. When she doesn't, he nods to her and carries on his way.

Katie watches Garth cross the street against the light, dodging the cars merging into traffic. He moves up Roxy in the direction of the Seville, his shuffling steps hurried. She waits in front of the buzzing neon pharmacy sign, not wanting to seem like she's following him and not questioning why she cares if it would appear that way. She mills about long enough to make Ahmed from Griffin Security eye her suspiciously. Katie doesn't notice Ahmed finger his walkie-talkie and drop his hand to his utility belt, resting it on his holstered 240 Lumen Guard Dog Tactical Flashlight. Indeed, Katie doesn't even know a flashlight could be tactical or what would make it so.

Standing in the traffic noise washing over the street, Katie thinks of Connor. She thinks of when they first met at the university. He was the teaching assistant for a class she was taking, and she had attended his office hours with questions about an upcoming exam. They went for coffee afterward and talked about everything but the class. Connor is handsome and charming, and she was flattered at being the center of his attention. He seemed so interested in her mind and thoughts. She immediately felt a connection with him, a chemistry that made her wonder if love at first sight could be real. It still seemed unbelievable that it could actually exist when all this time she had suspected it may just happen in romantic comedies and novels. Katie then thinks of the physicality of their relationship over the past three months, less a few days. Katie told him that she loved him, and lying in the tangle of sheets after a heated bout of love-making, he had merely grunted and was seemingly asleep.

In hindsight, beyond their first coffee together, there have been exactly two homemade dinners, three movie dates, and eight binge-drinking bar nights of booze and dancing (unlike most men, Connor is an amazingly sensual dancer, his body seeming to respond to her feelings). The rest of their time together has consisted of a near nightly rooting in Connor's apartment.

Katie is aware of her affliction of falling in love more quickly and for fewer reasons than most need. It's not that she doesn't realize the heartbreak this has caused in her life, but she refuses to quell her romantic heart because it brings her joy as well. She thinks back to the string of men she has happily introduced to her family, having them over to dinner to meet her parents and her sister. She remembers the immersive, warm comfort of everyone talking, everyone laughing around the table. Then she remembers the number of subsequent family dinners she has attended alone, either having called it off for one shortcoming or another or having been told that it was not her, it was him. These end in quiet conversations with her mom and sister, late in the night, tending to her broken heart while her dad sleeps in his chair in the living room. Above their quiet whispers around the kitchen table, they could hear TV proclamations from the living room, from "Jesus is the answer" to "Call the PartyBox now, hundreds of beautiful singles are on the line waiting for you."

Katie's sure there are other people in the world with her ability to fall in love. She sees her affliction as a good thing and refuses to become jaded by her many rejections. Her belief is that love doesn't make one weak; it does the opposite. She thinks that falling in love is her superpower. It makes her strong.

Today, she's intent on finding out if Connor Radley loves her back.

A horn bleats from the traffic on Roxy and jolts Katie from her reverie. She blinks, looks up the street, and doesn't see Garth lumbering anywhere amid the herd of pedestrians. She decides that she has waited long enough. It's time for reckoning. She will either get reciprocation of her feelings or go back to her apartment alone, eat the junk food she has just prepurchased in the pharmacy, purge Connor Radley from her thoughts, and start fresh tomorrow. With this firmed resolve, Katie sets off along the crowded sidewalk. At the corner, she waits for the light to turn in her favor and then crosses the street.

Ahmed of Griffin Security lets his muscles relax now that the threat has passed. There's a tinge of sadness that he didn't get to try out the moves he practiced with his tactical flashlight while standing shirtless in front of his bedroom mirror. He removes his hand from the flashlight's holster, and his fingertip slides from the corrugated plastic surface of the walkie-talkie button.

Katie cranes her neck and looks up at the twenty-seven floors of the Seville as she approaches.

He's up there, she thinks, in the concrete box at the top.

She can see the underside of his balcony and the little glass square of his apartment window. Then, too soon, she stands before the intercom keypad at the front doors. The doors are locked against vagrants, and beyond the street reflected in the glass stretches the lobby. It's dimly lit by rows of fluorescent lights and looks sad and empty.

Katie presses four buttons on the apartment intercom and waits while it rings. A few seconds pass before the speaker pops to life. There's a trembling inhalation, and then a timid voice comes through.

"Hello?"

Katie's distracted by a little boy bumping into her thigh. She looks into his surprised face until a man runs up and grabs the child under the arms.

"Gotcha, kiddo," he says and the child squeals and laughs at his dad. They carry on down the sidewalk.

Katie turns back to the intercom panel and hangs up. Wrong apartment number. She checks the directory. She had dialed Ridgestone, C., by accident, just one digit off and one line under Connor's. She runs her index finger across the names to double-check his buzzer number and then pokes the four numbers for Radley, C. The intercom rings twice before an answer comes through.

"Yep," Connor's voice crackles within the small grated speaker in the intercom box.

"It's me," Katie says.

There's a burst of static and then silence. Connor's voice blares through the speaker, much louder than before. "Who?"

"It's Katie."

There's another burst of static. It sounds like something being dragged over the mouthpiece on the other end.

The door buzzes, and the lock clicks.

CHAPTER
FOUR

In Which We Meet the Villain Connor Radley and the Evil Seductress Faye

Connor sits on his balcony wearing only his sweatpants. The concrete is cool under his bare feet, the soles of which are coated with a layer of dust and sand. It's a refreshing feeling, moderating the warm afternoon air. The plastic lawn chair in which he sits is sticky with sweat, so he peels his back from it by leaning forward and resting his elbows on his knees.

One hundred and twenty pages are stacked in his lap, and a ballpoint pen hangs from between his lips. One hundred and twelve pages have been stacked atop Ian's fishbowl and weighted down with a half-full coffee cup to fend off any errant breezes. Ian's bowl, in turn, rests on a folding card table, which is sidled up against the railing in the corner of the balcony. All of these items combined, coffee mug on paper pile on fishbowl on folding table on top-floor balcony, form a quiet shrine to the origin story of their being.

Connor is on the balcony because, in his small studio apartment, he feels the walls stifle his ability to edit.

The place is too small for his thoughts. He's working through the first round of comments on his thesis, which he received from his adviser, and he's on a self-imposed deadline to finish as quickly as possible and get the hell out of grad school. Connor finds it easier to think in the open air overlooking the expansive views offered to him from the balcony, so it has become his office. He has his lawn chair, a garage sale find and throwback to the seventies. It's made of hundreds of brown, burnt-almond, and dusty-green plastic tubes woven over an aluminum frame. He has his splintery, weathered card table, and he has Ian. Oh, and he has his coffee cup that reads "Paleoclimatologists do it in the dirt." A clever gift from Faye . . . or was it Deb who got it for him? Maybe Katie?

Connor glares at the page in front of him.

Each printed letter is a simple symbol meaning nothing on its own. Combined, the letters make words that also mean little without their neighbors. All of these words together, however, convey a greater meaning, detailing the assumptions of the statistical analysis used in his research. On its own, the section is interesting, as noted by the jottings of his adviser in the margins, but it grows more meaningful when considered in the larger context of the thesis. Likewise, without context in world prehistory, the findings of Connor's study, about the impacts of paleoclimatic fluctuations on the ancient human inhabitants of Idaho, would be less interesting than they inherently are.

But right now, Connor isn't thinking in such economies of perspective; he's busily learning more about less, losing the context of the big picture by trying to figure out what his supervisor had scrawled diagonally across an equation. His brow furrows. He thinks it reads, "Awkward. Do better." He ponders what such a vaguely savage statement could mean.

It's math. Math can't be awkward and, by its nature, is either right or wrong, so how could he do better? Connor chews on the end of his pen and shoots a glance past Ian to the buildings beyond.

Ian doesn't ponder any of this. He doesn't have the capacity to. He resides permanently in his bowl on the folding table overlooking the city for a reason. Connor tends to become bimaniacal when working on his thesis. His attentions focus to an unhealthy degree on editing and satisfying a chafingly powerful desire for sexual satisfaction. Connor feels embarrassed to be naked in front of the fish and definitely can't perform under his unblinking stare. For Ian's part, he's uninterested in Connor either way, clothed or naked, masturbating or copulating.

The cordless phone rings. Connor hears it, and Ian feels it as a frequency through the water.

Connor retrieves it from beside Ian's bowl, pokes the talk button, and holds it to his ear.

"Yep," Connor says into the receiver.

"It's me," comes a hollow voice, the static indicative of someone standing at the building's front door.

Connor isn't expecting anyone, and he can't place the voice. It's a female voice. It's definitely coming from the front door. The traffic noise rising to the balcony and that coming through the phone, the noisy motorcycle Dopplering past and the horn honking, all reach his ears in relative synchronicity.

"Who?" he asks.

"It's Katie."

Connor clasps his hand over the mouthpiece and says, "Shit."

Then he presses "9" on the cordless to release the lobby door and hangs up the phone.

Connor straightens the papers in his lap and then adds them to the stack atop Ian's bowl. He replaces the coffee-mug paperweight, less fearful of a smearing coffee ring stain than of a freak breeze kicking up and blowing the papers over the balcony railing. He stands and hikes up his sweatpants.

"Sit," Connor tells Ian as if he were a dog and not a goldfish.

Connor always wanted another dog. He grew up in the suburbs, a lonely boy in a neighborhood populated primarily by retirees, so his dog, Ian, had been his best friend. They had spent long, idle summers together, hanging out in the backyard or playing in the culvert that ran through a green space behind the house. Ian always waited for Connor after school. He seemingly knew what time the bell would ring. He occasionally misjudged it, however, and Connor would see him through the school window, sitting by the bike racks, sometimes waiting for hours.

Then, one morning, the school bus ran Ian over. Connor had been so devastated his parents didn't risk buying him another dog because they weren't sure he would survive its eventual death. So through the rest of his summers, Connor had read comics in the backyard or halfheartedly played in the culvert alone.

Connor had told Katie this story. She made that sympathetic smile that said "You poor thing" and "That's so cute" and "I feel for you" all at once. Then she bought him the goldfish Ian as a companion, to temper the memory of his traumatic loss.

"Here's someone to share your time with when I'm not here," she said, smiling her beautiful smile and presenting him with the plastic bag containing Ian.

Deep down, subconsciously, Connor has grown to believe that Ian the goldfish is spiritually linked to Ian the dog, perhaps even to the extent that the fish is the dog reincarnate.

The Seville on Roxy doesn't allow dogs or cats or Katie would have bought him one, he is sure. Pets are only permitted with the approval of the building superintendent, a globe of a man named Jimenez. And Jimenez never approves pets except for single fish in small bowls. He believes that animals don't belong inside, all pets are unclean, and large fish tanks pose too great a threat of leakage to the building and its occupants. Hence the limit of a one-gallon bowl.

Connor grabs the cordless phone and slides the balcony door open. He steps into the apartment. It takes a moment for his eyes to adjust from the sunshine. The air feels cool on his back where it had been sweating against the lawn chair.

After a few moments, he looks to the crumpled heap of pillows and sheets that crown his mattress and says,

"You have to go. Right now. My girlfriend is coming up."

Connor crosses the room, trips on a beer bottle on the way, staggers a bit, and then recovers. He shakes the bed. "Get your stuff and go. I'll call you later." He waits a moment before whipping the sheets from the bed and dropping them to the floor.

Faye moans and rolls onto her back. She lies before him on the mattress, unashamedly naked, unabashedly exposed, and unbelievably sexy. She blinks at Connor in the bright afternoon light.

CHAPTER
FIVE

In Which the Stoic Jimenez Tries to Fix the Elevator Despite Being Completely Unqualified to Do So

Jimenez leans back in his chair and sighs. He pushes the front two legs from the floor, leaving it to totter on the rear two. The chair creaks a loud response to his shifting weight. The little room that serves as his office is hot and loud and white, lit by old fluorescent tubes that hum overhead. There's a plastic placard embossed with the word "Maintenance" on the door, which is open, though it does nothing to freshen the stagnant air.

In the next room, the massive boiler burner sparks and roars to life every fifteen minutes or so. Behind its rusted metal grille, a blue jet of natural gas flame heats a vat of water for the occupants of the Seville on Roxy. The jet ignites with a pop and whomp. The noise can be heard through the painted cinder block walls, and it reverberates within the vent that runs between the two rooms.

Jimenez finds the sound of the mechanical monster next door both comforting and marvelous, a clockwork dragon heating a cauldron for the masses.

That machine is the heart, pumping blood through the building. It provides unquestioningly and is overlooked by all but Jimenez. The hot water travels through the radiator pipes that send waves of heat into everyone's apartment on the cool fall evenings. That water comes streaming out of the showerhead in the morning when tenants wash up for work and in the evenings when they clean themselves before bed. It washes their dishes and their clothes. It fills their buckets when they mop their floors on weekends. It's in the room with them when they have friends over, and it sits quietly in the pipes while they sleep, waiting for the next time it is called to use. It's a civilized and forgotten servant.

Like the boiler, the Seville on Roxy would slowly become decrepit and fall apart if not for the attentions of the stoic Jimenez. Like the boiler, Jimenez is an essential and oft-ignored component of the building's civility, without whom it would devolve swiftly and without recourse. Both reside in the basement, and both are heartbreakingly lonely.

At the moment of listening to the boiler ignite, Jimenez folds his meaty hands, hairy fingers interlocking. He stretches his arms over his head, exposing the musky smell of his armpits, to which he gives a quick sniff in a matter-of-fact fashion. If anyone had been with him, watching in his small office, his manner is one that says, "Yes, I did just sniff my armpits, and the results are mixed. On one hand, I smell. On the other, I worked hard all day and deserve to stink a little."

There are just two service requests left, each written on a little square of paper and skewered on a metal spike that sits by the old rotary phone on the corner of Jimenez's desk. Even though his workday technically ended an hour ago, Jimenez is not one to leave service requests unattended. Also, he loves the order he brings to the building. Like the boiler, his work goes unnoticed and unappreciated, but he takes pride in everything working smoothly, in making every resident's life a little easier.

He lets the chair drop back to all four legs and pulls the last two service requests from the spike.

The first one reads, "Leak under kitchen sink. Apartment 2507." He stuffs that one in his pocket. The other he crumples and throws into the garbage can. He knows what it says. He has been putting it off all day, and now its time has come.

With a sigh, he stands and grabs his tool belt from its hook near the door. He straps the belt on as he walks down an ashen-walled, dimly lit basement hallway and pushes his way through the stairwell door.

As he trudges up the stairs, amid the jangling clatter of the tools hanging from his belt, Jimenez ruminates on why he doesn't mind working late. Often, he stays in his basement office late into the evening, hours longer than he's bound to by his job description. In exchange for his work, Jimenez receives a modest salary and a subsidized apartment on the third floor. Over the years, he has more than earned his balcony over the parking garage entrance, his view of the alley, and the summer-time smells emanating from the Dumpster that sits under his bedroom window.

He knows the answer. He works so hard because he's lonely. There's no one to go home to and no reason he shouldn't stay late. Here, he feels needed. Here, he feels important, though few think of him when he isn't fixing their leaking faucet or mopping up the overflow from a clogged toilet.

I would only be missed if I wasn't here, Jimenez thinks. People would ask, "Where's that guy who always fixes stuff?" and, "Where's the super at? My sink is backing up with stuff that smells like old milk."

Jimenez reaches the landing, pushes the door, and steps through into the lobby. He stops and looks across the expanse of space to his adversaries, the elevators. One stopped working months ago and has been sitting with an "Out of Order" sign ever since. The other stopped working sometime this morning. It returned itself, empty, to the lobby level, and from then on it has sat there, unmoving. It still opens with a cheerful bing when people press the button. The doors slide closed after they board, but when they press the button for their floor, it sits motionless. Luckily, the door still opens to release them again.

Jimenez grew tired of the calls coming in from the residents and wrote a note in felt marker on one of his service request forms and taped it to the door. The note reads, "It don't work. Fixed soon. Use the stairs."

After taping up his note, Jimenez called the building manager.

"Marty, it's Jimenez. The other elevator's broke now too."

"Fix it," Marty said. It sounded like he was eating potato chips.

Jimenez thought for a moment. He knew very little about how elevators worked. "What if I can't?"

"Then I'll call someone who knows how. You give it a shot though," Marty said. "Technicians, man, those guys are expensive to hire out. Call me back. Let me know how it goes."

About half an hour ago, Jimenez was procrastinating by watering the plants in the lobby. He watched that home-schooled kid from the fifteenth floor cross the lobby from the stairwell. To Jimenez, the kid seemed nice enough, never caused any trouble, never vandalized the stairwell or threw stuff off the balcony. But there was something different about him, something missing.

As Jimenez watered the plants, the homeschooled kid shuffled across the lobby from the stairwell door and pressed the elevator button. The door binged and slid open. The kid shuffled inside. The door slid closed. Jimenez watered a few more plants and then grew curious about what the boy was doing in the unmoving elevator. He put down the canister and waited. Eventually the door slid open and the kid came out, looked around, and asked, "Excuse me, this isn't my floor. Where's my place?"

"Use the stairs, kid. Elevator's broke."

Jimenez has been putting off fixing the elevator all day. The stack of service requests dwindled by the hour as Jimenez worked his way through them. The lint trap in the Coin-O-Matic dryer isn't stuck anymore. The fire door to the stairwell on the seventeenth floor is no longer jammed. The pee smell on P1 has been dealt with and on and on until there were but the two request forms left. He has postponed this moment the best he could, but now it is time.

The door to the stairwell lets out a hiss as the hydraulic arm eases the door shut behind him. The latch clicks as Jimenez takes his first slow steps across the lobby, contemplating the elevator while he approaches. The tile floor glistens, and the blower unit circulates fresh air through the vents. Outside, through the security door, the traffic noise is hushed. Jimenez's hammer swings on a loop in his tool belt, thumping its dead weight against his thigh.

What tools does someone need to fix an elevator? Jimenez ponders and hikes his weighty belt back up onto his hips.

What's even wrong with it? Jimenez wonders as he presses the elevator button.

The doors slide open with a whisper, revealing the elevator's mirrored compartment. Jimenez glances at his reflection. Behind him, at the lobby door, he spots the big guy who lives up on the twenty-fifth floor. He wears a hard hat and carries a big black shopping bag. Jimenez pauses to nod an acknowledgment at the reflection of the man. The man nods back.

How hard can fixing an elevator be? Jimenez thinks as he steps into the compartment and starts to unscrew the brass screws on the panel.

The doors slide closed.

Jimenez leans the cover against the wall and then pokes around in the panel randomly, looking for some clue as to how the contraption works or what's wrong with it.

What can possibly go wrong? he thinks. It already isn't working, so it can't get any worse, right?

CHAPTER
SIX

In Which Petunia Delilah Feels a Peculiar Twinge in Her Nethers

With three weeks remaining until her due date, Dr. Ross instructed Petunia Delilah to avoid strenuous activity and anything else that might raise her blood pressure or agitate her. He said she's suffering from hyper-what's-it and should not take unnecessary risks with her health or the health of her baby. She couldn't salt her food, and Dr. Ross established a diet for her that is composed of equal parts of bland and boring. He gave her two lists of food, one on a green page and one on a red page. While his lips were moving, Petunia Delilah scanned the red page of forbidden foods and could only think how badly she wanted a fucking ice cream sandwich. And there it was on Dr. Ross's red page. Surprisingly, they are quite high in sodium.

Petunia Delilah has been horizontal all over the apartment. She lies on her back on the floor whenever the tingling numbness sparkles down her left leg. It's some pinched nerve, and she curses it. She lies on the couch, shifting as frequently as she flips channels in search of some fabled "good" daytime television show. She lies on the recliner out on the balcony, usually in mid-afternoon, when the sun is hot and before the rush hour traffic builds and too much noise percolates up the side of the building for her to enjoy the air anymore. She doesn't lie there often now though because it's difficult to get back on her feet without something to pull herself up on.

Right now, she lies in bed, propped up by a mountain of pillows and reading a dog-eared paperback. It's an old science fiction story in which the impeccably mannered heroes speak in complete sentences without contractions. Petunia Delilah likes to rub the brittle paper between her thumb and forefinger when she turns the pages. She likes the smell of old glue and yellowed paper because it's like touching the past.

Petunia Delilah stops reading and looks questioningly at the ceiling because she feels a peculiar twinge in her nethers. She knows they're down there, her nethers, somewhere where her legs meet her torso. They're there even though she hasn't seen them in a month unless aided by a mirror, her belly having grown too swollen and unwieldy for her to see them on her own.

And there it is again, the peculiar twinge. She cocks her head to one side and lowers the book to rest on her stomach.

She scootches to the edge of the bed and swings her legs to the floor. With a grunting effort she gets up and waddles from the bedroom to the bathroom, legs spindly and knees splayed like those of a cricket.

Dr. Ross prescribed bed rest after she passed out at her desk at work. She hadn't been doing anything strenuous, just the usual intake documents and registry, and the next thing she remembers is being in the hospital. The gap in consciousness between the two was a clumsy jump cut, not so much disturbing as it was awkward.

Apparently, the funeral home where she worked was abuzz with the news of her collapse. Of course, the first assumption about a nonresponsive body in a funeral home is that it has suffered death. In Petunia Delilah's case, an elderly couple attending the service of one of their recently departed friends knew better through their own hardened experiences with the reaper. They called the ambulance and stayed with her until the paramedics arrived.

The elderly couple, with no pressing engagements after the funeral service, even visited her in the hospital. They brought her flowers and chatted with her for an hour, their manners as impeccable as any hero's in an old science fiction book.

The funeral home director visited shortly after her collapse as well. He told her quite sternly and concernedly in his characteristic, mockable monotone, "You are on leave, Petunia Delilah. For your own good. Have a happy baby, and we will talk soon."

And so began the incarceration in her one-bedroom apartment.

Petunia Delilah turns sideways in the small bathroom. She unbuttons her nightie to her midsection and looks at the profile of her undercarriage in the medicine cabinet mirror. The skin is stretched and bulbous with some discoloration, nothing untoward; nothing has visibly changed with those peculiar twinges. She smiles, rubs a hand over her belly, and then buttons her nightie up again.

Danny, her boyfriend, affectionately refers to her belly as her fuck bubble.

She has looked at herself this way several times today, the peculiar twinges from her nethers sparking her hope of labor, a hope for the end of her discomfort and the even less bearable boredom.

The twinges have been happening since early morning. They woke her up, and she roused Danny in hopes that it was the start of her labor. They lay side by side, in the early-morning quiet, the city breathing softly outside the bedroom window, holding hands in quiet anticipation of the day to come.

But nothing happened.

Danny went to work, and Petunia Delilah read a book.

Petunia Delilah doesn't fear giving birth or the baby. Her midwife told her a truth: women have been giving birth for hundreds of thousands of years without modern medicine. It happens. If anything, Petunia Delilah is so purely excited for the experience that there is no room left for trepidation.

"With positive thoughts and calm emotion, giving birth is easy," Kimmy, her midwife, said. "Some of the things you think, they actually change your body. Good thoughts release bio-chemicals into your blood that can make the pain a happy experience. Thoughts become things."

Petunia Delilah isn't afraid to be on her own when her contractions start. In fact, she has longed for the experience and the cherubic company of the little one who will follow. She has had ample time to construct elaborate, gauzy fantasies of baking cookies and breastfeeding and nurturing because she has been horizontal for weeks in the one-bedroom apartment. She will kiss Danny every day when he comes home from the construction site. Danny will kiss her back and then kiss the baby on the forehead. They will eat supper together and laugh together and make such a great family.

Anyway, if she was to go into labor, Danny works just a few blocks away, pouring concrete for the Baineston on Roxy. He could be home in a few minutes. Petunia Delilah and Danny got new cell phones so she could call him if she needs anything. She glances at the wall clock above the toilet and thinks his shift will be over soon. He'll probably go for a few drinks with the guys though, before coming home.

Petunia Delilah turns from her reflection in the bathroom mirror and ambles into the kitchen. She opens the freezer and stares at the box of ice cream sandwiches for a moment before opening it. She runs her index finger over the stack of tightly packed sandwiches inside, entranced by the smooth, rhythmic bump of one sandwich to the next. Each wrapper emits a crackly static as she tickles it. They cool her fingertip, the chilled plastic silky to touch.

Six individually wrapped fucking ice cream sandwiches in my freezer, she thinks. And I can't even have one.

Petunia Delilah folds the box's cardboard flap closed, slams the freezer door, and turns the electric kettle on.

No coffee, no caffeinated tea, just these shrub clippings, she thinks.

She fingers through a ceramic jar of herbal tea sachets when it hits, the most peculiar of the peculiar twinges she has ever felt. She drops the jar. The base chips, and a spray of powdery ceramic ejecta stains the counter near the sink. The jar rolls noisily to one side and then back halfway again.

Petunia Delilah instinctively reaches down and cups her belly. She drops her hand lower to where it touches wet fabric, deceptively wet as the temperature of the fluid makes it barely distinguishable from her own skin, but there's an undeniable weight to the fabric that wasn't there moments ago. She watches a rusty puddle spreading on the linoleum from her feet and wonders why it's not clear, like Kimmy told her it would be.

My water broke, she thinks. It's happening. The baby's coming. I have to call Danny. Our baby is on the way.

Petunia Delilah and Danny have resisted Dr. Ross's encouragement for ultrasounds, amniocentesis, and even the scheduled C-section he recommended given the smallish nature of Petunia Delilah's pelvic girdle and her family's history of birthing trouble. They didn't want to learn anything from the doctor. They wanted to give birth naturally, without painkillers or radioactive pictures of their baby in her womb.

After all, as Kimmy the midwife pointed out, women have been giving birth for hundreds of thousands of years without modern medicine.

Not for the first time, Petunia Delilah wonders if it's going to be a boy or a girl. Kimmy says it will be a boy based on how she's carrying the fuck bubble. For some reason, Petunia Delilah is sure it will be a girl. She just feels it. She hasn't told Danny, and she hasn't told him she likes the names Chloe, Persephone, and Lavender. There will be time for that after.

With arms outstretched and legs a bow, walking like she had just dismounted a horse after a weeklong ride and propping herself against the walls like a drunk, Petunia Delilah makes her way to the bedroom. She can't help but smile as she gropes for the cell phone on the nightstand.

As another twinge shoots through her nethers, Petunia Delilah winces. It's an uncomfortable feeling but not as painful as she was led to believe by the baby classes they had attended. She speed-dials Danny. The phone rings three times before going to voice mail.

"You've reached Danny's phone. Leave a message."

Petunia waits for the beep and says, "Danny, the baby's coming. Where are you? Come home. Call me. I'm calling Kimmy."

CHAPTER
SEVEN

In Which Garth Returns to the Seville on Roxy with a Secret Cargo in Tow

"Oh, look it, look it, look it," Danny says, all the words blending together to make one manic sound. Danny stops feeding the concrete mixer and leans on his shovel. His eyes track a young woman walking by the chain-link fence. "Damn, that's fine. You know, I could watch that all day and find something new to love every second of it."

Garth swivels his head, following Danny's gaze. Garth catches a glimpse of her walking by the fence. She has short brown hair, mysterious kohl-encircled eyes, and a gorgeous figure, slender shoulders with a plumpness below her pinched waist. Fit but still soft, smooth skin over firm muscle with just a little layer of padding. The summer dress she wears ripples like water, offering sensuous hints of her body whenever the two meet. Each time her body presses against the fabric, it offers a tantalizing, electric snapshot of what's hidden beneath. The material pulls taut across her buttocks as she steps up one stair and into the drugstore next to the construction site.

That singular moment, nothing more than flesh pressing fabric smooth, that moment will haunt Garth for the rest of the afternoon and deep into his evening. In it, Garth sees all he has ever wanted, something so beautiful and strong but still distinctly feminine. A spontaneous marvel that's just there, unorchestrated, living in the universe.

Garth closes his eyes to the warmth sprouting in his chest and revels in her image seized by his imagination. He drinks deeply from the impression of her captured in the darkness of his eyelids. He can almost feel the tickle of the summer dress's fabric pressed against his skin and the slight give to the flesh slipping beneath it.

"Hey? Do I got the eye or what? I would tap that. Totally. Just spank it a few times. Make it jiggle a little bit." Danny's wishful voice breaks through Garth's peace.

Danny creeps into Garth's fantasy. Materializing out of a fog, there he is, naked Danny standing behind her, one hand smacking the woman's buttocks and spitting a quivering, goopy pendulum of saliva into his other hand before rubbing it on his prick.

It's fitting we're on this side of the fence, Garth thinks, and she's out there. Animals in here, all of us animals in this zoo.

"Shut up, would ya?" Garth grumbles, his eyes still closed, trying to rid himself of the vision of Danny behind the woman. He can't shake it. After a few frustrated seconds, he lets out a blast of air and opens his eyes. He can't get her back. He'll have to wait until he gets home to concentrate on her without the vile image of Danny to sully the fantasy.

Danny's already back to work, shoveling concrete mix in the spinning cement machine as if the woman was never a distraction. Garth takes a few moments, looks at his watch, and then glances up the street to the Seville on Roxy. That's where he lives. The Baineston on Roxy is the most convenient construction site he has ever worked on because he only has a few blocks walk home. Danny lives in the Seville too, with his girlfriend, though Danny and Garth hardly talk or see each other outside of the site. Garth knows Danny's girlfriend is pregnant because Danny talks about it a lot. He's excited to be having a baby with her. Garth knows that they live in an apartment on the eighth floor since that's where Danny got off the elevator the few times they rode it together. Other than that, Garth keeps to himself.

Garth loves living and working on Roxy because it's also close to one of his favorite stores, which is only two blocks in the opposite direction of the Seville. Almost daily, he slips away from the site and pops down the street during his lunch break. With so many coworkers around, he asked the storeowner if he could enter through the alley-side door. He couldn't risk being seen entering it, but he couldn't stay away from the shop.

The owner nodded that of course it was okay — "Garth, you are one of our best customers." And with that he handed Garth a package that had been wrapped in brown paper and then stuffed into an unmarked black plastic bag. His special order had come in that morning.

Garth was so excited he ran into the alley and squeezed the package, not daring to unwrap it to look at the contents. The package was the size of a phone book and yielded a bit when Garth squeezed it. The paper it was wrapped in crackled, and the plastic bag that held the package whispered sweetly as air escaped. Garth sprinted up the alley to the street, a huge grin on his face. He spent the short walk back to the site working on containing his excitement, repressing the urge to jump or run while fist-pumping. He had calmed his emotions by the time he saw the chain-link cage, reconstructing his hard facade of manual laborer machismo. He wolfed down his lunch in the remaining fifteen minutes, and by the time the break was over, Garth was his regular stony self and the package was safely tucked behind his dusty lunch box in his locker at the site office.

The afternoon crept by, and Garth couldn't keep his mind off the package. When he saw it in the store, he asked the clerk to double-wrap it and bag it. He was hesitant at first to bring it onto the site. He could have gone to pick it up after the final whistle blew, but the thought of waiting until after work to go pick it up was unbearable. He just wants to go home straight from the site with it, ride the elevator to his twenty-fifth-floor apartment, and hear the lock click as his door closes. The anticipation is so sweet and so unbearable he's torn between going home early to open the package and savoring the mounting temptation to do so.

All afternoon, Danny drones on. He points out the occasional hot woman walking by. Garth agrees some of them are attractive. For others, he wonders if Danny's putting on a show. Garth doesn't say much; he just grunts when Danny needs a prompt, which is rare. Danny's voice runs like the machinery in the background. It's a constant noise that, with time, Garth's mind has become desensitized to.

When the day ends, Garth goes to his locker, grabs his lunch box and the black plastic bag. The guys are talking casually, making plans to go get some beers and a burger at the nearby pub. It's all he can do not to sprint from the site, run blindly through the traffic on Roxy to the Seville, rocket up to his apartment, and slam and lock the door behind him, hugging the package to his heaving, winded chest, leaning back against the door, ready to explode with excitement.

Instead, he nods when someone tells him a joke he doesn't listen to and casually packs his safety vest and ear protection into his backpack like he's got no other plans. He says bye to the guys and no, sorry, can't go for beers tonight, got stuff to do, wave, wave, punch shoulder, and work on a contained walk toward the Seville. As he turns from waving, he bumps into her, the woman Danny pointed out, the woman in the summer dress and the kohl eyes on the other side of the fence. The perfect woman brushes into his side as she steps out of the drugstore.

"Sorry," she mumbles and stops in her tracks.

"It's okay." Garth smiles, overly conscious of his bulk, his belly, his hairy arms, his hairy chest, his hairy butt, his musty after-work smell, his greasy skin and sweaty hair, his apelike stature, his pendulous penis, his broad shoulders, his generally threatening manliness that he wishes were less . . . less . . . obvious at times like this.

In the span of his awkward self-assessment, Garth and the woman stand, staring at each other. Garth closes his eyes, again her image is imprinted behind his eyelids, and then he carries on toward the Seville. He squeezes the package to his chest. His heart pounds, about to burst.

This is going to be a magical evening.

And this time he can't suppress a quickly shuffling step. He doesn't wait for the light at the corner and crosses through traffic. He can't wait.

CHAPTER
EIGHT

In Which Claire the Shut-In Receives a Mysterious Buzz from the Front Door

Claire's apartment is immaculate. The late-afternoon sun shines through the eighth-floor window and streams in the balcony door, causing the whole apartment to glow like a celestial beacon of cleanliness. The stainless steel espresso machine on the kitchen counter is blinding. The tile backsplash reflects every bit of the daylight's intensity, becoming a second sun itself. In this brutal assault of light, not a blip of dust or a stray curly hair can be seen on any flat surface, not even under the couch or coffee table should one deign to look.

Claire hates those television shows about people who never leave their homes. They gather newspapers into swelling stacks and pile unwashed cans into tin mountains behind the stained easy chair. She had to stop watching because their dirty little paths that cut through the piles of plastic bags and old computer components made her furious. Not all shut-ins are like that.

No, Claire thinks, not "shut-ins." Technically, "agoraphobics," but she prefers the term "aggressively introverted individuals."

Those people on television, Claire thinks as she peels the cellophane wrapper off a sanitized, single-use plastic drinking cup, their places with the soup cans stacked on the counter and dirty dishes heaped in the sink, are the products of unhealthy minds. She pours bottled water into her cup, drinks, and places both the cup and bottle into the recycling bin. Claire opens a sanitizing hand wipe and swabs her palms, cleans between her fingers, and then dabs the backs of her hands.

Claire hasn't always been aggressively introverted. As a little girl, she rode her bike in suburban streets with the neighbor kids. She picked gravel from her scraped knees and dug up worms in the backyard. When she was older, she walked to school with friends and played on the playground during recess. In her early twenties, she attended the crowded lecture theaters and study halls of the local college. On Friday nights, she went to the sweaty, gyrating clubs with her friends and drank vodka slimes from spotted old-fashioned glasses. Occasionally, she would take a guy home, and if that was the case, they would almost always get it on. Once, after last call, she even wandered the bar, drinking the dregs from glasses and bottles left behind on the counters and tables. That night, she had been cripplingly inebriated. If asked, Claire would unconvincingly deny ever doing such a thing. If pressed, she would claim she doesn't remember doing that, which the look on her face would suggest might be true.

Then, in her late twenties, with her friends pairing off and breeding, disappearing from her life under the hefty obligations of children and mortgages, she began to think she really wasn't having that much fun. She started looking back at her childhood and youth and could only feel a vacuous space for people where a warm feeling of lifelong friendship and camaraderie should have swelled. If those bonds were so easy to break, if years of friendship could wither so easily, she didn't need them.

Claire stopped leaving her apartment.

Her apartment has two phone lines, one with a number that only her mother knows and the other a dedicated line for work. She orders her groceries online and has them delivered to her door. She watches movies and television series on the computer. She reads books downloaded from the Internet. Sometimes, for nostalgia's sake, she'll order a paperback or purchase a record and have it shipped to the apartment. She finds it easier not to leave the four walls. She prefers her ceiling to the sky and her floor to the ground.

The sun goes up and the sun goes down and Claire is happy. She has a safe bubble, a bright sunny apartment overlooking Roxy, where the bustle of humanity passes by, close enough for her to feel included, but not so close to need to be involved. She truly feels happy, more so than she can ever remember.

Still, needing to pay the bills, Claire finds it necessary to work. She does so in a great job, which she loves. It fulfills her minimal social needs, and she can telecommute. Her employer pays all her work expenses and even reimburses her for the space she uses for her home office. Living in a one-bedroom apartment, Claire has her computer and phone set up at the island in the kitchen.

Claire stands at the window, her hands on her hips, and watches traffic go by outside for a moment before returning to the island. She sits on her stool and glances at the computer, nine minutes left in her shift. The work line rings, and Claire taps a button to activate her hands-free earpiece.

"Hello?" Claire says. "And to whom am I speaking?"

A pause.

"Jason?" Claire continues, "Your name doesn't matter anymore, Jason. I'm going to call you Pig because that's what you are. Now ... tell me how fucking hard your cock is and where you want to put it." She nods to herself. Claire checks the clock, eight minutes until shift change. "Shut up, Pig. All you are to me is a hot pole to ride hard."

Eight minutes. Fast, but by no means a record. That's why they charge more for the first minute of phone time.

I can do this, she thinks, and then ... quiche for supper!

Claire is glad she didn't get the evening shift. Friday evenings are the busiest. She thinks it's odd that one night out of the week should be busier than any other when phone sex is involved, but it is. Friday always is. Perhaps it's the societal repression of urges for an entire week, a dam filling, swelling after a rainstorm, and needing to normalize its levels. Maybe it's just an urge for a natural stress relief. So many people calling in, getting off the hook, wanting to be humiliated, humiliating themselves, and then going out the next morning to brunch with their parents or to garage sales in search of secondhand clothes for their kids.

Friday nights are about lonely, slutty, filthy depravity for many, but for Claire they are about quiche. Her mother's recipe. The trick is using sparkling mineral water to make the dough. For some reason the crust turns out fluffier and less oily. Claire likes to think it's all the tiny bubbles that make it so but knows it's more likely to be some chemistry thing. Even if she had to work the Friday evening shift, she would make quiche.

Claire checks the clock, seven minutes left until she can log out.

"You're a mouthy little bitch, Pig. I think I'm going to have to stuff your mouth with my dirty panties to shut you up and then spank your ass red raw to punish you. Maybe I'm going to have to strap one on and drill you. Would you like that? Maybe I'll just rip open your —"

The phone rings.

Claire blinks.

It's the other phone. The one that shouldn't be ringing.

Pig's huffing is claustrophobia-inducing, grotesque, and close in her ear canal. His damp exhalations seemingly pant directly into her brain. She shivers.

The phone rings again.

49

Only her mother knows that number, and she only calls on Sunday mornings.

Claire's heart races.

"Hey, Jason, something just came up. I have to go," Claire says into the headset without taking her eyes off her personal phone. Watching for it to ring, terrified for it to ring. "I don't know . . . Finish yourself off for once," she says and hangs up.

Claire flinches when it rings again.

Something's wrong. Is Mom okay? Who else could it be, really?

Her arm shoots out, and she brings the phone to her ear and listens. Street noises come through the receiver. A car horn travels through the phone at the same time she hears it from her window. Someone is in front of the building, eight floors below, waiting at the intercom in the late-afternoon light. The building's shadow would be drawn out, casting a deep-blue shade on the sidewalk where the caller stands, waiting for her to say something.

"Hello?" she says, her voice trembling involuntarily.

There's the muffled sound of movement, quick movement. The voice on the other end growls, "Gotcha, kiddo." A pained and piercing scream comes over the line, followed by the static of a violent motion, like the sound of a fast punch.

The line goes dead.

Claire doesn't move. After several moments, the steady dial tone against her ear turns to a consistent beep. A bang comes from the hallway. Claire starts, slams the receiver into its cradle, and then dashes to check that her apartment door is locked. It is. It's never unlocked. She takes a deep breath and peers through the spy hole. There's nothing but the fish-eye tunnel of the lonely hallway stretching out from her door.

Satisfied the door is secure, she rushes to the window and looks down on the street. She's so desperate to see the front door that she almost touches the glass. She recoils from it as if it's fire. People bustle by on Roxy below, and Claire realizes any one of them could have made the call.

She cranes to see the front door, but because of the angle, she can't. She wishes she could go out onto the balcony. From there she would be able to lean over and see who's waiting for her.

CHAPTER
NINE

In Which Homeschooled Herman Finds the Consciousness That He Recently Misplaced

Sometimes, other kids make fun of Herman. He knows it's because he's smaller and smarter than the rest of them. He has been bumped ahead two grades in the last three years. He knows it's because he wears glasses and has little interest in physical activities like playing dodgeball during recess or football after school.

He also knows it's because he once told the other kids he can time travel and that the experience is nothing like it is in the movies. It doesn't involve flashing lights from the sky, a fusion-powered DeLorean, or slingshotting a spaceship around the sun. It happens in the brain, through a dimensionally unhinged consciousness. It's more a jumble of disorienting and confusing fragments than the present's clarity. Sometimes he sees the future, but mostly he sees the past. In hindsight, telling the other kids this was definitely a mistake.

It's not that the other kids are specifically making fun of Herman, as he often rationalizes; they are making fun of some of the things he says and does. The person he is at the core is not being ridiculed; it's the person they perceive him to be. Every time he says or does something weird, it's that specific thing they react to, not to Herman himself. Herman's self-aware enough to know that the hairbreadth distinction between the two is a coping mechanism.

Also, by extension, when other kids push Herman into the lockers or jeer when they see him, it is not truly him they are at odds with. It is more a comprehensive dislike for all that is different. This dislike is centered not with Herman but with a deeper, more primal fear of the unknown and a base-level animal hatred of the outlier.

Nobody likes a time traveler, Herman reasons. Why would they? He knows the past and has seen the future and is therefore a threat. They are trapped, stumbling around the three dimensions of geography, shackled by time and jealous that he is free to roam.

Really, they all time travel at a constant rate of one day, every day. But for Herman, the velocity of time can change, as can its direction. Herman has researched it. If they knew the things that Herman does, if they could manipulate the last, greatest dimension, they would also be considered a threat to the present.

It is just like that time I teleported, Herman thinks. Nobody but Grandpa believed me. I blacked out on the playground and woke up alone in the nurse's office. Everyone else just wanted me to prove it, that I could teleport.

"Do it again," they said. "Right now, dorkwad."

But it didn't work like that.

Oh, Herman thinks, if only it could be controlled, the time I would go to would be far away from this one.

The other kids are scared of Herman, and this fear is perceived as a threat, which is what Darrin Jespersen, in particular, was struggling with a year ago when he punched Herman in the ribs. They were clustered near the bike racks at school, just after the bell rang to signal the end of the day's classes. Darrin and his group of cronies backed Herman up against the rack. Darrin didn't say anything. He just punched Herman three times, and three ribs broke — well, two broke and one was just fractured, but it was all done in fear.

Darrin was scared of anything different, and Herman terrified him.

Herman has a habit of passing out in stressful situations. Herman knows it's a defense mechanism that stems from some early evolution. He researched it and found there are goats that pass out from confrontation. Some dogs and other animals do it too, like opossums. Playing dead decreases the instinctual drive of pursuing predators. That dark figure chasing Herman — sometimes his name is Darrin or Charlie, and once it was named Gail — that predator becomes uninterested when he falls unconscious. That hoary figure chasing him is hidden by the lack of rearward vision, and Herman knows that shadowed beast could fall upon him at any second and there's never time to glance back in the panic of the moment. So, sometimes a body that forces itself to collapse is the best defensive mechanism to have.

54

Without prey there's nothing to prey upon.

Quite often, Herman's bouts of blacking out are filled with vivid visions, which he doesn't remember because they are also followed by a span of memory loss. More accurately, they are bracketed with the loss of minutes and sometimes hours before and after collapsing, so like the memories, the traumas are also forgotten.

Sometimes the memories return in fits and starts, and sometimes they remain lost to his mind. If they do return, they are often in fragments and from perspectives not normally seen in the regular human experience. The memories return as details viewed from a great distance or, alternately, from microscopically close up. Rarely are they experienced from a safe or normal distance. Sounds are often missing or distorted into warped and folded tones. If words are heard, they're rarely discernible.

For example, at the bike racks, Herman collapsed after Darrin landed his first punch. The subsequent two impacts were not felt because Herman fell unconscious to the gravel. After that first blow, Herman knew only blackness. Darrin grew tired of punching an inert sack of meat, his primal mind became distracted by some other kid's movement on the playground, and off he went. His pack of minions followed.

"Herman," a voice came through the black. "Herman, are you okay?"

It was Grandpa's voice, disembodied in the dark unconscious, floating somewhere to the left of Herman's head.

Grandpa had been sitting in his car across the road, waiting to give Herman a ride home. He knew of Herman's idiosyncrasies, of his time travel and his singular bout of teleportation, and that he would never be the popular classmate. Grandpa had suffered similarly as a youth, but he had not known the extent of Herman's victimization by the other children until the day he witnessed what happened at the bike racks. Herman's grandpa, in reality more than a disembodied voice, saw the whole incident.

The following day, he demanded a meeting with the principal and, dissatisfied with the results of their meeting, withdrew Herman from the school. Herman's grandpa opted to teach Herman at home, to teach him as he had once been taught, passing on wisdom and ideas in the time-honored way, which was how Herman became Homeschooled Herman.

Presently, Herman wakes facedown on a cool tile floor. He likes the first moments of consciousness — he always does. It's a floating feeling of the blackness dissipating and the world drifting in a peacefully from a distance. The entire trauma that caused him to black out will return slowly, in a more manageable form than that in which it originally presented itself. However, for this peaceful span, Herman enjoys the calm of reality returning. Everything before this moment is gone. He isn't sure how he came to be prone and can't recall how he wound up here, wherever here is. He doesn't panic though because this is not an uncommon experience.

Those moments pass slowly. Herman admires the simple perspective of the grout line grid retreating from his eyes into a hazy distance. Slowly, sound comes back. The fluorescent lights above hum a hypnotic tone, and he can hear the soft sigh of the air moving, though he can't feel it move on his skin.

After a time, Herman pushes himself to a kneeling position. He sits on his heels. Then, a short while later, he stands.

Herman recognizes the tiny room. It's the elevator in his building. The mirrors all around reflect a version of himself, ever shrinking in every direction into an emerald-tinged infinity. He thinks for a minute to try to count how many Hermans are reflected but deems the task too monumental and entirely pointless.

Infinity is infinity, he thinks. It's not my business to try quantifying it, just to accept it.

The elevator is stationary, so Herman pushes the button to open the doors and they comply.

When he steps out, he sees the big superintendent watering the plants. There's a patch sewn to the super's bowling shirt that reads "Jimenez" in a swirly, cursive font.

"Where's my place?" Herman asks. He decides not to point out the plants the man waters are fake.

"Use the stairs, kid. Elevator's broke," Jimenez tells him, a look of confusion crossing his face.

Herman looks around and realizes he's still on the main floor of the Seville on Roxy. He makes his way across the lobby to the staircase.

The first fragments of the trauma that caused his blackout begin to return. Nothing concrete, nothing in sequence, just the feeling that something is very wrong. He pushes his way through the stairwell door and starts to ascend. His steps turn into a lope, which turn into a flat-out sprint as each memory starts layering upon the previous one.

CHAPTER
TEN

In Which We Rejoin Ian the Goldfish in His Perilous Plunge That Has Yet to Begin

Like an angel thrust down from heaven, like a meteorite rocketing through the troposphere, we left Ian a few hundred feet in the air, two floors down from where he once resided in the fishbowl on the balcony and twenty-five floors up from the sun-warmed, impossibly hard concrete of the sidewalk that runs in front of the Seville on Roxy.

"Now, what was I doing? Oh my, I can't breathe. Oh shit, I'm falling off a high-rise! Now . . . what was I doing?"

For as long as he can remember, Ian has yearned for freedom. As previously discussed, Ian is equipped with a goldfish brain and "as long as he can remember" covers a slender ribbon spanning only a fraction of a second. That being said, the desire for freedom is always there, suggesting it is deeper than a memory. It's embedded under his orange scales, residing deep in his cold, pink flesh and comprising an important facet of his essential character. Like dogs chase cats, like cats chase birds, fish long to fall. It's an instinct so deep in the roots of Ian's family tree that all goldfish have this yearning encoded by some long-ago ancestor.

Indeed, this need to move and explore new territory has been long entrenched in aquatic animals, and their successes have been documented in hundreds of events where they've fallen like heavy raindrops from the sky. There are thousands more such events that have not been witnessed by human eyes. Ian is not aware of this history beyond the drive in his muscles. History to Ian is the fishbowl he just left, the pink plastic castle sitting in the gravel, and his dim-witted, slightly annoying, but mostly lovable bowlmate, Troy the snail.

Regardless of Ian's perspective on time, from before the advent of the written word, recorded in ocher and charcoal on a cliff face, through the biblical scourges to just last year, there has been a long history of fish raining. It has occurred much too frequently and for far too long to be attributed to chance or fate or freak acts of nature. Be they frogs, toads, fish, or the occasional tentacled cephalopod, aquatic species have it in their nature to fall great distances onto far-flung locales. They often perish in the fall or from lack of water. They have expressed their longing for freedom as individuals, as in the case of Ian, or as schools of tens of thousands, as in the case of the more torrential fish rains.

Ian is not abnormal in his desire and should not be considered an anomaly.

The best minds of marine biology, when turned to the terrestrial endeavors of these fish, postulate the only logical explanation is one that has been dubbed the Dorothy complex, alternately the "No Place Like Home" hypothesis. To these researchers, it's obvious that a water funnel has sucked up these fish and transported them through the air over great distances in winds reaching upward of several hundred miles an hour to deposit them, intact and alive, inland.

It's obvious.

Calcutta, September 1839. Charles Tomlinson, in his book *The Rain-Cloud and the Snow-Storm: An Account of the Nature, Formation, Properties, Dangers, and Uses of Rain and Snow*, recounts a day when, around two o'clock in the afternoon, there was a rain shower with which descended a large number of live fish, all about three inches in length. It's stated that those that fell onto hard surfaces died on impact, but those landing in the grass of a nearby field survived and were quite lively. The fish came down with the rain, and it has been hypothesized that a waterspout sucked them up, only to deposit them on the village. If this were the case, why was only one species recorded?

Ian hasn't read the book, but he knows the answer. The fish were exploring. A vehicle of exploration, like a Soyuz rocket, is a use of rain clouds overlooked in Mr. Tomlinson's book. The oversight of this ingenuity is staggering.

It's obvious.

Two things Ian found particularly annoying about Troy the snail was his willing acceptance of his ecological niche and geographic restrictions. Troy was content to suck algae, day and night, with no grander thoughts than filling his seemingly bottomless radula and remaining oblivious to the wonders of the larger world outside the safety of the glass bowl.

Singapore, February 22,1861. Thousands of *Clarias batrachus* fell from the sky onto a village. The villagers said it sounded like old women beating their hut roofs with sticks. The villagers ate well for three days, harvesting fish from the streets, plucking them from ditches and puddles and trees, filling baskets as if picking berries from a bush, gorging themselves.

Were the fish sucked up in a water funnel as well? Were they magically transported by the rip-rending power of the funnel and later dumped inland, intact? Where were all the other kinds of sea creatures? There was not one snail or scrap of seaweed to be found.

Ian knows the answer even though he has never heard of the Singapore fish rain. It was a tragic end to an advanced scouting party looking for a new world. It was a dangerous endeavor the fish undertook.

One thing that Troy the snail got right is that an unadventurous life will secure one an impressively long life. But was it worth never leaving the gallon bowl for fear of the unknown? Ian doesn't think so. An entire life devoted to a fishbowl will make one die an old fish with not one adventure had.

Now, Rhode Island — that would have been something to see.

Rhode Island, May 1900, was the site of two exploratory fish expeditions. Perch and bullspouts fell from the sky in two separate thunderstorms. There are thousands of species in the northwestern Atlantic aquatic region. There are all kinds of fish and invertebrates and plants and crustaceans but only two species were present in the Rhode Island fish rain. Was it another selective and gentle waterspout, or were two species teaming up to search for a new territory?

Through the decades and up until this year, India, the southeastern United States, the Northern Territory of Australia, and the Philippines all have had their share of raining fish. And the list goes on. Scientists can posit their windstorms and water funnels and extreme weather as the vehicle, but they have forgotten how clever nature is.

It's obvious.

Let it be said that a fish will strive to find the highest point available in order to fall from it in an attempt to land somewhere else. They're noble explorers limited only by water, an atmosphere that always settles to the lowest spots, and though their souls strain toward the heights, it's for those low elevations that their bodies yearn. They are fearless adventurers caged by aquariums or restrained in bowls. They are repressed free spirits in search of the edge of the world, in pursuit of the unknown, and are predisposed to falling from great heights at much personal peril in order to find new territories.

In the hairbreadth of time it takes him to span the gap between the twenty-fourth and twentieth floors, Ian knows this. Even as the memory of Troy and the pink plastic castle and his fishbowl fade, this one certainty remains embedded and true. His basic desire to

63

explore, the very reason for his existence, has hung him in the sky.

Let boredom be to the snails!

And so Ian plummets toward the pavement.

CHAPTER
ELEVEN

In Which Katie Demands Satisfaction from the Elevator Button

The foyer door closes quietly behind Katie. The little hydraulic arm flexes, and the noise from cars passing by on the street outside becomes muted by a layer of glass and steel. As Katie crosses the lobby, she doesn't notice that the wilted brown potted plants have been replaced by a lush silk terrarium, nor does she notice how well the new silk plants have been watered. She doesn't notice how the tile has been polished to a high, reflective gloss and how there's not a scuff mark to be seen. However, the lingering smell of lemons, bleach, and vinegar in the air can't be missed.

Katie arrives at the elevators and presses the button with the arrow that once pointed at the ceiling but now misses it because, over time, it has become skewed about thirty degrees from vertical. The button now points to a sconce to the top right of the elevator door, and it clicks audibly when Katie pokes it. Katie waits in a silence that should be filled by the distant mechanical hum of the elevator moving. She glares at the button and then pokes it again. Waits. Then pokes it vigorously and repeatedly, the button sounding like an agitated cricket in the calm of the lobby.

The first press is to summon the elevator, wherever it hangs in the twenty-seven-story blackness of the shaft that vaults from here into the sky. The second press is because the button failed to illuminate from the first. It's a finicky thing. The opaque plastic lights up with a creamy glow from that second push. The last presses are frustration-induced jabs, violent pokings that eventually cause fingertip numbness.

Katie's emotions are all backed up, and she wants to get this over with. While the severe poking she subjects the button to does little to speed up the elevator's descent, it does vent a tiny toot of malcontentedness. She wants to be standing in front of Connor. She's impatient to confront him, have her resolution, and then move on with life. The afternoon has taken its time, slow seconds passing by to make up a minute and those minutes dripping by even more painfully to make an hour. All of them building to an end of her shift at the grocery store where she works, and each of them marking her passage from there to here. She didn't have the frame of mind to marvel how each second, on its own, was a useless freeze frame, but all of them compiled made something much more coherent.

Her finger jabs.

The first joint flexes backward, and the pink skin under her fingernail flashes white with each stab. It's a pacifying action, one that gives the same false sense of command over a helpless situation that floating seat cushions do on passenger jets crossing the frigid Atlantic at forty thousand feet. Those cushions won't do much in a five-hundred-mile-per-hour nosedive into the roiling ocean water. Even if, by some miracle, anyone survives, those cushions won't do much against the hypothermia and numbing freezing death that awaits the survivors. But it's comforting to know they're there, just in case. It's just like how, if Katie pictures the button being Connor's chest, she knows jabbing it won't change anything, but each word punctuated by a poke brings an elevated level of calm with it.

"You've" — jab — "neglected" — jab — "my" — jab — "feelings" — jab — "for" — jab — "too" — jab — "long." Sob. "I need to know you love me back." Jab.

Katie imagines Connor's smooth, deep voice stuttering out an answer. She pictures the stupid look on his handsome face, a look of surprise. It's the look of a trapped animal. His square jaw slack, the bow of his perfectly kissable lips hangs open. His voice, halting and hesitant, says, "Baby, uh, you know I do, uh, you're the greatest." Pause. "I think you're really great, uh."

She needs to hear him say the actual words, and she will tell him so.

"I love you. There are two things you can say right now." Jab. "Pick one and say it. I'll know if you're lying."

Katie doesn't know what he'll say, but she'll watch for that quick twitch or that momentary aversion of gaze signifying lying or avoidance. If he says the words back to her and if he really means them, she will make love to him right then. If he hesitates at the wrong spot, she will know. If he lies or can't say it back, she will take her toothbrush, her favorite coffee mug, and her pink nightshirt and go. She'll slam his apartment door as hard as she can on her way out. Damn the neighbors too.

The elevator chimes Katie's thoughts back to the lobby. The doors slowly part, revealing Jimenez standing there like the world's least appealing peep show dancer. He holds a screwdriver in one meaty fist and has a tiny golden screw cupped in the other. His tool belt has slipped off his hips and taken his pants down slightly as well. The smallest glimpse of his belly can be had, exposed from under his bowling shirt. Katie tries not to let her eye be drawn to the lobe of flesh, but she finds it hard to resist the spectacle.

Katie isn't sure what Jimenez's first name is. She's seen him around the building on occasion and knows his surname from his seemingly unending wardrobe of bowling shirts with the name "Jimenez" embroidered on an oval patch and sewn on the breast pocket. They've said a few words in passing and always share a smile or a nod when they see each other. He seems like a nice man.

Jimenez and Katie stare at each other for a moment, Jimenez with his eyebrows lifted and his forehead wrinkled, Katie with her finger still extended like a gunslinger's hip shot aimed at the elevator button. Each is seemingly surprised by the other's presence.

"Elevators are broke, lady," Jimenez says. "They ain't going up or down. You gotta use the stairs."

The stairs, Katie thinks. I have to hike up hundreds of stairs to the twenty-seventh floor. Then, most likely, have my heart broken, and then have to hike back down hundreds of stairs again, listening to the sounds of my own crying echoing back at me from the heights of the stairwell. Katie's emotions oscillate between self-pity and rage at Connor, a heady and unstable mix that leaves her uncertain of how much control she will be able to exert over herself.

Katie's stomach clenches when she thinks, Twenty-seven floors of hearing myself cry.

She feels like bawling right there, just to get it over with. The sooner she starts, the sooner she'll find catharsis, and then, done with it, her emotions will be free to heal as much as they can and move on. Instead, she stands with dry eyes, embarrassed and exposed in front of the building superintendent. Her upper lip wobbles into an unsteady smile, and she sighs. Her chin puckers once before she pulls herself together.

She will be strong.

She is prepared.

"Sorry," Jimenez says.

Katie realizes that there was a long and very awkward moment while she had been thinking, staring wordlessly at Jimenez.

Jimenez, the poor man, she thinks. I'm making this so hard on him. He's not to blame. He's such a nice guy too. He always says "Hi."

"Not your fault," Katie says and takes a moment to construct a more believable smile. "Thanks, I'll take the stairs."

Why did I thank him? Katie wonders as she crosses the lobby to the stairwell. He didn't do anything wrong, but he didn't do anything right either. He hadn't brought her good news.

She hears the elevator doors bing and slide closed again. Without looking back, she pushes through the stairwell door and starts her ascent.

CHAPTER
TWELVE

In Which the Evil Seductress Faye Bids Adieu to the Villain Connor Radley

Faye rolls onto her side. The mattress whispers under her. It doesn't creak or moan; it's just a mattress on the floor. The sheets feel amazing against her skin, a feather-soft embrace of her entire body that makes her achingly aware of every inch of naked flesh. A bead of sweat tickles a path from her armpit down the side of her breast. She shivers from the sensation and lets out a quivering breath at its touch. Her body is horribly spent but still beautifully charged.

The little studio apartment that crowns the Seville on Roxy is stiflingly hot. The air is stale and damp, like every breath of it has been used a hundred times. The late-afternoon sun streams through the balcony door, which is why she pulls the sheets up over her head, an attempt to fend off the light. She looks up, through the wrinkled tunnel of fabric, and she sees Connor Radley, barefoot and shirtless, his knobby spine curved, working on the pile of papers stacked on his lap. Just that glimpse of him is enough to spark her, a seed of desire to mount him mercilessly and ride him again until he's completely drained.

Faye sighs from beneath a pile of sheets that smells of a sweet mix of Connor's body and the heady heights of their sex, of their panting breaths and their sweaty skins, two organic fabrics sliding smoothly over one another. It's the smell of their sweat-damp hair being grasped, sprouting between a knuckled fist and being tugged to one side. It's the smell of the slippery bits between each other's legs colliding. It's the glorious mess their bodies made together. Faye's skin shares the same scent, as does her breath. She can still taste his skin. Faye made a point not to shower or brush her teeth. She wants to sleep through the afternoon immersed in nothing but the remnants of their time together.

It isn't a particularly pleasant scent, not one that would ever end up in an air freshener. It's more of a pungent animal smell than a pleasant floral one, but it does take her mind back to when they were writhing, fighting against the end of their pleasure, fighting against it together but driving one another closer to it with each thrusting second. The taste in her mouth is a fermented one but one that constantly reminds her where it came from. These two things combined, biochemical aphrodisiacs, make her wet again, and she pinches her knees together, happy to be so overwhelmingly aware of her sex, feeling so alive because of it.

The balcony door squeals and squeaks as it shimmies open along its track. Faye closes her eyes to the sounds of the people and traffic passing far below on Roxy. Connor's coming. She hears him moving around out there, outside of her bedsheet cocoon. She hopes it's time for round three. Time to feel his wiry body wrap around her, the heat of his skin against hers. A warm breeze breathes clean air into the apartment and caresses the sheets encasing her. The balcony door is left open, the stale air quickly fading in the fresh; the noise outside is now let in.

"You have to go. Right now." Connor shakes the bed. "My girlfriend is coming up." His voice is manic. "Get your stuff and go. I'll call you later."

Faye lies there and then moans when Connor pulls the covers from her. She opens her eyes to see his face, upside down, leaning over her from the head of the bed. His eyes drift from hers to her body. Faye smiles, stretches leisurely for his benefit, and then reaches up, looping her arms around his neck. She pulls him down for a kiss, with which he complies, but she can feel it's rushed. It's a shallow, worried, and hurried kiss, an "Okay, I'll kiss you but you better haul ass outta here right after" kiss.

The spell her body holds over him is broken, and he bustles off, out of her line of sight.

Faye rolls over on the mattress and watches him for a moment. Then she climbs out of bed and puts on the jeans she had folded and piled on the thrift-store nightstand. She looks from one side to the other. She can't remember if she was wearing panties before Connor ravaged her, so in the end, she doesn't worry much about it. Panties or not, it doesn't matter to her.

Connor walks around the room with a plastic shopping bag hanging from one hand, the other loading it with the sporadic wadded tissues and skin magazines and foreign articles of clothing. In the kitchenette, he peels off a condom that's draped over the edge of the cutlery drawer. Pinching it between thumb and forefinger, he swings the rubber like the limp corpse of some fish ... a bright-green, sour-apple-flavored, ribbed-for-her-pleasure, one-dollar, bar-washroom-vending-machine fish.

If Faye ever were to wonder what she was doing with Connor, which she never has to do, she would just have to look at him to know. It's simple. He's the best sex toy a girl could ever want. God designed him as a tool with the sole purpose of making her come. He's a few years older and almost a foot taller than she is. He's thin with a tight sheath of skin covering an anatomy lesson of musculature. He's handsome, square-chinned, and perfectly hung for her tastes, pendulous but not gargantuan. He's strong enough to throw her around the room when she wants it that way but not so strong that he's a threat. Sometimes he can be an asshole, but she never questions her desire or asks more of him than what he can provide.

That's how she knows they're perfect for each other. Neither wants to change the other. It's all about using the right tool for the right job.

Never use a spoon to cut a steak, Faye thinks, looking around again at the mess.

"I can't find my shirt," she says. "Or my water bottle."

Connor sighs and grabs a pink nightshirt from the kitchen counter. "Here, wear this." He crosses the room. "And here —" He grabs her wide-necked sports bottle from the coffee table. It gurgles when he hands it to her. Faye slips the nightshirt over her head, finger-combs her hair back, and finds an elastic in her jeans pocket to secure it out of her face. She fixes it back in a ponytail.

Within a few minutes they are at the apartment door, Connor still shirtless and besweatpanted, Faye wearing jeans and the pink nightshirt. Him, shoeless with hairy toe knuckles, and her, slipping on her flats. Her hand rests on his shoulder for support, sliding down to his chest for balance. Her heart fluttering at the feel of his button nipple under her palm, him resisting heroically, though betrayed by the growth straining against his sweatpants.

Finally, to punctuate the moment, he leans forward to kiss her. He says, "Take the stairs, my girlfriend will be coming up in the elevator." Then, in response to her strained look, he begs with a drawn-out "Please."

Faye smiles, nods, and is two steps toward the stairwell door when he calls after her. She stops, smiles to herself, and spins on a heel to face him. The hallway lights flicker off, leaving her illuminated by the sunshine coming through the apartment door and him as an angular silhouette in the light.

"Faye, baby. Here," Connor says. The lights come on again, and he's holding the plastic shopping bag full of garbage out to her. The sticky sour-apple condom is pressed, flat and wet, against the opaque plastic.

"Could you drop this in the garbage chute on your way?" he asks.

CHAPTER
THIRTEEN

In Which Jimenez Dares to Disconnect the Blue Wire but Leaves the Red Wire Attached

There's a distant, repetitive clicking. It sounds like some agitated desert insect has wound up behind the elevator wall. Jimenez blows on the exposed end of a fine copper wire sheathed in black plastic and cocks his head to one side, listening and wondering if an insect infestation will be the next task scribbled on a service request and skewered on the metal spike on his desk tomorrow morning. He ponders the noise for a moment and then bends the end of the wire into a hook by curling it over the shaft of a screwdriver. He loops the hook over the thread of a screw in the elevator's service panel and tightens it until the wire makes contact.

The current flows, the gears grind, and the elevator doors slide open. The clicking noise stops, and Jimenez looks up from the panel to see Katie standing there, a gun finger pointing at the elevator button, hovering before the next poke of the up arrow.

Jimenez knows Katie, not conversationally or as a friend but he has seen her around and has always liked her. There were the times they passed in the lobby and said "Hi," and there was the time she locked herself out of the apartment and came to him, wearing only a pink nightshirt. Jimenez had averted his eyes to afford her privacy, but it had been hard not to gawk. He is fond of her, not in a romantic way but in wanting to protect her from the world. She's very pretty and always greets him when she passes him watering the plants in the lobby.

What she's doing with the *pendejo* from the twenty-seventh floor, he can't guess. Yes, that guy is tall and lithe and handsome and has straight, very white teeth, but it's obvious he doesn't love her — that and Marty has sent Jimenez to his door, twice in the past six months, to collect on bounced rent checks. Jimenez has also watched him cross the lobby with other girls. Jimenez saw how he touched their lower backs, an open palm at the base of their spines, just north of where the swell of their buttocks waned. There was no mistaking his intent, no way to misinterpret how he leaned in to talk to them, arching his body to whisper something sweet in their ears, the soft press of his breath against their skin, goose bumps rising from the sensual tickle of his words, more felt than heard. Probably the same words for each girl. Probably the same ones he used to trick the affections of this poor one now poking at the elevator button.

Jimenez thinks of loneliness and how it seems to harbor in good people like himself and this girl at the elevator door, this girl who's destined to find out the truth about her *pendejo* boyfriend and all the other women he's had up to that apartment at the top of the building.

Jimenez doesn't really know if Katie's lonely, but if she continues investing herself in guys like the one on the twenty-seventh floor, she will wind up there. There's such a fragile, thin veneer of illusion between the words "together" and "alone."

This girl is looking for her boyfriend and looking for the elevator to take her to him.

"Elevators are broke, lady," Jimenez says and thinks how, if he were younger and more handsome, he would ask her out for a coffee. Then, holding her hand across the table, a flaky pastry pushed to one side, he'd tell her everything about that *pendejo* and comfort her when she cried. He would buy her another pastry to make her feel better. There'd be crumbs in the corners of her mouth and tears in the corners of her eyes when he told her of the tough fibers of the heart and how they could grow so thin and ache without another. As she licked the icing from the fork, he would tell her how wonderfully those fibers thrum when they do finally find another who is like-hearted.

Instead of all this, he says, "They ain't going up or down. You gotta use the stairs."

Sometimes he curses his fumbling English. Sometimes he curses other people who can't understand the beauty of his Spanish when he speaks it, how eloquent and romantic his mind can be. Instead, he has to settle for this stumbling grammar and these inadequate words. Even though Jimenez speaks it well, he feels his ideas become trapped in a cage of English. He finds the

78

language very practical, but it's not made for the same beauty as his mother tongue.

"Oh," Katie says. Her face falls, and Jimenez's heart falls with it. He can see this is a compounding hurt, and instead of sheltering her as he wanted to, he has inflicted more. She's not disproportionally upset that the elevators aren't working. He can see that it's just one more thing piled on the others, making the weight of her problems an ever-growing burden.

"Sorry" is all he can offer.

"Not your fault," she says and waves a dismissive hand at the thought. "Thanks, I'll take the stairs."

He watches her go toward the stairwell entrance before the elevator doors slide closed, blocking out the world of the lobby. Jimenez stands for a moment, sighs, rolls his shoulders, and then looks at himself in the mirrors on either side of the elevator. They reflect him back and forth into a murky green infinity, reminding him that he's the only one in that depth of forever. He's alone in the mirror. He wonders if any of those other Jimenezes are unconditionally happy. With one last glance at the infinity of Jimenezes fading into an immeasurable distance, he turns his attention back to the elevator panel.

So it's not the black wire, Jimenez thinks, and his eyes stroll from one border of the service panel to the opposite one. There must be fifty wires here. None look loose, overloaded, or compromised in any way. All these tiny components work together toward making the elevator function, but when one fails, the whole thing screams to a halt. Jimenez scratches his head at how the simplest failure of one part could keep the whole complex machine from working.

That's if the problem is even here amid this nest of copper and plastic, he thinks.

The blue wire next, Jimenez thinks. If I go through each of them, one by one, I can rule out those that are live from the one that has a fault. It may take the rest of the afternoon and evening, but what else is there to do? Go up to my lonely apartment with its single bed, pull a frozen dinner out, and microwave it to an edible temperature? Then, leaving the lights off, sit in the strengthening darkness and watch the city lights flicking on as the sun fails, each illuminated window with someone behind it, eating supper or getting ready to do it all over again tomorrow?

I've got nowhere to be, he thinks. There're only fifty wires.

Jimenez unscrews the blue wire and pulls it from its connector. The elevator goes dark. Jimenez stands in the blackness for a moment before pulling his flashlight from his tool belt. He switches it on. The elevator is lit in a dull amber glow for a few seconds before it falls into darkness again. He shakes the flashlight, and it rattles a response. A dim beam flickers twice. The batteries are dead.

Jimenez pokes blindly at a few buttons on the panel, aiming for where he thinks the button to open the door is. Nothing happens. He systematically pokes his way through each button on the panel. Nothing happens. He gropes at the doors and tries prying the two sliding slabs by wedging his fingers in the gap and pulling them apart. He strains. They budge a bit, allowing a faint fingernail of light to break through from the lobby. Jimenez strains again. His fingers slip, and the doors slap shut. They are locked tight, and the darkness is complete again.

Jimenez curses under his breath and then draws his fingers slowly along the panel, feeling for the screw he removed the blue wire from. Once, his fingertip snags on a sharp metal edge, and then he thinks he finds it, the connector screw. He places the blue wire against it and there's a blinding flash of light and an electric snap. Jimenez jolts, his arm snaps tight in a contraction, and he drops the wire.

A single yellow spark flares, and the panel catches fire.

CHAPTER
FOURTEEN

In Which Garth Finds the Center of Unadulterated Loneliness in the Stairwell

Garth keys himself through the doors and into the lobby of the Seville. He bustles across the gleaming tile floor and up to the elevator doors. He draws up short and contemplates a small square of paper taped to the metal that reads, "It don't work. Fixed soon. Use the stairs." Garth looks around for someone to share this inconvenience with, a comrade to roll his eyes and shake his head with, but the lobby's empty. People pass by outside, a stroboscopic light flickering between their bodies as they move about their day.

Garth wishes he hadn't rented on the twenty-fifth floor. That's a lot of stairs to climb. Ground floor seems fine in this situation.

Then again, the climb will do me good, Garth thinks, trying to convince himself that this is okay. Not like I have anything else going on, and not like I can't do with the exercise.

And so, he makes his way to the stairwell, pushes through the door into the dimly lit column of stairs, and begins his ascent.

Garth climbs a flight and switches back, moving up the ascending zigzag, his backpack slung over one shoulder and the package wedged under his arm. He holds the handrail as he climbs, then pauses for a moment at the sign on the stairwell wall. It's a plastic sheet bolted to the cinder block under a bulbous, yellowed light covered by a wire cage. The light flickers off, plunging the stairwell into darkness. A scrabbling ruckus echoes up from the dark below. It's a panicked sound from somewhere farther down the stairwell.

The lights pop on again. Hazy, weak, and jaundiced at first, the shadows dance as they stutter to life.

The sign on the wall reads that it's the sixth floor. Nineteen to go. Garth puffs, shifts the package from under one arm to the other. The chore of climbing the building has taken a bit of the excitement out of the contents. No, Garth thinks. It just heightens the anticipation of his eager fingers fumbling with the tape that seals it closed to the world, revealing it slowly, peeling back one corner of the paper at a time. The anticipation is half of the excitement, he reasons.

And Garth carries onward, upward.

The shuffling, scraping noise from below grows louder and Garth pauses midflight to see what it's about. A kid goes sprinting by, springing up two steps at a time on skinny, coiled legs. He shoots the space between Garth and the opposite wall, narrowly missing both in the maneuver. He doesn't slow down or look back. He doesn't excuse himself or apologize.

"Easy there, kid," Garth calls, but the kid keeps running, disappearing around the next landing, out of sight and becoming only echoing noises of huffing breath, footfalls slapping, and the occasional grunt. He hears a door open and then latch shut, and again the stairwell falls silent. Garth absorbs the stillness for a moment.

After the explosive presence of the kid, the absence of movement in his wake strikes Garth with a deep hollow of loneliness. In the middle of a city, on a bustling street full of life, here alone in a concrete shaft encased by a building filled with people, a creeping sense of insignificance leaches into his mood as he renews his ascent. In every direction from where he passes the sign for the eighth floor, there are people. He's gift wrapped in a building of them. They walk above his head, sit below his feet, nap to his left, and pour a cup of tea to his right. Hundreds of them in every direction, yet he knows none of them. He knows nothing of their lives, and he knows none of their names. They're all strangers to him. Outside of this wrapping is a city full of them, a city spilling over with people, hundreds and hundreds of thousands of them. From his apartment window, he can see the buildings, lights stretching to the horizon as the sunsets, all those little dwellings so alone and stacked together, making up this city. Too many people to know and none know him.

This stairwell, he thinks, it's the center of unadulterated loneliness, and I'm in the middle of it.

How is it possible to barely know anyone in a world full of people? Garth wonders. How is it that no one really knows me after thirty-seven years? The paper package crinkles in the bag as he shifts it again from under one arm to the other.

That kid, he thinks, he just came and went. All I know is his skinny little legs and his red Cushes, and then he is gone. And what am I to him? A fat guy in a stairwell blocking the way to his computer games or his supper with his mom or wherever he was rushing to.

And then I'm gone.

Like I was never even here in the first place.

Garth draws a deep breath to steady his heart and gives the package a squeeze, pinching it between the crook of his arm and his torso. It gives a reassuring crackle in return. He takes it in both hands and gives it another squeeze. The softness compresses to a point, and then he can feel something solid and hard in the middle. He repeats the motion and decides he has to run up the remaining flights. He needs to move through this horrible space as quickly as he can. He needs to get to his apartment and recapture the full excitement he had felt before the stairwell sucked it out of him.

He runs.

A city full of people and a world full of billions, and this is who I am. How could there be only one me?

Who could I be if I weren't me? Garth wonders as he hoofs up the stairs. Who in these walls, who in the city but myself? Nobody knows this Garth, so what is to say the story would be any different for another Garth?

That little kid who ran by me a few seconds ago? That little kid is just starting out and getting to know the world. I could be just starting out again, learning of all the wonders and monotony and thrills and fears.

That young woman that Danny and I saw walking past at the construction site, that woman goes into the drugstore and buys . . . what? Buys chocolates and fashion magazines and whatever else a woman buys in a drugstore? If I were her, I would know how it feels to be stared at, to overhear snippets of Danny talking, knowing he's talking about me.

Is that any less a lonely place to be than having eyes pass you by entirely? Still nobody really knows you, not like you know yourself.

Garth pants and puffs. Within a few flights, his sprint up the stairs slows to a forced lumbering. The back of his shirt, even in the short exertion of three floors, is damp with sweat. He wheezes to bring enough air in. He's fat. He snorts derisively at himself, at his big body moving up the stairs, slowing with each step, running out of energy already.

I couldn't be anyone else, he thinks. I can't even imagine them, and I can barely be myself.

By the eleventh floor he has slowed to a plodding pace, one step at a time. When he reaches a landing between flights, he stops again to catch his breath. He pulls the package from under his arm and holds it in one hand. The black plastic bag has slid halfway off, exposing folded brown paper secured with a piece of clear tape at the join. The sweat from his armpit has soaked the paper a deep shade of chocolate in an elongate, uneven smear. He hopes none of his after-work, underarm smells have seeped through. He runs a flat hand over one side, smoothing out the wrinkles in the paper.

86

Garth smiles and starts moving again, ignoring his thrumming heart and strained breath. He carries onward, upward, past the sign that reads "Floor 12." By the sixteenth floor, he needs a rest again. A cramp has formed, stabbing him in the side with each breath he takes. He's too big and inert by nature to carry on like this without a break. He rests against the wall and leans forward to put his hands on his knees.

For a moment, he thinks about what would happen if his heart stopped right then. What would they make of him and the package? What would they make of his overexertion, his excitement so obvious it would transcend his death? He decides it wouldn't matter because he'd be dead and has never been egomaniacal enough to think that his meager legacy matters for anything or to anyone.

Garth huffs a deep breath and then continues, onward and upward.

CHAPTER
FIFTEEN

In Which Petunia Delilah Learns That Birthing Can Become Complicated and That Her Housekeeping Skills Could Use Honing

A film of perspiration slicks Petunia Delilah's forehead. Her body is stressed, involuntarily working on something, momentarily separated from her consciousness as it goes about its task.

Surely, Danny will call back quickly. She glances at her watch. He should be done with work by now, but maybe they had to finish something up. Maybe he just didn't hear the call over the noise of the construction site. It can be so loud she often hears them from the balcony. He'll notice the missed call, check his message, and come sprinting back to help her. She pictures him running up Roxy and dialing her number. His hard hat falls to the sidewalk behind him with a clatter, but he doesn't stop to get it. He's telling her he's a block away, he's in the lobby, he's in the elevator, he's at the apartment door.

"Baby," he would say, "this is the happiest day of my life and it's all because of you. I love you so much."

She dials the cell phone again, mashing the numbers that will connect her to her midwife, Kimmy, who lives with her partner a few blocks away, just off Roxy. Kimmy will help. Everything will be fine when Kimmy shows up. The baby will come, and Danny will run in to find her lying on the bed with his new child nestled against her bosom and her, finally, eating a fucking ice cream sandwich.

The phone rings five times. Just when she thinks it's going to go to voice mail, a tentative "Hello?" comes from the other end.

It's not Kimmy. Shit, Petunia Delilah thinks, what was her partner's name? Meg or Mel or something like that.

"Get Kimmy," Petunia Delilah grunts. "Tell her it's Pet, and she has to come help me, the baby's coming right now."

There are three dull beeps.

Petunia Delilah pulls the phone from her ear and glares at it. The screen is blank. She pokes a button and is rewarded with the image of an empty battery. She had neglected to charge it for days.

How much of that phone call got through? she wonders as she fumbles around the nightstand, frantic hands focused on finding her phone charger and cursing herself for letting the battery run down. Kimmy's probably trying to call her back right now. She lets out a blast of air from her nose, a snuffle of frustration at her oversight.

Surely, Kimmy will head over as soon as she gets the message. Even if she can't call back, Meg/Mel will tell her it sounded desperate. Kimmy'll grab her satchel and load it into the basket on the front of her bike. She'll pedal over the few blocks to the Seville, chain up her bike, and, with the focus of a trained professional midwife, dash through the foyer, rocket up the elevator, and burst through her apartment door, yelling, "Be calm. I'm here. Everything will be all right."

Petunia Delilah pauses, closes her eyes, and takes a deep breath as the next contraction seizes her body. Breathe through it, she tells herself in the dark behind her eyelids. Just like Kimmy taught you. There's a honk from outside, so she focuses on that. Distracting her mind from the mounting wave of pain of her body clenching. As it intensifies, she wonders if a home birth was a wise choice. Any kind of painkillers would be welcome right now, and the contractions have just started. Slowly the pain crests and passes. She opens her eyes again.

That wasn't so bad, she thinks. Now . . . where's the charger? Petunia Delilah glances at Danny's nightstand on the other side of the bed. It is not there. She riffles the sheets. The old science fiction book she was reading minutes earlier falls to the floor, and the bookmark she had loosely inserted slides from the pages.

"No," Petunia Delilah moans, looking at the bookmark and feeling like crying. She stands, staring, the bedsheets crumpled in one fist. She can't remember what page she was on.

"No," she says again, louder this time, and feebly slams her sheets onto the bed, which, being sheets, return an unsatisfying slamming noise. She can't even remember what was going on in the story, and she was just reading it.

The next contraction causes Petunia Delilah to drop the cell phone, which she was clutching in the death grip of her left hand. It causes her to double over and then fall to her knees, an automatic response of a body in pain desperate to find a position to alleviate it. Petunia Delilah finds that position on all fours, kneeling beside the bed, beside her dropped cell phone and the book. It's an animal posture, an indecent one, she thinks, but a somewhat relieving one.

Look at all the dust, Petunia Delilah thinks as, from this vantage, she can see under the bed. Weeks of debris have built up under there. There's a candy bar wrapper, a paper clip, an unopened condom, and tens of other bits silhouetted by the light coming from the other side of the bed. Since before her diagnosis of hyper-what's-it and her prescribed bed rest, she has not cleaned under there, and Danny sure as hell never has. An unopened condom? How long has it been since this place was cleaned? Since before the stick turned blue, at least. Come to think of it, Danny never helps with the cleaning, the bastard.

Petunia Delilah clenches her teeth as the pain mounts again, and she thinks, All that will change. He's not going to get away with it anymore. She pounds the floor twice with the heel of her hand. Her pain peaks, and she lets out an exasperated squeal and a sharp exhale. He's going to do his fair share from now on.

She opens her eyes, and there it is, under the bed, the phone charger.

Petunia Delilah grabs it and the phone and props herself into a kneeling position before using the bed as support in her struggle back to her feet. She stands for a moment, sadly contemplating the novel again before waddling down the hall toward the kitchen. It's the only place with a plug that she can reach without having to bend over. Maybe she'll help herself to a fucking ice cream sandwich while she waits for it to charge enough to use it. It couldn't do any harm now. The baby's coming anyway.

In the first few steps, however, she knows something is going horribly wrong. Never having gone through childbirth before, Petunia Delilah doesn't know how she knows, but she feels something inside her is amiss. While there are waves of contractions passing over her body, they're pretty close together already. They're also unsatisfyingly irregular and weak compared with what she has been told to expect.

Surely, she thinks, there should be some pressure from her nethers. So far, all the action is bodily, and there's not much sensation coming from down there.

As she passes the bathroom, she leans on the doorframe and flips the light switch. The lights flicker on and then blink out. She stands in the dark for a second before they come on again. In the mirror, her nightie drapes wet across her splayed knees. She's drenched in sweat, and she notices a shadow of stubble under her arm, her armpit exposed by how she leans on the doorframe. She wishes she had shaved that. She wishes she wasn't looking such a fright — surely the midwife will judge her unkempt and unhygienic. Then she thinks, It's Kimmy. Surely she's got hairy pits and a scruffy cootch.

Petunia Delilah feels so unattractive, though she recognizes this as a random, unfounded thought. She knows she's having a baby and nobody cares about armpit stubble, or dust under the bed for that matter, but she's felt so unattractive for so long it would be nice to just feel pretty again. She longs for a minute of attention to be on her, not just her womb. She wants to be seen as a woman again, not just some incubator with legs.

The next contraction is upon her. She leans forward, both arms stiff and grasping the edge of the sink. She lets the phone and charger slide into the basin with a clatter, scared she will crush them if she keeps them in her hand. The battery pops out of the back of the phone and rattles around against the porcelain. In the mirror, through the part in her hair, her scalp is bright red with the exertion. Her arms are knotted, tense cords of muscle. A string of spittle hangs from her mouth. A purple-green vein juts out of her neck, and another tracks a jagged ridge across her forehead.

As the contraction peaks, Petunia Delilah gives the sink a shake, rattling it against the wall. When the pain wanes, she reaches down to her thigh and walks her fingers against her skin, bunching up her nightie, inching it up with each finger stroke, until she holds the fabric gathered up in a hand. She draws the fabric above her belly and looks in the mirror, like she has many times in the past few weeks. Unlike those times though, she's not fascinated by what she sees, she is not intrigued by the shape of her belly or its contents, nor is she filled with a warm anticipation for the baby's arrival.

With the glance in the mirror, she knows the cell phone and the charger won't bring help to her in time. It will take minutes to get a minimal charge on the phone before she can even use it. Then, who knows how long it will be until help comes.

In the mirror, Petunia Delilah is pale and glossy, and she looks terrified. Her eyes are wide and puffy; her mouth is pinched and drawn, leaning with one arm against the sink and the other holding her bunched-up nightie above her waist.

In the mirror, at the hinge where Petunia Delilah's bowed legs meet, below her distended belly button, and protruding from the base of the dark tangle of her pubic hair is a single, waxy blue, tiny little foot with five perfect little toes.

CHAPTER
SIXTEEN

In Which Claire the Shut-In Immerses Herself in an Edible History

Ice-cold mineral water. So cold it needs to have little crystal shards floating at the surface. That's the trick Claire's mother passed on to her for the most exquisite quiche crust ever. There is none better. The recipe has been handed through generations of Claire's relatives, one to the next, lifetimes of experimentation and tweaking the mixture and adjusting the timing, and after decades, here it is, the perfect pastry.

She feels them with her in the kitchen; those daughters and wives and mothers, they are all with her whenever she makes the quiche. A yellowed index card with faded pencil markings passed from mother to daughter. A translucent spot on the card, an artifact from a specific moment in a sunlit kitchen when a drop of oil went astray. She feels them, just in from working the dusty fields of France, roughly milled flour dusting their hands as they work the crust. The recipe handed from grandmother to granddaughter on a blue-lined sheet of paper, rough along the edge where it was torn from the binding of a journal. A smudge in the ink where a grandmother wiped flour from the page with the side of her damp hand. Claire feels them under the coal-dust skies in the cities of a brand New World, stretching their fingers over a wooden rolling pin after a monthlong boat trip. The result of their recipe is an edible history.

Claire cleans as she goes. She brushes excess flour from the counter into the sink with a rectangle of paper towel. Her very first job as a teenager was working the chicken station at the fast-food place a few blocks from where her mother still lives. Her extensive training in chicken instilled a need for cleanliness. The clean-as-you-go mantra only grew more entrenched in her as time passed. That job was also the inception of her taste for men in uniform. Claire hasn't prepared or eaten chicken since she quit, but she has always dated men in uniform.

That's where she met Matt, her first crush. Matt lifted weights every day and was on the high school football team. Matt worked the same shifts that she did. He looked so good in his work uniform. The company logo bent so slightly around the curve of his sculpted pectoral muscle. An embroidered little man in a waiter's uniform dashed away from Matt's armpit and toward the cleft in his chest, carrying a burger the size of his head on a platter. Three embroidered steam lines on the logo implied the food was fresh and piping hot.

She watched Matt for hours across the kitchen from her chicken station. His wiry forearms, cables of muscle wrapped in smooth skin, rippled when he pulled patties from the burger steamer. She watched when he spun to put an order under the heat lamp. The way the poly-cotton-blend trousers stretched tight across the muscle of his buttocks when he twisted at the waist drew her eyes like quick movements draw those of a predator.

Claire looks at her arms. A fine dusting of flour and salt is caught in the sparse fuzz of blond hair. She stirs the ingredients in a large bowl, mixing it thoroughly and thinking about the span of time that has passed since Matt and how she looks older now even though it feels like not a week has passed. A twinge of melancholy catches in her stomach. The time has passed, she realizes. Every hour of it. Has Matt grown fat, lost his hair, or lost his tan?

Matt's tan was beautiful, accentuated by the tangerine glow of the heat lamp near the burger steamer. Claire pictured him, his tan in perfect contrast to the pale skin underneath his clothes. His visor and shirt lay crumpled on her bedroom floor. Those poly-cotton-blend trousers, a patty-smelling grease stain on the hip from where he always wiped his hand, were draped over the corner of the nightstand. He held his boxers in one hand, the musky scent of his heat-lamp sweat clinging to the fabric, and she just watched him. She would have him stand there, turn one way and then angle the other, so she could see him differently in the light streaming through her bedroom window. The way the light played across the bends and curves of his body was entrancing.

All she had to do was close her eyes and there he was, in uniform, placing a burger in the rack. His left forearm, the one he let hang out the car window when he drove, was a darker shade of bronze.

They had dated. They had taken their meals and breaks together, huddled in the tiny staff area near the back door with the sound of the cooler fan running behind their talking. One summer night, when they had propped open the door to the parking lot to try to cool down the kitchen, Matt sat on a plastic crate across from her, coloring a kid's meal place mat with crayons. It was a thick-lined map of the world. Matt shaded some African country orange.

"What country is that?" Claire asked.

"Don't know." Matt continued to color. Without looking up he asked, "Want to go there with me?"

Claire said she did and, because of her youth, it was easy to mean it. She would have gone with him. He drove her home after work that night. They kissed in front of her house. They felt each other's bodies through their uniforms, which still carried the smell of fast food, the scent of canola oil from the deep fryer.

Canola oil, Claire thinks. That's the other trick. Never use canola oil for the crust. A quarter cup of olive oil. It's a heavier, more brutish oil, but it brings a palette with it that the blank-canvas taste of the dainty canola oil lacks. Also, the fragrance of olive oil doesn't carry the same memories that the thin golden canola does.

It doesn't remind her of the string of unfulfilling men in uniform who followed Matt, nor does it remind her of how much time has passed since she felt that . . . thing inside her chest that she felt for Matt. She worries that the giddy, overpowering feeling of Matt has blackened, shriveled up, and blown away into dust.

The oven chimes that it's preheated. Then the power flickers, the lights go off, and the oven dies. As quickly as it happened, it hums back to life and the oven chimes again. The clock flashes a row of eights, and Claire starts poking buttons to reset it.

She and Matt were so young. The country he asked her to visit was Gabon. She looked it up. They never went to Gabon together. They didn't talk about it again. Instead, they went to different colleges in different parts of the country and drifted apart. Their geography just didn't work.

Then there were the uniformed men who followed. All wonderful in their own right, but none was Matt. None was as young or so captivating, and with each passing day, she found it harder to reclaim that immersion she had found in him. Claire realized it was a change in herself. She loved with less ease and more caution as the days passed by. She would no longer go to Gabon as she once would have when casually asked the question.

There was Peter, the ice cream guy with his gaily striped red-and-white uniform. His hands were always cool, and his eyes were full of light, as if he were a child. Ming, the mailman, sported a regal deep-blue uniform. He would leave before sunup and be home by noon. He had amazing calves, solid like rocks, and a lilting voice she could listen to for hours. Chuck, the hospital janitor, wore a stark, crisp white button-down shirt and linen pants. Claire loved the way he smelled. His skin like almonds, always fresh like after a shower.

And there was Ahmed, the security guard. His uniform was a sleek, tailored black. Ahmed made her nervous in a way she liked, but for only a short time. It was the way he would practice hand-to-hand combat in the mirror, shirtless, swinging his flashlight around like a baton and clubbing invisible assailants. Ahmed's violence had never transposed itself onto Claire, but she grew increasingly untrusting of its presence in the apartment. He did not take it well when she left.

Claire shakes Ahmed from her thoughts and glances at the phone. She thinks back on the strange call from the front door and tries to ignore the unease that settles over her.

"Gotcha, kiddo," the voice said just before the fast static noise that sounded like violence. Surely it was a misdialed number, but even so, it was from the front door, so close to home that she can't help but think that someone in her building was in obvious and serious trouble. It is unsettling, the thought of that so close to her. But what can she do?

The oven chimes again, reminding her that it's preheated to four hundred degrees Fahrenheit and awaiting a quiche.

CHAPTER
SEVENTEEN

In Which Homeschooled Herman Makes a Startling Discovery

Herman's heart hammers against his chest, battering against his rib cage with both fists. His shoe squeaks like a startled bird as he spins on the ball of his foot. The small plastic sign riveted to the cinder block wall reads "Floor 6." The lights blink off, the stairwell goes dark, and the sign blacks out of sight. Herman stumbles on a stair, and a thought flashes through his mind: Has it happened again? Am I still here? He grabs for the railing and finds it in the dark but not before grazing his shin on a concrete riser.

No, he thinks, I'm still here. The pain tells me so. He draws a quick breath through his teeth to fight off a yelp from his injured shin.

The lights flash on again, and with them, a mountain of a man blinks into existence half a flight ahead of him. The big man stops, leans on the railing, and then looks over his shoulder. He's huffing from the exertion of his climb. There are damp moats under his arms and a sweaty V shape between his shoulder blades. There's a gap between him and the wall, and without breaking his stride, Herman slides through that space between flesh and concrete. Herman's vision is jaunty with movement, but his mind is smooth with autonomic motion. It feels like he's floating, moving without thought, just pure action.

"Easy there, kid," the man says.

The voice fades to echoes behind Herman as he rounds the next landing and launches up another flight of stairs.

Herman knows he has to slow down soon. He isn't fit enough to be sprinting up stairs for too long. His attentions have always been geared toward the academic at the expense of the physical. This has left him weedy and weak. He always has believed the body to be an appendix, an organ that society has outgrown and civilization has now rendered useless in favor of the brain. He realizes now that this deduction was a mistake.

How could I have been so blind to sit out of every gym class? he thinks. Was "social dance" really too strenuous? He realizes now that one never knows when one needs strong legs.

Ten more floors, two flights of stairs each, twenty in total, Herman thinks, vaulting up the next flight. The distance isn't that far, but he feels like he can't cover it fast enough. His legs burn with exertion. His lungs strain to provide oxygen to his muscles. Herman knows something is wrong in his apartment.

Don't let it be true, his thoughts beg. A tear streams from the corner of his eye and traces a glistening arc over the curve of his cheek.

He can't remember the last time he felt such fear and anxiety. He wills his body not to collapse. He wills his mind to focus, cursing it as useless at this crucial point when it was needed more than ever.

As it often does, his mind starts releasing contorted images and filling in the gaps of time and place from his recent blackout. They filter back in disjointed bits and pieces, a puzzle he has to construct an image from. Herman remembers being upstairs, in the apartment. Grandpa was there, sitting in the living room, reading the paper. A cup of tea sat on the side table, releasing a wispy thread of steam into the late-afternoon light.

Herman was working on a trigonometry assignment Grandpa had given him. The calculations of angles and lengths flash through his mind as a series of numbers on a page. The memory of his desk, the page on it, the equations scrawled across the paper, some crossed out and others circled. The pencil strokes were clear and magnified, viewed from so close they were pockmarked, thick graphite lines striking out across the fibrous expanse of paper. The tip of the pencil was a waxy moon rock from this magnified perspective.

There was silence. The ticking clock in the living room, the street noise crawling into the apartment from outside, the whirring of the fridge's compressor from the kitchen, all those usual noises that the brain typically ignored, they were absent. It was all quiet outside. The only sounds came from inside Herman. Herman breathing. Herman's blood rushing in pulsing fits through his body. Herman inhaling as he pushed his chair back from the desk and stood. Herman huffing

103

and rasping his way up one flight and to the next. The sound of his breathing is exaggerated by the close spaces of the stairwell, reverberating off the hard surfaces. The sound of his pulse deafens his ears.

There are voices in the stairwell, coming from above or below he can't tell. What they're saying, he can't tell. Echoes contort the sounds. Voices bounce off the walls so many times that they become garbled and unclear. Voices thick in the air all around, his memory drags one out of the din and into clarity. It's his own voice in the silence of his apartment, sounding muffled in the flesh and bone of his own head, calling out after a moment's pondering.

"Grandpa," it said. Herman stood, waiting for a response that didn't come.

The quiet in the apartment was unsettling. All the sounds in the world had been turned off. The automatic sounds of the apartment, the clock, the bustle of the lady in the apartment next door, the ticking of the radiator, all were absent. Herman knew something was wrong. His body knew too. This breed of silence often came before the blackness.

"Grandpa? Are you there?" His voice was small.

Another moment passed.

Again, no response.

Herman dropped his pencil to the desk. It rolled across the piece of paper, tracking a kaleidoscope of scribbled equations before falling to the floor. It didn't emit the clatter it should have, just the motion. Herman heard his breathing, felt the friction of his chest, the constriction of the air passing through the hollows of his body.

The sign on the wall reads "Floor 15." Herman pushes the bar on the door, depressing the latch to release the bolt to shoulder the door and fly through the frame into the hallway. The lights are dim and the carpet is dark. Apartment numbers, brass numerals tacked to the doors, tick by his vision. As he runs up the hall, he grabs at his shoelace necklace and pulls the apartment key from under his shirt. The metal is warmed to body temperature, courtesy of its resting against his chest.

Herman wonders how he wound up in the elevator, how it had come to rest on the lobby floor, and, most important, why both of these things came to be. Those were the significant gaps in his recollection. The method and purpose of his movements during his blackout are still lost to him. However, he suspects he will find the reasons when he opens the apartment door.

The elevator.

He remembers the elevator didn't come when he pressed the button. He had wanted to take it to the lobby, but there were no sounds, no machinery noises in the elevator shaft, no wheels running or cables grinding behind the steel doors when he summoned it. Yet he was in the elevator on the lobby level when he awoke.

Herman remembers the apartment door isn't locked as he reaches for the handle. He left without locking it. That part he remembers as he flings open the door.

Herman runs past the hallway closet, past the kitchen, and into the living room.

Grandpa's reading light is on. Steam no longer rises from the teacup sitting on the side table. At that moment, his fragmented memory and his reality merge. He has been here in this place at this specific time before. He has traveled back in time to the point of his discovery.

Grandpa sits in his recliner, his newspaper in his lap and his arm draped over the side of the armrest. Anyone fresh upon the scene would see an old man who has fallen asleep reading the paper in his favorite chair. Herman has been here before though, and the reading lamp casts Grandpa's slack mouth and stubble-covered chin in a high-contrast, wrinkly death mask.

Grandpa's dead, Herman remembers. And it's my fault.

Herman blacks out. His body hits the floor with the carelessness of the completely unconscious.

CHAPTER
EIGHTEEN

In Which Ian Learns of the Final Betrayal of His Body

We left the little nugget of Ian's body pinned perilously to the sky, hanging somewhere in the nothingness alongside the twentieth floor of the Seville on Roxy. We left him contemplating, in the fleeting way that only a goldfish can, his species' desire for freedom and the golden era of that quest for new territory, the early days of fish rainings. We also left him stoutly resolute that jumping from the balcony was a sound and reasonable choice for a goldfish to make.

And so, just one drop in the torrential downpour of fish rainings, Ian continues his descent. However, what started off as a leisurely tumble through the air has quickly become a more harrowing and dreadful experience. Having passed through the strata of Connor Radley's thesis, he has no further aesthetically pleasing distractions like those peaceful pages still fluttering around above him. Ian catches glimpses of the pages up there, flickering on and off as they waft in the breezeless, failing afternoon light. It's a peaceful image that's in stark contrast to the feel of the wind shear buffeting Ian's lateral line, the pinstripe of sensory epithelial cells that runs down the length of every fish's body.

The lateral line is, firstly, a physiological adaptation to sense changes in water turbulence and aid in schooling with fellow fish. Coincidentally, and still unbeknownst to science, it's also a means to judge airspeed. The feeling of the wind on his lateral line is not unpleasant. It's akin to being in the middle of a big school of fellow fish. A warm feeling of brotherhood and camaraderie floods through Ian's mind, and if his musculature were equipped to smile, he would. While incapable of higher thought, Ian is reactionary on a base level, and the feeling of friendship and family is something he understands.

Presently, Ian twists sidelong to the ground. By the nature of his physiology, this leaves one eye staring at the wide-open sky, with its fluttering pages and balconies passing by, and the other eye on his destination, the hard ground below. In turn, this leaves his brain conflicted. Is he to be calmed by the peaceful enormity of the crystal-blue sky and the beautifully clear day? If this is the case, Ian wishes he had eyelids to squint against the brilliance of the late-afternoon sun. Alternately, is he to be in absolute terror of the approaching sidewalk? If this is the case, Ian wishes he had eyelids to close in fright against the impending doom. Ian isn't sure which he is supposed to feel. The result is a middling emotional state, that fine point between absolute panicked fear and complete transcendental calm.

Seven stories have passed since Ian began his descent, and already he is moving at quite a speed. He has fallen roughly a quarter the distance between his bowl and the pavement. Rounding up by a few milliseconds, that is roughly one second into his fall. In this short distance, he has already reached a speed of twenty-two miles per hour. To this point, there's a steadily building headwind, which Ian finds increasingly uncomfortable, primarily due to its drying qualities. Again, he finds his lack of eyelids and tear ducts to be quite a disadvantage.

In the manic shaking and trembling of his vision induced by the fall, his earthbound eye registers something interesting far below on the street. It offers a welcome distraction from the gumbo of confusing sensations he experiences. Ian sees flashing red lights strobing the building-shadowed street below.

When did that get there? he wonders. Has it always been there, or did it just arrive?

The lights are attached to a little box with large black numbers painted on the roof. An ambulance has pulled to the curb in front of the Seville. Traffic on Roxy has slowed in response, clotting up as it approaches the vehicle and then freeing up afterward. The aesthetic grips Ian's mind for the moment. The perspective of it fascinates him. From this height, there's a reassurance from a vehicle that indicates dire trouble, attesting to the fact that, from a distance, even a disaster can look peaceful.

The bustle below has slowed, calmed in the presence of the emergency vehicle, creating a coursing, multicolored thread of cars free to flow once past the ambulance. Somewhere, there's an injured person or some other crisis. Viewed from up here, the spinning bank of red lights is tranquil, rhythmically flashing off the shadowed metal and glass and concrete and all the other hard surfaces below. They say that help has arrived. Cars slow to a crawl, and the little specks of people walking the sidewalk mill about. They stop in groups and wonder what is going on.

Ian can see the clusters of them. He wishes that Troy the snail were with him to share the sight. Even though Troy is infuriatingly dim-witted, Ian feels that he would have liked to see this and would have enjoyed the experience.

Ian is torn from the scene when, as he falls past the eighteenth floor, he discovers the final betrayal of his body. His instinct for freedom has led to several such revelations so far. Even in the short second of his flight, the experience has been more edifying than the months he spent in his bowl. He not only has found that he can't breathe in this atmosphere but also that eyelids are handy devices and evolution has left him ill prepared for flight. Now he learns that the aerodynamic nature of his body, which allows him to slice through water so effortlessly, with the right amount of wind shear transforms him into a streamlined, nose-down golden rocket. It pushes his tail to the sky and forces his head ground-ward. The turbulence compels his body to wiggle in a fashion not dissimilar to swimming in a strong current. No longer does he tumble. His descent

110

becomes much more sinister and direct through the shrieking air.

He can no longer see the bright-blue sky or the milling, growing crowd below him. He's bracketed by buildings, towers of concrete, metal, and glass screaming by, and can't see anything save the blurred and rhythmic tick-tick of the balconies and windows passing by from nose to tail. With the speed and determination of a bomb, he plummets past the seventeenth floor into another, terrifying cycle of his memory.

In this cycle, Ian thinks, Now . . . what was I doing?

He will again realize that he's falling, and within moments, he will meet the sidewalk at the building's entrance.

CHAPTER
NINETEEN

In Which Our Heroine Katie Finds the Magic of Love in the Cleaning Supply Room Under the Stairs

Life and all the sounds associated with it are muffled and distorted in the stairwell. The concrete walls act to trap the noises in and keep all the other life noises out. Katie thinks of her heart in the same way. It lets in the love and the pain, and it doesn't let anything else through. She has never truly gotten over her past heartbreaks. Every time, her heart just cracks a little more. It never heals; it's something she has just learned to live with.

She met Connor during his office hours in his tiny, shared office under the stairs in the anthropology department. It was a dusty old building built more than a century ago, a collage of crumbling honey-colored brick, rippled glass windows, and the incongruous modernity of air-conditioning units and energy-efficient lighting.

Connor's office was tucked in a ground-floor corner of the building. There were two desks, one crammed under the sloping rise of the underbelly of the staircase and the other wedged between a couple of vertical pipes. One pipe consistently radiated heat, and the other made trickling sounds whenever someone flushed a toilet or ran a tap in the men's washroom on the floor above.

There were books stacked on every flat surface, photocopied papers piled on the floor, and coffee cups scattered in a random constellation around the room. It was stuffy and musty with the smells of dust and old paper. The lighting was dim and yellow, cast from two desk lamps and a weak, naked bulb overhead. There was no number or name emblazoned on the office door, just the worn stenciled words "Cleaning Supplies."

The door was open, but Katie still knocked.

Connor spun in his seat to face her. "Welcome." His eyes lit up when they fell upon her. "Come in."

"Your office is hard to find," Katie said and took a step into the cramped room. Connor smiled and stood, crouching slightly because his height exceeded that of the ceiling. He took her proffered hand and shook it when Katie introduced herself.

He said, "I know who you are."

It felt good that he knew her because there were more than three hundred students in the class. It made her feel less lonely in the crowd. They stood closer than strangers normally do because of the cramped quarters. They stood close enough that she could feel his breath on her skin. It smelled like spearmint, or perhaps it was bubble mint, Katie thought.

"Yep, crammed under the stairs. An obscure space for two obscure grad students working on obscure projects," he said and smiled again, his lips a perfect bow backed by straight white teeth. "They don't know where to put me, so here I am, tucked out of sight with Lonnie."

He gestured with his chin at the guy sitting at the desk wedged under the lowest part of the stairs. Katie hadn't noticed he was there, working silently in the laptop-screen glow. Her eyes had been on Connor the whole time. Connor still held her hand.

Lonnie looked like he had been at that computer for days without even taking a break for a shower. He behaved as if she and Connor weren't there, to the point he passed gas in the tiny space. It could only have been Lonnie. Katie knew from Connor's reaction it wasn't him. Lonnie carried on pecking at the keyboard as if nothing was amiss.

With a wince at the fouled air, Connor asked, "Do you want to go somewhere else? Maybe I can buy you a coffee?" And with those words, so began Katie's next adventure in love.

Katie slips from her reverie when the Seville stairwell goes dark. It's as pitch as only a windowless concrete column can be. In the dark, she refuses to now think of Connor as her next downfall, her next failed relationship. She will not wind up at her mother's house, sitting late into the night, sobbing out vague, monosyllabic questions like "Why?" and "How?" — questions to which she knows there are no answers.

114

No, there is every possibility that Connor will say, "I love you," back to her. It isn't out of the realm of reason that he has been repressing the expression of his feelings. Some people are so in love they can't say it because they're afraid to scare off the objects of their affection with the intensity of their emotions. Some people are timid about sharing themselves, as if it makes them weak or vulnerable. Maybe Connor is that guy, vulnerable and shy.

The stairwell lights come back on.

Katie sighs at the sign in front of her. "Floor 8." She takes the next flight of stairs two at a time, the plastic bag from the pharmacy swinging from her hand. There are noises, people moving above her in the stairwell. She leans over the railing and peers up, the spiral of railing ascending into a fuzzy space far overhead.

They had gone off campus for a coffee. Katie had asked all her questions about the upcoming exam on the short walk to the coffee shop. Connor had answered her diligently and attentively, seeming to want to help her more than anything. By the time they had settled into their chairs with steaming cups resting on the table between them, the sun was setting and the shop was bustling with the dinner crowd.

"I loved that dog," Connor said, his voice raised over the clamor of other conversations. "And when he got hit by the bus, I cried for, shit, must have been a week at least."

Katie made a sympathetic mewling even though she was smiling. She reached a hand across the table and put it on his.

115

Connor looked at Katie and chuckled. "Why are you laughing? It was really traumatic."

"No, no," she said but still couldn't wipe the smile from her face. "It's not that. It's just so horrible. And to get hit by the school bus. I can see you, little kid Connor, all sad and alone. It's terrible."

"That was the loneliest summer of my life. There really weren't any other kids in the neighborhood my age. Mostly just old folks. My parents had me late in their lives. I was a surprise. That's how my mom put it. That word doesn't have the same connotations as 'accident' does."

"You poor guy," Katie remembers saying. "And your parents didn't get you another dog."

"Nope," Connor said. "They saw how hard it was for me to get over Ian, and I think they thought I couldn't survive the death of another pet. They were probably right."

She went back to Connor's apartment that night. After they had writhed together, after he had fallen asleep, she lay awake with her hand on his head, his soft hair sprouting between her fingers, and thought she might fall in love with him. And she did. How could she not? He seemed perfect. He was handsome and seemed to have a great heart. A good guy, a little down-and-out but so willing to give his all for her to make her happy. That's how it seemed then, but as time passed, she has craved a more concrete affirmation of her affection.

Connor doesn't have much, but he does what he can with it. The fact that he gives so completely and willingly when he has very little to give makes it seem so much more significant. Just last night, she brought a bottle of wine, and they stayed up drinking and talking into the night. Then, with some soft music playing in the apartment, they dragged his mattress across the floor and positioned it in front of the balcony door.

"I want us to do it among the stars," he told her. "This is the best I can do halfway between the ground and the sky."

It was romantic. He seemed ashamed he couldn't offer more, but what he did offer was more than enough. There, held aloft by the Seville on Roxy like an offering to the sky, they made love. Afterward, she noticed that the city lights were too bright and she couldn't see the stars. It didn't matter though; they lay in each other's arms and looked out over the twinkling city instead.

"I love you," she said. Her heart tumbled, nervous in her chest. She wanted to hear the words back. After all they had shared, there was no reason he shouldn't be able to say the words.

Connor grunted a satisfied and unconscious noise. It seemed, though he had been awake a moment before, now he was deep asleep.

CHAPTER
TWENTY

In Which the Villain Connor Radley Sees the Signs and They Are Everywhere

Connor watches Faye wander down the hall. She seems unsteady on her feet, like she's distracted, dreamy, or drunk. He likes the way her ass fills her jeans, how it moves with her unsteady gait. He especially likes the crease in the material at the base of her buttocks. He sighs before taking two steps backward into his apartment and closing the door.

Connor takes a deep breath and turns to confront the mess in the apartment. He picks up a wandering path of dog-eared pornography, errant clothes, and miscellaneous garbage from the apartment door to the balcony door. By the time he gets there, he has a garland of unopened condoms draped over his arm, a bundle of clothes tucked between his elbow and his hip, and a bouquet of tissues wadded up in his hand.

He pauses at the view out the balcony door.

Ian swims in his bowl, tracking lazy circles in one direction and then, seemingly on a whim, switching to the other. The snail is a brown dot halfway up the glass.

Ian stops to peck at it a few times and then continues his swim. The castle sits as a reminder of harder, more primitive times, not that castles were ever pink, made of plastic, or sunken into the ocean.

Connor revels for a moment in the absurdity of the castle, the miniature archers manning the walk, puzzling over how their tiny arrows could take down this giant goldfish floating by their walls.

The thesis papers stacked on the fishbowl ripple in a stirring of air, weighted in place by the coffee mug against the gentle pull and push of the breeze.

Connor sniffs the air in the apartment. It stinks of hours of sweat, exertion, and spunk. He decides against sliding the door closed. It's as warm outside as it is inside anyway. He stands with his hand on the door handle, looking out on the balcony. Something is amiss and keeps him stuck in place, puzzling him into inaction.

What is it? he wonders. There's something deeply wrong here, and I can't put my finger on it.

The fresh air washes over him and into the apartment, as if it is attempting to cleanse all that has happened there since he moved in. It brushes past his naked skin, an invisible caress stroking him. Connor takes a deep breath and closes his eyes, attempting to clear the scene from his mind, clear his palate so he can see it with refreshed eyes and pinpoint the problem. He exhales fully and opens his eyes to scrutinize the balcony again.

It's a simple scene before him and nothing that should cause him such concern, especially considering the state of the apartment at his back. But for some reason it cripples him.

The mug reads, "Paleoclimatologists do it in the dirt."

He is filled with such deep self-reproach that he thinks of leaving the apartment and never coming back. Whatever is out there on the balcony makes him want to flee, to just go to the elevator, press the down button, and ride it to the lobby. He'd drop his keys in the super's mailbox, shoulder through the front door, and keep walking. Across the street, across the neighborhood, past the city limits, and right on across the continent, walking away from everything he has and, by association in his mind, everything he is. Walking past highway truck stops and billboards for casinos, past small-town corner stores and dusty gas station parking lots. Eventually he would reach an ocean town, cross the sand-sprinkled boardwalk and ribbon of beach, and just keep going, wading out into the water until the sand dropped away beneath his feet. Then he'd swim, the water turning from a pale blue to black as the continental shelf slid away, plunging into the hollow depths full of unknown monsters, the alien kinds with dangly bioluminescent baubles hanging from organic filaments before their eyes. His body would become a mere speck of humanity hovering over an almost infinite depth of nothing. His movements would be so small in the water that, no matter how violently he thrashed, they'd have no impact. His legs would kick themselves into exhaustion, and eventually he'd fade into nothing, disappearing as if he never even happened.

Then Connor figures out it isn't the apartment he wants to flee; it's something much more difficult to escape. He wants to flee himself. As soon as he realizes this, he knows it's the coffee mug that makes him feel this way. That kitschy custom mug with a dried coffee kiss on the rim.

The mug was a gift from Katie. Not from any of the other girls. She had it made at a specialty place where they also print novelty shirts, buttons, and stickers. Ian's also a gift from Katie. She bought the fish for him after he told her about his dog and growing up alone in a community of retirees.

And now she's coming up the building to see him, riding the quivering elevator to his door. She wants to see him, wants to know more about him. She cares about him. And while she's riding the elevator up, Faye's descending the stairs. His infidelity is safely secret.

Connor turns his back to the balcony and sees the empty bottle of wine on the kitchen counter. Katie had brought it. They drank it together and then pulled his mattress to the balcony door to look out at the thousands of city lights in the dark. Connor told her that he wanted to make love to her under the stars, but the city lights were too bright to see them.

Sure, he'd still banged her there on the mattress on the floor in front of the glass doors. He had wanted them to be near the window because he thought the couple in the next building over was watching them through the telescope he had seen in their apartment. And the couple in the apartment across the way *did* watch them doing it. Twice. But he and Katie had talked late into the night after they both came, and he had fallen asleep to the soft music of her voice.

A tea bag sits on the side of the sink.

The next morning she made tea before she went to work.

Now, the reminder of her sits there in a salt flat moat of Earl Grey residue.

These pieces of her are around all the time. Everything reminds Connor of her.

She's here in the waxy yellow Q-tip in his bathroom garbage can and the strand of hair on the tile in the shower. She's here in the glamour magazine draped over the edge of the couch. They'd done the "Are you too picky about your guy?" quiz together. Katie, yes. Connor, no.

Connor's stomach clenches with regret. How could he have missed the point? He is a tiny archer in the pink castle watching the giant goldfish float past the turrets. It is so obvious. The continental shelf, the infinite black below, the inconsequential speck of him in the vastness of it all; him, he could be so much more with her. With her, he wouldn't walk away. With her, he was safe and at home floating in the deep black below.

All of this stuff she has left in his apartment, the constant reminder of her presence in his life, makes this ocean a little less lonely. And looking at it all, he finally realizes he doesn't mind any of it. She has been in his life for such a short time, but all of these bits of her

122

make something bigger. She is the most beautiful and wonderful thing, and how could he not have seen that?

Why does Faye even exist in my life?

Why is there a Deb in it, also?

He looks at the porno magazines in one hand, the tissues in the other, and they tell him that he has wronged her. They highlight his shame and make him long to be better for Katie. They make him realize he is committed to her.

What's wrong with me that a Katie isn't enough?

Faye, great in the sack, sure.

Deb, very great in the sack, legendary.

Both of them are. That is it. Nothing more. The only difference is that one is a blonde and one is a ginger. Deb and Faye, interchangeable bodies with varying availability.

Katie, also great in the sack, beautiful, with a laugh that never fails to make him crack up, and, he thinks, she could really be something more. Connor thinks back to when they dragged the mattress in front of the window and talked, looking out at the city night. There was no struggle to fill the gaps in their conversation. There was no trial of thinking of something to say. In fact, it was three in the morning before he knew it.

That means something, right?

Looking around the apartment, there are so many more pieces of Katie scattered about his space and he likes it. That has never happened with a woman before.

So why do Faye and Deb exist in my life?

His reaction to Katie calling and coming up exposes what is important to him. It reflects what he truly feels.

He couldn't get caught with Faye because it would hurt Katie, which means that Katie is more important than anyone else and that is something that hasn't happened before. Ever.

Could this be what love is about? Connor wonders. He wonders if this could be a sign, an abrupt "This is love" in flashing neon.

Or is love more gradual? Something a person grows into.

Is it a sign? I need a sign.

Then the apartment goes silent. The bedside lamp goes dark. The fridge's compressor stops running. There's a distinct silence that falls over the building, more of a feeling than a lack of noise. The quiet buzz of everything electrical is gone, not that it was noticeable in its presence, but it is definitely noticeable in its absence.

Connor listens to the traffic hum far below on the street.

Connor knows something is wrong with him.

Connor knows something has to change, but he has only just started to figure what that is.

The floor lamp in the corner of the room comes on again, and the fridge clicks and starts to whir. The stove clock flashes a row of green eights.

I love Katie, Connor thinks. And I have never been so sure of anything before.

CHAPTER
TWENTY-ONE

In Which the Evil Seductress Faye Discards the Remnants of Her Love and Begins a Very Long Descent

Faye opens the door to the garbage room. Its hinges squawk horribly, and the handle is tacky with filth. It swings shut again behind her, and she wipes her hand on the pink nightshirt. The walls are painted an off-white color and sport variously hued smears and stains splattered with increasing density near the metal trapdoor in the wall blocking the garbage chute. Faye lifts the hem of the pink nightshirt and uses it as a glove to open the trapdoor. She gags on the smell that emanates from the darkness below. It's a warm, fetid exhalation that breaks like a rotting liquid against her face.

She drops the garbage bag into the chute. The sight of the sour-apple condom, wet and plastered against the side of the opaque plastic bag as it disappears into the offal of the dark chute, makes her yearn to wash her hands. The soft sound of the bag bouncing from wall to wall fades, and Faye lets the handle slip from her grasp. The trapdoor bangs shut, the sound amplified in the small space. Faye uses the hem of the nightshirt again to open the door, and when she steps into the hallway, she takes a deep breath and lets it out through her nose, trying to expel the sticky smell in her nostrils.

Faye follows the signs to the stairwell. She has never been in the stairwell of the Seville and no wonder — Connor's on the top floor. She always takes the elevator, but this time she will take the stairs, just as Connor asked, just so she won't risk a chance run-in with his girlfriend.

Not that I would be able to tell her from any other chick I see in the building, Faye thinks.

Faye knows of her existence, and she knows her name because Connor talks about her, but she has never even seen the girlfriend. In her mind, Katie is a generic girl with legs and arms and breasts and eyes and hair. Nothing more specific than that.

Faye knows Connor has other women on the go in addition to herself and this girlfriend. It doesn't bother her much as their relationship is strictly physical. Faye has other lovers on the table too. She talks about them openly in front of Connor just to see him squirm, which he does.

Faye believes there are different people out there for different reasons, each serving a purpose in her life. No one could be expected to satisfy her every need. Some are great to talk to, and some are great to go to bed with. Some are there to help her move heavy stuff, and some are meant to go to the movies with. She thinks herself too complex and men too simple for her to be tempted by any single one of them . . . exclusively.

126

Twenty-seven floors' worth of stairs to the lobby, Faye thinks as she steps onto the landing. She wonders why she agreed to hike down the building. Connor will pay for this. This and having to play garbagewoman are the limits of her affections for him.

No, she thinks, not affections, more lust. They are the limits of her lust. "Affections" implies there is something deeper than the simple physical attraction they share, something more than their bodies periodically colliding.

She lets a sigh escape into the stairwell, and the stairwell sighs back to her. To her right is one half flight heading up to a trapdoor to the roof. There's a latch and a padlock on the little hatch. To the left is the beginning of her descent, wide open and spiraling downward. Leaning over the rail and looking down the column of space between the flights of stairs, an Archimedean whorl of handrail stretches out below her and shrinks with the depth. She catches a glimpse of a hand grasping the rail several floors below. It was a flash, gone as quickly as it had appeared, and it makes her wonder if the fleeting appendage existed in the first place or if it was a trick of her mind.

Twenty-seven fucking floors, Faye thinks as she takes the first step. She wonders if she should count them all and hold that number against Connor for some reward. Then she thinks twice of counting stairs, even for one flight. It would get boring. Totally not worth it. She can make him pay without the final count.

"Take the stairs," he said.

"Fuck off" was her initial reaction, but she had stayed that in one of the few bouts of self-control she could remember suffering.

Normally, Faye would have told Connor off, but he had been so cute, his face begging, his body all sexy and lanky like some sweaty man-animal bike courier after a long August shift. His skin coated with a matte of old sweat from their grappling. The curves of his musculature and the way his sweatpants hung off his hips, no shirt, and desperately pleading on top of that. It was hot. *He* was hot, and his body was amazing and those sweatpants were packing heat.

She swishes one knee past the other as she descends, just to remind herself of the feeling of him, the feeling of his pressure on her inner thighs.

Connor's only one of three current lovers. There's that guy in the university library. Faye isn't sure of his name, but he's always in the psychology section, at that study corral in the corner that's blocked from the stacks of books by a fabric partition. He has round, wire-framed glasses and always has a well-groomed beard to accentuate his sharp jawline. He's always reading books and is so sexy in a geeky way. They never talk, just fuck quickly and quietly behind that partition. It's the library after all.

Then there's Janine at the pool. Faye had never dug on a chick before, but she does on Janine. Janine's so civilized except that she makes shrieking animal noises when they have sex. Like a baboon. She has an amazing body too, toned by swimming miles every day, one pool length at a time. Sometimes, Faye goes to the campus pool to see if Janine's there, which she often is. Faye sits in the bleachers and watches the smooth, repetitive motion of her cutting through the water. Sometimes they swim together, no talking, just the cathartic repetitions of movement and the burbling whisper of water past her ears. It calms her mind. Janine is a great break because Faye's beginning to find men exhausting.

And then there's Connor, whom she finds exhausting in every way, both good and bad and sometimes both at the same time.

Faye inadvertently moans at the memory of him as she passes a plastic square affixed to the wall that reads "Floor 21." She unscrews the lid from her water bottle and takes a swig. There are noises of other people in the stairwell. There are murmurs and footsteps and the muted metallic rings of hands slapping the banister. There's the soft scraping sound of Faye screwing the lid back on the water bottle. She wipes her mouth with the back of her hand.

She can't tell if the sounds are above or below because the noises bounce around the concrete walls so much. She adds another satisfied sigh to the sounds. She smiles. Nobody could mistake that noise; it's the full-bodied sigh of postcoital satisfaction, and Faye wants people to know she just had one of the longest, hardest, and most epic fu —

Faye stumbles midflight. A shot of adrenaline shocks her heart, and she grasps the railing. Her water bottle falls from her hand and bounces a punctuated clatter down the steps. She steadies herself and then chuckles at her distraction.

The clatter of her water bottle stops abruptly.

"Are you okay?" A voice comes from the landing below.

Faye looks down to see a large, round man standing there. He's clutching a package to his chest with one arm and holds her water bottle in his other hand. His toes are slightly turned in, giving him a nervous, childlike stance, which is in conflict with his size, his scruffy facial hair, and his massive arms.

"Yes," Faye replies, "I just lost my balance for a moment. Missed a step."

"I know what you mean," the man says. "That's all it takes."

CHAPTER
TWENTY-TWO

In Which Jimenez Witnesses a Spontaneous Creation in the Blackness

The fire starts as a blue electrical flash the size of a pinhead. It's a tiny, perfect nova with a halo of light and star's arms stretching out in four directions. It emits a simple crackling pop. The noise reminds Jimenez of his *abuelita*'s old transistor radio. It popped and crackled the same way when she turned it on to listen to the news most nights after dinner. Within the elevator, it's a modest sound considering the magnitude of its consequence.

The spark seems to float in the darkness of the elevator compartment, hovering in midair and geometrically reflected outward for an eternity by the mirrors. There, it makes its own cerulean constellation, an array of bright-blue dots stretching out to infinity, uncountable brilliant spots giving depth to the complete black. It's a spontaneous creation in the dark. Had the mechanics behind its origin been unknown, it would have seemed miraculous in both existence and beauty.

But Jimenez knows the reason for it sharing this space, and he is scared.

When the reason for a thing's being is illuminated, it doesn't hold the same mystery it does when it is unknown, which is both a wonderful and a horrible revelation. It's wonderful because it's like peeking into the universe and understanding a tiny bit of its complexity. It's also horrible because a little bit of magic is removed from the world with each discovery.

The electric shock that comes with the light causes Jimenez's arm to seize. The current passes through his muscles from fingertips to shoulder, then travels a course down the side of his body to the floor, painfully locking them all for a moment. In that contraction, Jimenez drops the wires. He regains control over his arm and shakes it out to the side, as if to flick off the residual electricity and to reassert control over that which is his. What's left behind is a burning muscle exhaustion that aches deep in his tissue. But Jimenez has little time to contemplate his arm.

Within seconds, the spark blossoms. The pinhead of light swells to the size of a match's flame. The elevator doesn't remain dark for long. The flame illuminates the elevator compartment in a blinding contrast of deep shadow and harsh light that bullies the colors from Jimenez's vision and forces him to squint against its brilliance. It continues to grow from there, sprouting fingers and tongues, a living creature licking the space for anything to fuel its hungry growth. It travels a short way up the wall, feeding itself and leaving a black charred waste in its wake. It crackles and sparks as it goes.

Jimenez pulls his work gloves from his back pocket and swats at the flame. With each swipe, it seems the fire dodges to the side and works to defend itself, to grab the gloves and envelop them in a wave of flame. But it never seems able to gain a strong enough grasp of them. It flares in defiance and spawns bits of flaming debris that fall to the floor. Jimenez stomps on the debris while continuing to bat the fire with his gloves.

Jimenez can see clearly now. The blackness is replaced by the firelight and by the reflection of it in the mirrors. The small compartment quickly heats up, and his brow beads with sweat. In the compounded light, he lashes out, swiping at the fire again and again. The flames growl and strobe with each stroke. They fade and flare and snarl at the attacks. Jimenez's sleeve momentarily erupts in flame but is extinguished by a quick and violent shake.

The air rapidly becomes opaque in the flickering light. A cloud of acrid smoke rolls to the ceiling, at first a delicate, curling wisp, then an inch thick and then quickly a foot deep. Jimenez coughs and holds his arm across his face, the crook of his elbow to his mouth, breathing through the cloth. He relentlessly continues his assault with the other. The smoke is vile, industrial chemicals choking with burning plastics. It's thick and biting in his throat, gagging him every time he tries to inhale. Hacking and sputtering for breath, Jimenez is forced to his knees as the cottony layer of smoke roils its way down from the ceiling of the elevator compartment. Short moments later, he has to crouch so his head is not fully in the cloud.

In a few more seconds, he knows, he will succumb to asphyxiation. It won't take long, Jimenez thinks; this space is so small, and the air is so poisoned.

When they find me, he thinks, it will be with blackened work gloves in my hand and a charred sleeve. They'll find me, my eyes red and swollen from irritants, and I'll be either partially or fully charred, depending on how hungry this fire really is. They will say, "He fought a good fight, but it wasn't enough." Then they will ask, "Does anyone know who this burned man is?" And people will shrug.

When they go through my belongings, they'll find all the artifacts of a lonely man without a family, without a love, and without a friend. They will pity me. The only evidence left of my life will be two frozen dinners in my freezer and the old romance novel on my nightstand, a worn copy of Dee-Dee Drake's *Love's Secret Sniper*. The old romances, when they are about love and not just sex, they're the best.

His mind races while he tries to put out the fire, picturing a couple of workmen clearing out his apartment. They'll hear the parking garage door rumble and feel its vibrations through the floor, and they'll shake their heads sadly at the sound. All of my stuff will probably fit in one box, he thinks. Maybe two. Not even a yard sale's worth. Combined, it'll be a lonely testament to a life half lived and a death by asphyxiation in an elevator.

134

When they look for someone to give my pitiable life insurance payout to, they'll find no one. It's willed to a charity. When they look for someone to write my life into an obituary, there will be no one. There will be nothing left of my life to outlive me. And so I will fully fade away into the murky currents of time.

I can't let them find that life, Jimenez thinks. I won't.

He doubles his efforts, batting the flames twice as fast, pushing his gloves into the fire in a bid to smother it. His hand becomes a blur of motion in the hazy, strobing light. The fire grows dimmer and dimmer as he makes headway.

And then all goes dark. A subdued crackling comes from the wall, cooling down from where the fire fed from it.

There's still no air.

Jimenez hacks and coughs. He wipes the back of his arm across his face. Tears stream from his stinging eyes, his body attempting to flush the irritants from them. Smoke is everywhere and his lungs scream for a breath of fresh air. Jimenez feels light-headed, and he can't recall the last breath of clean air he had. Whenever it was, it's now stale within him and due for exhalation. Yet he holds it because there's nothing to replace it with.

Jimenez remembers the access hatch through the ceiling of the elevator.

In the airless black, he gropes his way across the floor and then up the wall. He finds the handrail that runs at waist height around the circumference of the elevator and follows it to a corner. Then he clambers up onto it, his butt jammed into the corner, his feet standing on perpendicular railings and his arm braced against the ceiling. He runs the desperate fingers of his free hand along the ceiling until he finds a seam. The hatch is almost directly above his head. He pushes on it, but it doesn't budge. He hammers it with his fist, and after a few forceful blows, the little door releases and swings upward on its hinge.

Jimenez is too large a man to fit through the hatch, but after a few moments, his nose tells him that the elevator compartment is clearing. The smoke dissipates into the dark column of the elevator shaft. He can breathe again, which he does shallowly at first and then more deeply when he deems the air clear enough. It still stinks, but it's not choking anymore.

Jimenez pops his head through the hatch. A dim light creeps through the cracks in the second-floor elevator door a short distance above. In the shallow light, not more than an arm's length from the opening, Jimenez spies a breaker switch angled horizontally toward the elevator's roof. He blinks to clear his eyes and then squints at it. It's greasy and dusty on the underside, which, he reasons, is the opposite of what it should be. He wedges his arm and shoulder through the hatch and flips the breaker. The elevator lights flash on, and the compartment hops once as power surges through it again. The sound echoes up the hollow black expanse above him.

Jimenez lowers himself back into the elevator and swings the hatch closed behind him.

136

A few more moments and Jimenez is left with nothing from the incident but a foul taste in his mouth and the tang of burned plastic clinging in his nose. His gloves are grilled, and his shirtsleeve is charred, but the skin underneath, though a little pink, is otherwise unharmed.

He examines the panel. Things are charred, but everything still seems connected to where it should be. He replaces the cover and screws it into place. Most of the evidence of the fire is hidden, save a dissipating smear of charcoal sneaking from under the corner of the panel.

Then, he pushes a button.

The doors slide open.

Jimenez sighs and sniffs his clothes. He needs to change. His sleeve is scorched, and he smells like an industrial fire. He pokes the panel a few times, depressing the button for the third floor. It fails to illuminate on the first press but does so with the second.

The elevator doors slide closed again.

Jimenez smiles and waves a hand feebly as if it will clear the bad smell out of the elevator. He puts his hands into his pockets and leans backward to admire his work. In his pocket, his left hand encounters a folded piece of paper.

He pulls it out and reads, "Leak under kitchen sink. Apartment 2507."

That should be easy.

CHAPTER
TWENTY-THREE

In Which Garth Encounters the Evil Seductress Faye and Completes the Long Journey to His Apartment

Garth can't take another step. His leg muscles fire tremulously, twitching awkwardly from overstimulation.

I'm going to feel this tomorrow, Garth thinks to himself, wondering if he'll even be able to walk or if he'll be crippled with fatigue when the sun rises on the morning.

He leans against the wall, the concrete cool through the sweat-damp fabric pressed to his lower back. He grips the black plastic bag in one hand and places the other against his hip in an attempt to stretch the cramp out of his side. This is the twentieth floor. Only five more to go and already Garth has sworn several oaths to get in better shape, tone down the beer consumption at night, and sign the organ donor form from his life insurance company should he survive his ascent. And, like the same resolutions he swore for the New Year, he's certain he will fulfill none of them. He recognizes them for what they are, coping mechanisms.

Garth's attention is drawn upward by a scuffling shamble and a short exclamation. A beautiful young woman at the top of the flight misses a step and stumbles. She starts to topple forward, her body leaning precariously beyond balance and threatening to fall headlong down the concrete stairs. Garth lunges forward to catch her but realizes he's too far away. At best, he will be able to slow her tumble by the time she reaches the base of the stairs, but she would have to suffer several bounces first.

Luckily, the woman's hand darts to one side, grabs the railing, and she's able to regain her footing. She loses grasp of her water bottle, however, and it rattles down the stairs to come to rest at Garth's feet. The woman pauses with arms outstretched and legs awkwardly splayed, but manages to remain upright. Then she stands and takes a breath. She seems to chuckle at her misstep, as if chiding herself.

Garth picks up her water bottle before asking, "Are you okay?" With his other hand, he hugs his package to his chest.

The shocked look on her face tells him she hadn't seen him. She recovers from her momentary loss of composure and replies, "Yes, I just lost my balance for a moment. Missed a step."

She continues down the stairs toward him, one hand gripping the railing now. She moves with graceful fluidity, one foot landing in front of the other, her ankles nearly touching with each step and her hips swaying like a model's on a runway. Even though she wears canvas deck shoes, blue jeans, and a wrinkled pink nightshirt, she is stunning. Her hair is pulled into a messy ponytail, but it looks like it shouldn't be any other way. She isn't wearing makeup and doesn't need to. Her skin is smooth and evenly toned, her beauty entirely natural. She looks like she may have just climbed out of bed but could have thrown on a gown for a formal night on the town as easily as she had thrown on a pink nightshirt to clamber down a dingy stairwell.

"I know what you mean." Garth thinks of the truth of that statement, the momentary loss of balance, the missed step. "That's all it takes," he adds.

She nods, but he can tell the meaning is lost on her. Maybe he endowed too much significance in his words. He feels an embarrassed flush rise on his cheeks from being so melodramatic. He can tell she is distracted and hopes she won't notice.

"I'm Garth," he says when she reaches the landing where he rests. He holds out the water bottle for her to take.

"Faye," the woman says, contemplating him for a moment before taking the bottle. She offers a hand for him to shake.

Garth takes her delicate hand in his ham fist and pumps it twice with short, awkward movements. He holds his elbows tight to his sides while he does so she won't notice the rings of sweat soaking his shirt. He's sure he stinks, and he's sure she doesn't.

"Quite a climb," he says and laughs. "This is my third rest break."

"Hell of a thing, hiking up this many stairs to get to an apartment," Faye agrees. "Or hiking down so many to get away from one," she adds, glancing up the stairwell behind her, as if to check she's not being followed.

"You live here?" Garth asks.

Faye laughs. "No, I don't. I was just visiting." Then she adds, "Working on a class assignment with a study buddy."

Faye and Garth look at each other for a moment. Faye's eyes size up Garth's plastic bag. Garth assesses the mess of Faye's hair. They appraise each other silently and decide there are secrets being withheld, intimate secrets that make the other untrustworthy. When neither speaks, Faye steps past Garth and carries on down the stairs without looking back.

"Good to meet you, Garth," she says with a flick of her hand over her shoulder. "You take 'er easy."

"You too, Faye," Garth says. "Watch your steps going down."

There comes an "Uh-huh" from Faye's direction. She nods.

Garth watches her until she disappears around the corner half a flight down from the landing. Then he bolts up the last five floors to his apartment. He's elated to reach the little sign on the wall that reads "Floor 25." Exiting the stairwell feels like being reborn, like a pall being lifted from his mood. The excitement he felt earlier percolates within him again, and he steps into the twenty-fifth-floor hallway with lighter feet than those that climbed the building. It's a homecoming, and as the stairwell door latches with a click behind him, Garth feels his spirits rise. He has made it. He's close to home now. He catches himself walking toward his apartment with such jaunty steps that he's almost skipping.

At the end of the hall, in front of the door on the left, he fumbles with his keys and then successfully navigates the lock, the knob, and the door. Inside, he slips his backpack from his shoulders and tosses it into the hallway closet. It lands against the wall with a loud thud. His hard hat. Garth kicks his work boots off on top of the backpack and then closes the closet door. Down the hall and into the kitchen, Garth pauses to give the room a once-over.

There's a glass in the sink into which the faucet drips. He left it empty this morning, but now it's overflowing. The dripping sound turned from a flat smacking noise into a more full-bodied plunking sound at some point during the day. There's a toaster in the corner of the counter and a few crumbs near it, but all in all, Garth thinks, everything is pretty tidy but not so tidy it seems staged.

Garth puts the package down beside the sink and then checks the cabinet underneath. When he opens the door, a short piece of dental floss falls from where it was wedged between the cabinet and the door. Garth shakes his head, tweezes it from the floor with his thumb and forefinger, and puts it in the garbage can. He closes the cabinet door.

He snatches the package from the counter and makes his way to his bedroom, pausing for a moment to admire the view through his sliding balcony door. It's an expansive view of the buildings across Roxy and as far as the eye can see. It's one of the reasons he agreed to pay two hundred dollars a month over his budget when he signed the lease for the apartment. It's the one thing he can never walk by and not pause to take it in because it is different with every second. The light always changes, and there is always something moving out there. It is living artwork.

Garth continues to the bedroom and draws the curtains closed. The room is plunged into near darkness; only a sliver of light sneaks between the wall and the curtain. He then flicks on the bedside lamp. He pulls the package from the plastic bag and places it on the bed, admiring how the brown paper forms a pleasing contrast to his light-blue comforter. He straightens the package, squaring it to the bed, and steps back to admire the new aesthetic. His admiration only lasts a short while before his excitement wins out. He's waited this long and shakes with anticipation now the wait is over.

Sliding a trembling finger under the tape that fastens the paper together, Garth releases the hold it has.

With eager hands, he unwraps the package.

CHAPTER
TWENTY-FOUR

In Which the Tripod Petunia Delilah Goes Door Knocking

Petunia Delilah lets the wet fabric of her nightgown slip slowly from her fingers. By pleats, one length at a time, it falls heavily in fits and starts back down to her knees. The fabric feels cool against her skin, for which she's thankful because her body burns with stress. She watches the hem of her nightgown fall to place in the bathroom mirror. Her hair is matted flat with sweat; bolts of it cling to her forehead and cheeks. Her skin is pale, but her cheeks are flushed pink. Dark-purple rings hang under her eyes.

I need help right now, she thinks.

I can't do this on my own.

I can't get help in here, and I need it, she thinks.

I have to leave the apartment to find it.

Slowly, bracing herself with arms to doorframes and walls, she turns her back on her reflection and waddles to her apartment door. By the time she reaches the door, she knows there's more than a foot protruding from her nethers. There is a limb, one she fears to inspect but knows is there because it swings with her movements and hits the inside of her thigh. Once, the little leg moved on its own, giving her a kick. Each time she feels it, she grimaces in terror. She wants her baby to be okay more than anything.

At the apartment door, she slides the chain from its track and undoes the dead bolt, opens it, and steps into the hallway. The door swings shut and locks behind her. The handle locks automatically. She hadn't thought about that before the door closed. Hopefully she won't have to go back in because the key is hanging on a key-shaped hook just inside the door.

The hallway is dimly lit. The bulb in the sconce beside her apartment door is burned out. It has been like that for weeks, and she intended to put a service request into the building superintendent but never got around to it. She hasn't left the apartment in as long so was never reminded that it needed to get done. The hallway is quiet save for the subdued hum of the vents circulating air from either end. Often, in the hallway, she could hear people talking or a television set babbling behind a door. Right now, there are no such noises.

She looks down the length of the corridor and it seems so much longer than it ever has, as if it became elongated as soon as she needed it to be short.

With one forearm sliding along the wall for balance, Petunia Delilah takes her first tottering steps toward the neighbor's apartment door. Her other arm is crook-elbowed and tucked against the side of her belly. It seems to take an eternity, but she puts her head down and shuffles along, concentrating on anything but her pain and her predicament. The carpet is gritty. The occasional pebble sticks to the soles of her bare feet, only to be brushed off again a few steps later. Then her forearm rests on a doorjamb. She looks up. Above the spy hole, bolted to the brown painted door, are tarnished brass numerals spelling the apartment number: 802.

Petunia Delilah squares herself to the door and then leans forward against it, arm against doorframe and forehead to arm.

"Hello," Petunia Delilah says, her voice a raspy gurgle that bounces down the empty hallway.

She knocks on the door and says "Hello" again.

Petunia Delilah waits for a moment. There's no answer.

Why would anyone be home? she reasons with herself. It's still too early for people to be home. They're probably just packing up their desks or hanging their tool belts, getting ready to leave work. Nobody with a day job would be home yet; just pregnant ladies suffering from hyper-what's-it are home at this time of day.

Petunia Delilah is scared and alone. A mounting contraction forces her to suck air sharply between her teeth. She clenches the breath tightly in her lungs when it peaks and exhales slowly as it ebbs. It wasn't a bad one. There have been worse.

She pounds on the door with the heel of her hand. It rattles in the frame.

"If you're home, please, open the door." She turns her head, holds an ear to the door, and doesn't hear anything.

146

"I need help," she says quietly, to herself more than anyone.

The paint is cool and soothing against her cheek, so she rests there a minute, listening to the whooshing of her pulse in her ears. She's exhausted, but she knows she has so much farther to go before she can rest. This is just starting, and she's already so tired. The baby needs help, and she's not sure she has the strength to make it. She's terrified that she will fail this, her first real test of motherhood: bringing her baby into the world. She isn't sure she could live with herself if she fails.

There's no one else but me, she thinks.

It takes effort to focus, right herself to stand, and continue on her way.

Forearm to wall, sliding along the paint with the sound of a talkative snake, Petunia Delilah works her way down the hallway. Ahead of her, another apartment door, the stairwell door, then more apartment doors. Right now, one foot, the other foot, then back to the first one. She hopes the next apartment is the one, that someone is home, and that the someone is an obstetrician on her day off who won't mind dealing with a breech-birthing lady pounding on the door to her inner-city, one-bedroom apartment.

And here it is, a brass 803 bolted to the door. Again, Petunia Delilah leans on the door, her feet spread shoulder width apart, slightly alleviating her discomfort.

A knock, knock, knock and a quiet "Hello."

Nothing.

Petunia Delilah pounds on it with her fist. She wants to knock the door from its hinges, push it right out of the frame, whether someone is home or not. She wants their phone. She wants help. She wants this to be someone else's problem too. One way or the other, she wants this baby out of her body and safely into her arms. She wants it all to be over, and she wants that to happen right now. Then she wants a fucking ice cream sandwich.

She pounds and yells, "Hello. Anybody in there? Open the fucking door." And by the end of the sentence, she's sobbing.

The sconce next to the door shines a lonely light in the dim hallway. It quivers as Petunia Delilah lays into the door. She cries and pounds and makes a noise that she finally notices she's making but doesn't know for how long. Her mouth hangs open, her lips wet, her cheeks wet, and a hoarse exhalation escaping from her.

And there's no answer.

She feels like sitting down with her back to the door of Apartment 803, just for a few moments, just so she can gather her strength. But no, she knows the baby's life, and maybe even her own, are in her hands alone. She will not give up. Down the hallway, not far but too far for her, glows a red "Exit" sign, illuminated on the ceiling and pointing at the stairwell door. Beyond that, the door for Apartment 804.

"Onward." She laughs as she cries. With one hand, she pulls the hem of her nightgown above her knees, making it easier for her to walk. Her legs are so heavy, but she moves them regardless.

One foot, the other foot, back to the first one.

Forearm to wall for support, whispering as her skin slides along the smooth paint, halfway between Apartment 803 and the "Exit" sign, the stairwell door explodes open. Petunia Delilah freezes where she stands when a small body flops through the doorframe and lands on the carpet, dead still, unmoving, maybe not even breathing. She can't tell.

She watches.

It's a boy.

Is he breathing?

He isn't moving.

Is he even alive?

The hydraulic arm hisses, and the door clicks shut, sparking her into motion.

The boy's chest rises and falls with a breath. He is alive.

"Hello?" she says. "You there. Boy on the floor, are you okay?"

The boy doesn't move.

Petunia Delilah shuffles forward a few steps and asks the boy again.

He lies there, face to carpet and limbs akimbo.

The leg between her legs twitches, tapping gently against the inside of her thigh. It sparks her to cry again because it reminds her of the situation she's in.

When she reaches the boy, she pokes at him with her toe. He doesn't move so she kicks him in the shoulder. He still doesn't move, and Petunia Delilah takes a step around him, intending to leave him there. She takes another step, and the boy burbles pathetically. Petunia

Delilah stops. It's obvious he needs help, and if he were to die there on the floor, she would never forgive herself. So she squats, an arm on the wall to steady herself on the way down and the other outstretched to grab the boy by the leg.

"Okay," she says. "We can do this. Come on, little unconscious kid. All three of us. Off we go."

And she takes a step toward Apartment 804, dragging the boy by the ankle behind her.

CHAPTER
TWENTY-FIVE

In Which Claire the Shut-In Loses Her Job, Gains Some Groceries, and Calculates How Horny the City Is

The oven chimes. It's preheated and awaiting quiche.

Claire blinks and then bustles across the kitchen, scoops the quiche from where it rests on the counter, and puts it in the oven. She takes a roll of paper towels from the drawer beside the oven and grabs a spray cleaner from under the kitchen sink. She busies herself to distraction by spraying and wiping and scrubbing the flat surfaces of the kitchen, rubbing them vigorously into cleandom. She spins and sprays and wipes repeatedly, every corner, until the countertop shines. Afterward, she washes her hands again, sits on her stool at the island, and pours herself a glass of wine.

With the mysterious call from the lobby door still playing in her mind, she huffs and drinks the half balloon of wine down in one gulp. A phone call this afternoon, bizarre, she thinks. I've had only two calls in total through the past week. And both of those were from Mom. Those calls had been scheduled, normal,

151

and social. They were "Hi, honey. How was your week?" and "Lovely weather and the forecast looks good for the rest of the week." None of this weirdness. What did it mean? "Gotcha, kiddo." Claire shakes her head, grabs the bottle, and glugs her wineglass full again. She takes another liberal swig from it.

The stove clock ticks backward, the green numbers slipping past the ten-minute mark. Less than ten minutes until the temperature has to be reduced. The quiche is starting to talk, a peaceful sound like a lethargic rain on wet ground as it bubbles behind the oven door.

Claire taps the keyboard on her laptop and the screen flashes to life. The call-manager program from work is still open. Her last call is recorded there. Pig, she thinks back on it. What was his real name? Jason, she recalls. Two minutes and thirty-eight seconds. That was how long she spent on the phone with him. Poor guy. She blushes remembering how she told him to finish himself off for once. The job often calls for doling out a little humiliation, but Claire tries never to be judgmental or cruel, and what she said to Jason was just mean.

She recognized his voice from past calls, a few a week at the least, one a day at the most. She couldn't remember exactly. With one hand cupped around the bell of the wineglass, Claire uses the other to casually scroll back through her call log. Nine calls in the three hours since her lunch break and five calls in the two hours before that. Fourteen lonely guys today. One hour and fifty-one minutes of dirty talking. A light-traffic day. Even so, Claire tries to do the best job she can, and it can be exhausting coming up with creative ways to get guys off. It is a cerebral challenge with a physical payoff that often leaves her completely spent.

Claire glances at the oven clock, seven minutes and thirty-nine seconds left and counting. She leans a cheek on the palm of her hand and pokes at her computer with the fingers of the other.

Fourteen guys, Claire thinks, in a five-hour day. She thinks about the nine other women working for the PartyBox and figures, if they take a similar volume through their shifts, that's one hundred and forty calls daily. A light-traffic day though . . . carry that out through the year. Claire clicks open the computer's calculator and starts multiplying lonely guys by time . . . That's more than fifty-one thousand calls in a year.

That is one lonely city. Claire swirls her wine and holds it to her nose. She inhales and then takes a shallow sip. She tilts her head in contemplation. Blowsy, foxy, and hard. Cinnamon, leather, and tobacco. She looks over the rim of the bell, out at the buildings across the street from her apartment. Nobody is home, not from the windows she can see through and what she can see in them. She takes another sip and sighs. The oven clock counts down past the four-minute mark.

Claire yawns, clinks the wineglass onto the counter, and turns her attention back to the computer.

So, given there are just over a million people in the city and roughly half of them are guys, if every guy called the line once, her company could cycle through the city's entire population of men in ten years. So, in the long run, she will have whispered sexual fantasies into the ears of thousands of men every year. She knows the assumptions of her exercise are absurd to the point that the result is utterly inaccurate, but still she can't help but feel a little dirty. She had never thought of the numbers. Then there are many other companies offering to service this city, and she knows not every guy calls.

Still, something so seemingly simple as human companionship is really quite the opposite. It should be easy to find each other, yet her job indicates it's not. The number of people having trouble making that connection is staggering. This is one lonely city on a very lonely planet.

The timer on the oven chimes and startles Claire from her reverie. The warm, savory aroma is growing stronger, starting to fill her apartment. Claire smiles as it blankets her. She has a sip of wine and then takes a momentary hiatus from the kitchen island to turn the oven's heat down to three hundred degrees.

She resets the timer for half an hour.

Claire can't help but flick on the oven light and peer in. Under the pale-yellow light, through the spotless oven window, sits the quiche. The top has taken on a custard consistency, and the crust is starting to tan nicely. Tiny bubbles start to jewel the sliver of space where the crust meets the pan. Claire smiles at herself for becoming so enamored with the pie. For Claire, food is something so visceral and magical that she can't help herself. It's the perfect intersection of all the senses, and her body consistently quivers when she immerses herself in the acts of cooking and eating.

Claire thinks it odd that humans, those talking dirty on the phone and stumbling heartbreakingly through paid interpersonal interactions, would be the same animals to create such a thing. In her college career, she took an anthropology class that defined humans above all other animals as the ones that use tools. Then it was discovered that chimpanzees use sticks to pull termites from their mounds.

Claire's quiche, in her mind, is the defining characteristic of humankind. That ability to combine ingredients into other nourishing and wholly satisfying culinary creations. A mixture to stimulate smell, touch, taste, and sight all at once. Spending time collecting and assembling all the ingredients is beyond simple survival. Monkeys don't do it. Bears just eat their berries and rotty dead things. Birds peck at whatever is around, and dogs like meat from the bone. And on and on and on. Not one other animal could create a quiche, so, Claire thinks with a smile, it's through quiche that human beings are defined.

The computer chimes that she has received email.

Claire peeks in the oven once more before returning to her seat in front of the computer screen. There are two emails awaiting her attention. She clicks on the first — it's from her grocery delivery company. It details her order for tomorrow and asks her to confirm or change the items. She scans through the list, deletes a bag of oatmeal and the almond milk. In their place she adds a half dozen eggs and some organic orange juice before sending it back to the grocer.

The second is from Gabby, Claire's boss at the PartyBox. The email is addressed to her and the other nine women working the phones. Gabby starts off by apologizing and then writes that everyone is fired.

Claire sighs and reads on.

Of course, there is the mandatory two weeks' notice in which Gabby will happily give them the contact information for a placement agency that can help them find alternate, gainful employment. She apologizes to everyone again and then explains that the franchise has been under fiscal review and it is prudent to centralize the call center and outsource the phone-sex trade. All future call volume will be handled by a company in Manila. She informs everyone that, currently, the new call center employees are undergoing extensive training for the job. The last paragraph thanks them for their hard work and for their efforts making the last few years as successful as they have been. She ends the email with "Regards, Gabby."

Claire blinks, takes a sip of wine, and scans the email again.

"Fuck."

CHAPTER
TWENTY-SIX

In Which Homeschooled Herman Witnesses His First Life-Altering Moment

Herman spotted his grandpa in the audience, smiling and clapping quietly. Grandpa struggled his way to his feet, from a chair one row back from the front and set a little to stage left. The stage lights dimmed, and the floor lights came up in a dramatic sweep. The room was packed to the walls. People stood at the back and sat on the stairs bracketing the bank of seats. Every seat was occupied, and the constant cough or sniffle jumping around the room attested to the capacity crowd.

Other than that roaming, intermittent human noise, the theater was still. There was also the quiet shuffling sound of Grandpa's dry hands clapping softly together. Grandpa's fingers were gnarled at the joints and painful with arthritis. For him, the noise he made was a resounding applause to go with his standing ovation.

Herman looked out over the rows of uninterested faces. He had lip-synched the best he could to Bonnie Tyler's "Total Eclipse of the Heart." He had given it his all. He had thrown his hands out in front of himself, curled his splayed fingers into tightly grasped fists in all the right places. He raised them, pleading to the lights in all the right places. He shook bodily at all the right times, when the cannons fired about halfway through his performance. He moved his whole body and used the entire stage throughout his performance. He worked hard to just let emotion take over, and when it did, he flowed with the power of it. By the end of the seven-minute epic, when he stood to receive his applause, his chest was heaving from the exertion. He had become so immersed in the song that tears streamed from his eyes when the falsetto voice at the end swelled. He hoped that no one could see him cry under the bright stage lights.

It would not be enough to win the competition, however. Darrin Jespersen won for lip-synching some Nickelback song. It must have been his air guitar, Herman thought and had to admit it had been pretty good. While Herman's efforts would not be enough to garner any more than Grandpa's raspy-clap standing ovation and the uninterested looks of dozens of parents who were only there to support their own kids, it would earn him the beating near the bike racks that would eventually cause Grandpa to withdraw him from school.

Herman has vague recollections of the stairwell door opening, of being in the stairwell. The shadows stick like thick black honey in the corners, and there are dark scuffs on the walls. The railing is painted pale blue on the underside and worn to a shiny silver from years of caresses. Years of soft touches could wear away even the hardest surface. Herman floats as much as falls down the stairs. He's not sure how long he's in the stairwell because time doesn't matter when one disengages from it and moves independent of its control.

As if in a dream, time stretches out above and below him, a column he can easily move through and get off at any time. Flights of runs and risers twisting back on themselves, time becomes a serrated corkscrew edge heading up into the future and down into the past. The elevator jumps between the two, slipping the column from the beginning to the end, stopping on demand or randomly at any floor in between. Time is dog's years versus tortoise's years. Time is always happening, all at once.

If you live half as long, is the time you spend twice as important?

Herman knows it is.

Dogs know it too.

And if you have too much of it, you get tired of it. It loses meaning.

Herman drifts through a door, not even sure if he opens it or just passes through it, not even sure where it leads, and then he sees a new terror. A woman staggers toward him. She speaks a cottony noise at him, but he can't figure out what she says. One of her arms is propped against the wall, and the other reaches out for him, fingers splayed, grasping. She walks stiff-legged, like the dead if they could walk. It's all too much to process. Herman's vision slides opaque and turns sideways.

★ ★ ★

Grandpa slid a piece of paper in front of Herman. It was a blank white page except for two dots that Grandpa had marked on opposite corners.

"How far apart are these dots?" he asked. "Tell me but don't measure the distance — you don't need to."

They had been working on a trigonometry lesson together, and Herman's mind had been keenly tuned to the beauty of Pythagoras's numbers for the past twenty minutes. Grandpa was always innovative with his lessons. It was a standard 8.5-by-11 sheet of paper, so, Herman reasoned, it was not a question of how far apart the dots were; it was a question of what was the hypotenuse of a triangularly bisected sheet of standard letter paper. Herman scribbled out an equation and completed it.

"Those two dots are approximately 13.9 inches apart," Herman said, a proud smile on his face.

"That's one answer," Grandpa said. "What's another?"

Herman was puzzled. Grandpa smiled encouragingly at him.

The math was absolute, Herman thought. There were no two ways to add or square a number; there was only one way. "There's only one answer." He checked his sums again while Grandpa watched. There could only be one answer. "They're 13.9 inches apart."

"That's true — there's nothing wrong with your arithmetic. There's something wrong with how you see the question."

Herman stared at the page, his eyes dancing between the two dots and tracing imagined lines back and forth across the blank white page. He frowned.

Grandpa patted him on the shoulder, stood, and said, "I'll leave you to it." As he walked to the door, he said, "The distance between the two is variable. Those two dots can be the same dot, or they can be anywhere up to fourteen inches apart, like you think. Now tell me how that could be." Grandpa left Herman's room.

Herman put the eraser on the end of the pencil in his mouth and sunk his teeth into its flesh. Time passed and the kettle wailed in the kitchen. Herman furrowed his brow, trying to make sense of the distance between the dots. Grandpa shuffled around the apartment. A short while later, Herman heard the rustle of the newspaper from the living room.

And then, Herman was in the car, watching to make sure his sister didn't cross the invisible line demarcating his side from hers on the seat between them. She was sneaky. She thought it was funny to cross the line, and it kind of was for some reason Herman couldn't pinpoint.

Her strategy was to wait until he looked out the window at a motorbike or a big truck, and then she'd slip her fingers across. By the time he looked, they would be back on her side, but the remnant contraction of her arm would tell the history of her intrusion. He tried to slap her hand whenever it crossed over. He never slapped too hard though, just enough to shock but not enough to hurt. Most of the time she got away with it and giggled at her cunning evasiveness. He pretended to be mad, but she knew he wasn't, that he was just playing. When he did get her, she squealed in surprise and Mom or Dad glanced in the rearview mirror or turned around to tell them to behave.

The radio was on, playing some song Herman didn't know and didn't think about as anything more than background noise. The tune mixed with the white hiss of the air passing by the car and the sound of the tires on the road. They were traveling the highway.

They were on vacation, touring the coast and zigzagging inland to sightsee and visit friends, here and there along the way. They had camped on a beach last night. As the sun set, Dad struck up a fire and they cooked hotdogs on sticks they had cut from willow branches near the shore. They had sticky fingers from roasting marshmallows for dessert.

Over the water, the sky turned shades of bruise and apricot. The reflection of the water made it look like the sky had melted to the horizon. The wind picked up as the sun dropped below the horizon and the fire flared sideways and roared for a while. Then it was calm again, there was sand in Herman's marshmallow, and the sky grew a deep indigo before black. He looked up to see the stars. Then they had slept in a tent, which Herman thought was uncivilized. He didn't sleep well because of the sound of the water and the ripples from the breeze stroking the nylon walls.

The next morning, they stopped at a drive-through for juice, breakfast sandwiches, and hash browns. Dad passed the orders out from the driver's seat, and when everyone was settled and satisfied, they merged back onto the highway.

The next stop was the city to visit Grandpa in his apartment. Herman had been here before, in the past, in this car driving this road with the blurred green of the pine trees running a dynamic backdrop to the roadside litter and ditch puddles. The pale blue-gray of the hot summer sky was the same now as it had been then. The songs that played on the radio were the same.

The DJ babbled mindlessly.

Herman slapped at his sister's hand and then grew sad because he knew what was going to happen.

Dad slumped forward against the chest strap of his seat belt. His hands slid from the steering wheel and the cruise control kept the car moving at a steady speed. Mom looked up from the crossword she was doing. Then, she looked at Dad as the car drifted across the yellow centerline.

The paint on the pavement did nothing to stop them from drifting into the lanes of oncoming traffic.

CHAPTER
TWENTY-SEVEN

In Which Ian the Goldfish Realizes He Is Falling

There comes a point in every goldfish's descent when he realizes he's falling — again. In fact, there come several points in a goldfish's descent when this revelation is had.

Ian is at this point once again as he whizzes past the seventeenth-floor balcony. There's a bikini-clad lady sitting on a plastic folding chair on the safe side of the railing. A book in one hand, a cup of coffee in the other, and the sun warming her gym-firmed tummy. Her face is blissfully calm. Her eyes trace the lines of text in her book. She enjoys the warmth of the waning afternoon light, and she relishes the racy nature of the smutty prose she reads. The book cover is adorned with a curvy vixen in a billowy pink gown parted seductively to expose her cleavage, in the embrace of a be-six-packed man-stallion. One of her knees is drawn up to his waist. She clings to him like he clings to the rope of a timber tall ship. The woman on the balcony is so engrossed in the words she doesn't see Ian, at best a mere blip in her peripheral vision, at worst a rocketing inch and a half of fish flesh passing by unnoticed, in the span of a blink.

What Ian takes from the scene is the peaceful escape within a novel's pages. Even though the calm of the woman is in sharp contrast to the near constant terror that threatens Ian, the goldfish shares a fleeting moment of camaraderie with her. Her escape through the words on a page is akin to his plight, though a lot safer. Ian didn't have the choices for adventure and exploration that the woman sunning herself does. Ian can't read Dee-Dee Drake's *Love's Secret Sniper*. Ian can't imagine, and Ian had no one to talk to in his bowl save for Troy. And while the goldfish and the snail were friends through circumstance of geography, Troy was not a good communicator. Ian usually just wound up nipping at his shell for hours to amuse himself, trying to pull Troy from the glass, dislodging him from his algae dinner. There was the odd time that Troy became unseated, and Ian felt an immense satisfaction when he did.

Within a few hours though, Troy would be back on the wall of the bowl, slurping up the vegetation. Indeed, Ian found Troy to be a wholly disappointing roommate, though this was not a revelation by any stretch given Troy's brain was composed of a mere few ganglia.

Now firmly below the woman on the balcony, Ian glances into the apartment as he flashes past the sixteenth floor. Nobody is home, and Ian, for a moment, thinks about how sad an empty home is. An empty home is a lonely box awaiting life to bring it to its full potential. The coffee cups sit in the cupboard;

Ian thinks and then stops himself. It would be cliché and erroneous to say "collecting dust" because the verb is an active one and the cups are inert.

The tap drip-drip-drips into the sink. Given a thousand years, it will erode a hole through the stainless steel with its soft but persistent caresses. The milk in the fridge moves, second by second, toward its "best before" date. It is an inevitable reminder of time passing and how, through the very act of existence, the unmarred, unspoiled purpose of things moves inexorably toward expiration.

Ian thinks of his fishbowl, now empty save for the algae, the pink plastic castle, and Troy slipping across the glass with his interminable munching. Ian thinks of what a lonely thing Troy's shell would be without the chewy organic mass of Troy to inhabit it. Ian won't miss the sound of Troy eating. He won't miss the constant slurping and sucking noises, the ripping noise Troy makes day and night as he sucks the algae from the walls. He won't miss that chiefly because his fishbowl is no longer even a memory for him.

Ian is distracted from his thoughts by something he spies through the dust-streaked glass of the balcony sliding door to the apartment he passes on the fifteenth floor. In the fraction of a second it takes, his mind captures a still life of the goings-on inside.

There's a gangly boy standing in the background, framed by the light of the kitchen behind him. He has knobby arms and a skinny neck, seemingly too fragile for the weight of the head it's forced to support. The boy stands, slump-shouldered, in shadowed contrast to

166

the light reflecting off the white cabinets and the white appliances behind him. There's a reading lamp in the foreground, its stem curved like a question mark and its apex casting a cone of amber light upon the slack arm of an old man sitting in an armchair.

The old man wears a blue knit cardigan and has a crocheted blanket draped across his lap. He sits, askew to one side as if sleeping carelessly, slumping with an arm slung over the armrest. The old man's knuckles are swollen with arthritis, and his fingers are warped from a lifetime of use. A newspaper has fallen across his knee; a sheaf remains draped there, and others have fallen to a disheveled pile on the floor. The pile has created a scruffy paper volcano on the carpet. It looks rugged in the lamp's light, with crumpled crevasses and jutting ridges. The space between the boy and the old man seems vast for some reason, and the feeling of that space is mirrored in the expression on the boy's face. It's a look of loss and helplessness. It's as if the distance across the small living room is a space too large for him to cross, as if there is something so fundamentally awry in the apartment that the boy can't close the gap between them even if he should want to.

The boy's expression shifts in a flash when he sees Ian passing in a vertical line in front of the sliding balcony door. Before Ian slips below the level of the balcony, the boy's body convulses in a nascent sprint toward the window. In his speedy descent, Ian only sees the start of a step before he's out of eyeshot. And then the boy is gone, the old man is gone, and the moment is gone. It was a singular instant never to be repeated. Ian does not have the mental capacity to recognize the honor of witnessing the intimate scene within the apartment on the fifteenth floor. The time and space will never again align into that moment, ever.

Ian carries on downward past the fourteenth floor. Now, he thinks, what was I doing?

CHAPTER
TWENTY-EIGHT

In Which Our Heroine Katie Is Lifted Heavenward, but Only a Short Part of the Total Distance

Katie pauses on the tenth-floor landing. She pulls a sharp breath into her lungs and puts her hands on her hips to do a shallow back bend. Her brow is starting to bead with perspiration from the effort of the climb. Katie is in good shape — she jogs three times a week and swims every weekend — but the vertical exertion is enough to raise her heart rate.

She glances at the sign on the wall.

Seventeen floors to go, she thinks.

Connor is up there waiting for her. Resolution for her desire is up there waiting. Katie doesn't pause for long, just three shallow back bends and a few deep, forced breaths. Her purpose of mind drives her to continue upward, moving closer to the sky.

"I want us to be closer to the sky," Connor told her last night in his apartment. "I want us to do it among the stars."

Then, once they were spent, Katie said it, "I love you," to a sleeping Connor in a dark night apartment.

169

On their first date, they had wandered from the coffee shop near the university to his apartment. The evening was beautiful and warm. They had taken a meandering route while the shadows grew longer, down the hill from the university, through a park with fountains and laughing children, and into the city. Their shadows pivoted and gyrated on the pavement as they walked under the street lamps or whenever car headlights swept their bodies. Katie and Connor didn't notice any of this. Their gazes alternated from each other's eyes to their feet, from each other's eyes to the traffic passing by. Their voices ebbed and flowed against the city's nighttime murmur.

The sun had set, but the air was still hot and would remain so throughout the night. It was a heat that robbed sleep and forced people from their apartments and town houses. They sat on their front steps or balconies, some smoking cigarettes or just reclining in the dark, some drinking beers. All of them talking quietly to shadowed companions, a burbling sigh in the dark.

And Katie laughed when Connor joked.

And Connor listened when Katie told of her parents' forty years of marriage.

They suffered together through an awkward sweetness in front of the Seville on Roxy when Connor asked her up to his apartment. In hindsight, those heart-pounding, uncomfortable seconds of daring and acceptance were tragically short. It could only happen once in a relationship, that exhilarating instant of reward or rejection, a gamble that grew less thrilling as the heart grew complacent with experience.

They rode the elevator and didn't speak again, both silent in anticipation of what was to come and committed to the intent of the visit. Not a word was said until they were in Connor's apartment with the door closed to the hallway behind them. Outside, a sweeping view of the honey-colored patchwork of city lights in the night.

"It's beautiful," Katie whispered, looking to the window.

Connor left the apartment lights off that first night, and their bodies melded in the dark. Their fingers read each other's skin like braille, beautifully together even up until last night.

They both crossed the small space to the balcony door.

"I want us to be closer to the sky," he said and wrapped himself around her from behind, his arms around her waist and his chin on her shoulder. "But the best I can do is this, here, halfway between the ground and the sky."

His breath tickled her neck like his words did her ears. She thought those words romantic. He seemed ashamed he couldn't offer her more than a nice view and a tiny bachelor apartment, but for Katie, it was more than enough. Impossible promises were only made sweeter by the sincerity of their intent followed by wholehearted failures of their attainment. She didn't need him to be rich or successful or to steal the stars from the sky for her. She needed him to do stuff like this.

"We're just a little bit closer to heaven," he said.

She thought it a heartwarmingly cheesy thing to say. Even so, she was grateful that he was trying. Katie had thought to tell him that it was corny, to laugh and make a joke of it, but she couldn't bring herself to belittle his efforts. They were embarrassingly cute and the firmness of his body behind hers was irresistible. She could feel his heart beat where his chest was pressed against her shoulder blades, and the warmth between them became a dampness from the heat of their shared skins.

In the dull amber glow of the city outside, they each grabbed a corner of the mattress and slid it across the apartment to the balcony doors. Katie's mind raced, the taste of wine sweet on her tongue. She was in love with him. She knew it and it was overwhelming. It was this piled on top of all his other attentions, this last thing, this beautiful notion, the gesture of him wanting to make things perfect for her, to do something special for her.

He was readjusting the sheets over the mattress, pulling the edges taut and tucking them under, when Katie pinched the hem of her shirt and slowly lifted the fabric. She watched him as she did; his body, a silhouette haloed by light from the city, stopped fussing and watched her reveal herself to him. At first, Katie felt self-conscious and she stood covering her stomach with her hands. Then, she saw his face, its expression outlined by the city lights, and she saw that blissful look of desire. She lifted her arms behind her and released the clasp of her bra. Slowly, she pulled it from her shoulders and slid it down her arms, letting gravity take it to the floor. And then he removed his shirt and slid his pants from his hips, then his underwear. They stood at opposite ends of the bed, neither speaking, each naked for the other in the soft glow coming through the balcony door.

"I want to see you," he said and flipped on a light.

Katie thought to protest but was flattered from it by the look of sheer admiration on Connor's face. That, and by the detail of his body that the light now afforded her. A warmth spread between her legs, and her heart pounded relentlessly with anticipation.

Connor moved first, sidling onto the bed with one bent knee and the other foot still on the floor. He reached out to her, and she took his hand and lay beside him. He propped himself on an elbow and caressed her with a hand as soft as the air, from her cheek, floating down her chin and down her neck. His hand continued to her breast, not lingering long before carrying on down past her stomach and down farther still. There, held aloft by the Seville on Roxy like an offering to the sky, they made love.

He took amazing command over her body. At times their writhing was soft and passionate, and at others it was heated and violent. He had whispered. She had moaned. He had spanked, and she had scratched. At one point, Katie remembers screaming at the ceiling. At another, Connor had grunted in her ear that his cock belonged to her. By the time they had both come, many of the apartment lights outside had been turned off. It was that short hour, neither late night nor early morning, in which it seemed the whole city slept.

Lying on her side and looking out the balcony door, with Connor's body mirroring hers from behind and his arm draped across her waist, she noticed that she couldn't see the stars. Even at this hour, the city glow canceled out the sky. It didn't matter though; she lay in Connor's arms and looked out over the twinkling buildings instead. Those things said in the heat of passion were overlooked with embarrassment once sane minds prevailed. Katie did love Connor, but she had never wanted to own his cock, even though he had offered it so easily. She thought of how odd it was to offer ownership of parts of one's body rather than a commitment of one's feelings.

Why was one so much easier than the other?

"I love you," she said into the quiet of the apartment. She needed the words back from him.

Connor grunted.

Surely he had heard, she thought.

She could feel his belly rising and falling, exerting a gentle, pulsing pressure against the small of her back. His breath was a soft and steady rhythm on her neck. It seemed, though he had been awake a moment before, he had fallen asleep.

Katie rounds the stairs between the thirteenth and fourteenth floors, her mind deep in reminiscence. There's a noise from above, and she looks up to see a woman her age coming down the stairs toward her. Katie freezes midstep. The woman wears her pink nightshirt. Katie left it at Connor's a week ago, and now, here it is, covering the perky breasts and toned body of this woman.

Katie chokes on a bit of vomit but swallows it back down. With the sour taste of bile in her mouth, she glares at the woman in her nightshirt and wonders which she will lose control of first, her fury or her sorrow.

CHAPTER
TWENTY-NINE

In Which the Villain Connor Radley Judges His Heart and Finds It Wanting

Is it that simple? Connor wonders to himself.

He stands still, back to the balcony, and contemplates his tiny apartment.

Is it that easy to love someone? Is the feeling that simple? Surely it has to be more complex. Every time people talk about it, they say it's this huge, life-changing emotion. But this is a subtler feeling than that. She's everywhere, sure, in the things she has touched and left behind, but everything triggers a memory. It's like he can see her, hear her, smell her everywhere. He thinks about her when she's gone, and he cares not to hurt her. He does want to make her happy.

Are these things love?

Of course he wants to spend time with her and learn about her and ask her to move in . . . Is that true? He hadn't thought about it before now.

Do I want to ask her to move in with me?

Connor's eyes scan the apartment. He thought love would be a freight train of emotion, something huge and unwieldy and devastating. He sees everything Katie has touched in the apartment. The things she has moved and he remembers when she moved them. He sees the things she left behind. He remembers what she said when they were sitting on the couch together or while they were lying on the mattress. She's always here in his mind.

Connor's eyes drift to the bathroom. The door is open, and there's a clutter of toiletries on the counter. A facecloth is crumpled in the corner against the wall. The condom wrapper on the floor, the peeled edge curled like a dried orange rind. The toothpaste and the toothbrushes sit in a cup by the basin. Two toothbrushes.

The toothbrushes, Connor thinks. Christ, I let Faye use Katie's toothbrush. I told her it was for her.

This horrible shame, he wonders. Is this love?

The feeling that everything isn't good enough for Katie, the feeling that no matter how good he is, it can't be what she deserves, that is love. Everything he has done up until that point isn't good enough. Katie doesn't deserve Deb and Faye, and neither of them offers him a more fulfilling existence than Katie does.

But Deb, oh dirty Deb. She let him do things to her that most girls he asked wouldn't. And she seemed to enjoy it too. He would have been too shy to ask such things, but she pretty much begged him for it. She loved it. In fact, a few of those things had been her idea from the start. Connor hadn't even conceived of a few of them, which was surprising because where sex is involved, he has contemplated almost everything.

Connor blinks against the thought, trying to erase the images of Deb from his memory.

He decides that even Deb's kinks aren't worth hurting Katie. Deb's not enough. He can forgo her for a lifetime with Katie. Then he thinks differently, maybe not . . . Deb and Faye were outstanding; it's a lot to give up. He settles on his first thought again: Katie deserves better, and he has to deliver it to her.

And if he does, and if she loves him back, maybe she would let him try those things that Deb did. Surely love has its rewards along with its sacrifices.

Connor grabs another plastic bag from underneath the sink and starts rushing around the room. His goal: to make it a place Katie will want to stay tonight and, eventually, a place she will want to stay with him for years to come.

He hustles to the washroom and grabs the toothbrush from the cup. Katie will get a new one. He pinches the condom wrapper from the floor. From now on, the only wrappers that belong on the floor are those from making love with Katie. He grabs a hair band from the doorknob and an ankle sock with a pompom on it from behind the toilet. He uses it to wipe an errant hair from the toilet rim, not even sure whose it was. He scans the bathroom and decides it's good.

Connor moves on to the living room, his panic rising. There's so much to clean from the space in such a short time. As he tidies, he feels like crying and wonders how long he has felt this way about Katie. Maybe since the first day he talked to her, when she

178

came by his cramped little office under the stairs during his office hours a week before the midterm exam.

When he saw her coming, he told Lonnie, his officemate, that he needed an excuse to ask her out. Lonnie shrugged and said he could make that happen.

She was beautiful, standing awkwardly in the door. She was not thin and lanky like most of the other women in the class. She was soft and curvaceous and her smile — oh, how he remembered her smile. Connor usually knows the exact words to say to a woman. It is as if that is his superpower, how the words will just come to him and how they will ultimately lead a woman to his bed. But in Katie's case, he couldn't think of much to say. It was as if she were the supervillain to his superhero, that she possessed the exact opposite powers that could nullify his sex ray.

Connor had pretended not to notice how she derailed him; desperation reeks of neediness, and women don't like that. Confidence is needed.

"Welcome," he said. It sounded forced, lame. He was crippled in her presence. "Come in."

Connor can't remember exactly what was said, but he knows he wasn't as smooth as he usually is. He stammered out inanities and was repulsed by his own incoherence. She had him flustered, and he wondered if she knew it. It was usually so easy. Still, she seemed to want to chat with him and it seemed about more than the upcoming midterm. Or had he just wanted to believe that?

And then Lonnie oozed his distinctive stink into the small office.

Katie's face curled in response.

That was his cue. "Can I buy you a coffee?"

And she agreed.

The short walk off campus was a blur. They chatted as they passed the computer sciences building. Connor waved at a student who waved at him as she walked by. She seemed to want to stop and chat, but Connor and Katie passed her by, engrossed as they were in conversation. They waited together at the corner in front of the university entrance for the light to change in their favor.

The next thing Connor clearly remembers is they were both sitting at a small bistro table by the window. The light was fading from the day, and everything outside was cast in a flat gray. Inside, there was the bustle, chatter, and clatter of a busy coffee shop, but as they talked, it all seemed to fade into the background. It was as if everything else shrunk away and all that was left was this beautiful creature across the table from him.

"I didn't know at the time that my parents were swingers," he said. "How could I? I mean, I was just a kid. In hindsight, it was the eighties and there was a lot of that going on in the neighborhood. I guess that's why my parents always wanted me out of the house. I was encouraged to spend long days outside playing with my dog, Ian."

Katie laughed.

"What?" Connor asked.

"Your dog's name was Ian?"

"It was." Connor feigned offense. He wanted her to understand, but he couldn't be mad at her. "Why's that funny?"

"I don't know. Ian's a person's name, I guess. Not a dog's name." She chuckled.

"Yeah, well." Connor fiddled with his mug. "He was my friend."

Katie reached across the table and put her hand on his. Her palm was warm on the back of his hand, and he looked at her. She met his gaze for a few moments and then looked down at her coffee. She drew back her hand and seemed close to apologizing.

"No," Connor said. "It's okay."

He cocked his head, seeking out her eyes again, and when Katie looked up, he smiled.

"I wish I had a group of friends growing up, but Ian was all I had. He was a good buddy. Sometimes it's all you can do, give a dog a human name and make him a friend. Make your reality fit your dreams however you can. Kids do it all the time with things they don't get. A little self-delusion can be a good thing. I had a good childhood with Ian, better than it would have been without him."

They held hands across the table and talked. Their coffees grew cold and stayed untouched because neither wanted to break contact. Later, they went back to his apartment and talked some more. Later still, they made love. Connor now knows that is what it was.

Connor knows what he had been blind to then. His habits with women were stronger than this realization, and it took until now to figure it out. He stuffs the plastic bag of debris into the closet by the door and closes it with the resolution that he is done with Faye and Deb. From now on, there's only Katie. He knows it because he really feels it, and that's a certainty he's never felt before.

Connor is going to tell Katie that he loves her.

CHAPTER
THIRTY

In Which Faye Reminisces About the Rooting and Body Parts Connor Has Given Her

"My cock belongs to you," Connor grunted two nights ago as he pistoned atop Faye, his hips colliding with hers with a meaty smacking sound, both of their bodies slick with sweat and their muscles quaking together. The mattress had been stripped of most of its sheets and covers as they had twirled upon it, and now it was bare against her back.

Faye rolled her eyes. She'd heard that one before. What would she do with it, put it on the mantel with the others? Perhaps mount it on the wall? How stupid the offer sounded.

She wrapped her legs around his waist and her arms around his neck. She pulled his body down onto hers. He felt amazing inside her, his skin sliding across hers, but what really elevated the titillation of the whole encounter was the couple in the apartment across the way, taking turns watching them fuck in front of the balcony door. She could see them — too far away to make out any of their details, a bug in a window with a telescope proboscis pointed their way. She made her best porn face in their direction and then stared directly at them. She wanted them to know she knew they were there.

Faye had suspected what was happening when they dragged the bed from the corner of the apartment to the balcony door. She had smirked when he told her he wanted to do it under the stars with her but then turned the lights on, spotlighting his apartment to the city outside and blinding them to the night's sky. And she had outright laughed when he offered her the stars while adjusting the bed to offer the best exposure to the night.

Faye told him to "quit being such an idiot and fuck me."

Then she stripped, stripped him, and started in on him with no further discussion.

She thought of his earlier offerings of the sky and the stars, and when he added his cock to the list, she said, "You're so giving." Then she stuck fingers in his mouth, two of them, knuckle deep, pinning his tongue down to keep him from saying anything else. He gagged a bit but didn't seem to mind. She felt the warm, wet tube of muscle wriggle under the pads of her fingers, and his breathing past the obstruction sounded like an overrun dog. She didn't need him to talk.

In no time, a strand of warm saliva traced a slimy path down the back of her hand to her wrist. It beaded there in preparation of making the trek down her forearm. Then, Connor bit down on her fingers, not hard enough to break skin but hard enough to send a

184

jolt of pain up her arm, making her gasp with the shock, which, in turn, pushed her into a back-arching orgasm. Her seizing body caused him to convulse inside her and then collapse with his belly against hers, his cheek to hers.

Faye lay for a moment, breathing under the weight of him and feeling his pulsating retreat from inside her. She turned her head to the city view just in time to see the apartment with the telescope go dark and disappear into the surrounding night.

Faye catches the stairwell railing with both hands again, righting herself. In her distraction, she missed another step and almost fell onto the landing under the sign that reads "Floor 16." Faye's heart races from the adrenaline spike of her stumble. She smirks at her clumsiness but can't scold her sex-addled mind to pay more attention. She's too distracted by the lingering feel of him all over her skin, and she can't escape the smell of the nightshirt she wears, still damp in spots from their last session and steeped in their secret scents.

Faye's mind wanders to Connor's girlfriend. She's anonymous to Faye. A woman without face or form but with a strong enough presence in both of their lives to make her take the stairs and Connor bustle around like a maniac, trying to keep his apartment from tattling on him.

What did that mean? Faye wonders if Connor would afford her the same subterfuge, and after a moment she thinks it unlikely. Faye knows of the girlfriend and the other woman. It's obvious the girlfriend doesn't know about them.

Connor talked about both of them to her. He had asked her to do the same things that the one named Deb let him do, and while Faye thinks of herself as sexually liberated, she couldn't allow it. She was afraid she would look at herself differently for the rest of her life. She knows there are some things a person does that they have to live with every day.

What was that saying? she thinks. Once you're fucked, you can never be unfucked. Or something like that.

And what had Connor said about Katie? He told her about what they talked about. He told her the funny things Katie said, how she was going to introduce him to her family even though they had only been together a short while. He actually seemed excited by the prospect. There was that fish that lived on the balcony — she had given it to him and given it its stupid name. Connor talked about the things that they did together but never about what they did between the covers.

He loves her, Faye realizes. He just doesn't know it yet because his cock gets in the way. Once he recognizes it, he's going to be crushed under the weight of Deb and me. With hindsight, he'll track back to when he fell for her, add up all the times he cheated her of his feelings, and he'll collapse with the knowledge of how badly he's fucked up. Then he'll have to hide or fess up, and either way, Deb and I will be a forcibly forgotten past.

Faye feels a twinge of pity for him because, while Connor is a low-down cheater, he's more a good-hearted but unthinking victim of his cock, the one that he gives away so generously and freely. Regardless, there will be consequences. Not even that thing Deb lets him do can help him avoid the train wreck he's in for.

Faye wonders how many times Connor has scrambled to avoid a meeting between the three of them. Has Deb ever taken the stairs while she rode up in the elevator? Has she ever seen one of them entering the building while she was leaving? Then, she wonders if there are only three. She knows of Deb and the girlfriend, but could there be more? Oh yeah. There could be, she decides.

Faye had always attributed the feminine debris in the apartment to be from one of the other two. The coral lipstick she had thought was the girlfriend's because, really, who wears coral anymore? The nineties are long gone. The scarlet panties draped over the toaster, those would be Deb's. Faye could tell just from the way they were torn. Connor had never torn her panties off.

Faye thinks, just to add to Connor's impending emotional train wreck, that she will propose the three of them get together. Connor's mind would explode at the idea. Faye could picture his eager nod, and she has been intrigued by the stories of Deb's perverse proclivities for a while now. Who even thinks of that stuff?

Then there's this pink nightshirt she wears. She thinks about it for an entire flight of stairs but can't decide whose it is. The pink nightshirt — they had writhed all over it during their heated coupling. It had been in bed with them when they started. Connor laid it down on the floor so the carpet wouldn't leave friction burns on her knees. He placed it on the bathroom counter so her ass wouldn't get cold. He had taken her in there because he wanted to watch their struggle reflected in the mirror. He had placed her on it in the kitchen and somehow it stuck to her back as she took him up against the apartment door, grunting and sweating together in the hottest, sweatiest, and most epic fu —

What are you staring at, bitch? Faye wonders when she sees a woman standing half a flight down, her face a contorted mix of emotion.

Faye glares back in a primal, alpha-female sort of way, but doesn't notice that this woman is actually staring at the pink nightshirt. Faye thinks this woman is about to say something, but then she just bolts past, spins on the landing, and runs up the next flight, disappearing from sight. The noise of her footfalls slaps against the walls as she ascends.

CHAPTER
THIRTY-ONE

In Which Jimenez Gets All Slicked Up and Smellin' Good

The button for the third floor doesn't illuminate with the first press. Jimenez pokes it again before the lobby slides out of view, shrinking with the crack between the elevator doors. He wipes a soot smear from the third-floor button with the heel of his hand. Jimenez examines the panel; only the top corner is visibly charred. In hindsight, the fire was only a small one. The perceived size of it swelled in the dark with the panic of the moment.

A three-floor test drive, Jimenez thinks. Just to make sure everything is working properly. What's the worst that could happen?

Jimenez stands, eyes locked on the floor number displaying above the door. It doesn't move from "L." The elevator doesn't move, so he stabs the button again. The compartment shudders, and the lights flicker a little. A grinding metal wail echoes from outside the compartment, but the extra weight on the soles of Jimenez's feet tells him it's moving.

"It is," he says and smiles to himself. "It's working like a charm."

He watches the number above the door tick by the "2" and settle on the "3." The doors slide open and Jimenez frowns. The elevator has stopped a foot above the third-floor hallway. Jimenez presses the door-closed button and jabs at the third floor one again. The elevator free-falls a foot and halts with a bouncing jolt. Jimenez steadies himself with an arm against the wall. When the doors open again, the elevator is level with the third-floor hallway.

"Like a charm," Jimenez mumbles to himself.

The elevator still smells of smoke, so Jimenez unhooks his key loop and picks an odd-looking, peg-shaped key from among the others. He inserts it into the maintenance lock and turns it until the button lines up with the small, embossed letters that spell "Open" so the doors will remain open, the elevator locked in place.

"That will give you the time to air out your stink a bit," Jimenez tells the elevator as he steps off. He hoists up his tool belt because it has slipped from his hips. It jangles all the way up the hall to his apartment. He spins a few more keys around his key loop before finding the one for his door. He opens it, steps in, and flips on a light.

Little natural light comes into the apartment from outside because it faces the alley side of the building. There's a view of an office building's parking garage across the lane, a tall, close structure that blocks out any hope of the sky. At best, the light coming through the window warms from a cold blue to a cool blue by midday. It doesn't bother Jimenez though; the rent for

190

the place is cheap, and he only really comes to the apartment to sleep. The rest of his life is spent in the building working or out of it wandering around the city, going to an old movie theater or dancing. He considers the world to be his apartment and this apartment to be his bedroom.

Jimenez slips his shoes off at the door and empties his pockets. About fifty cents in change clatters against the kitchen counter. There's also a business card for a silk plant place, a crinkly cellophane wrapper from a hard candy, and the last service request — that leak under the kitchen sink. He looks around his small galley kitchen. There's a two-burner stove with its tiny oven, the fridge that holds his microwave dinners, and a microwave oven in the corner. The laminate counter is scratched near the sink from a previous occupant's careless butchery, and the veneer is chipped along the edge from some past trauma.

Jimenez strips his shirt off and examines the burned fabric on the sleeve. He pokes a finger through the hole, and it comes out the other side, coated in black ash. He realizes he's lucky he bought cotton instead of that cheaper plastic stuff that would have just melted and fused to his arm. He drops his shirt to the counter and then examines his arm. A bald patch emits the distinctive smell of burned hair and the skin is a little pink, but other than that, he seems unscathed.

He shakes his head and looks at the shirt crumpled on the counter. It was a good shirt.

Can't be fixed, he thinks, shrugs, and then throws it in the trash bin under the sink. He gathers the corners of the garbage bag and ties them together. The shirt, three microwave dinner boxes, a couple bags from instant oatmeal, and an empty carton of milk attest to the past three days. Jimenez crosses the living room, slides the balcony door open, and leans over the railing to drop the bag into the Dumpster below.

Back inside, Jimenez pulls off his undershirt and wanders into the bathroom, where he throws it into his hamper. He unbuckles his tool belt and puts it on the vanity counter and then lets his pants fall to the floor. He looks at his reflection in the mirror. He's a solid man with a furry, firm, round belly and thick arms. His briefs hang baggy under his tummy, the elastic on them long since worn out. The fabric is threadbare, and the dark patch of his pubes shows through.

Jimenez slaps his belly twice, strips off his underwear, and drops it into the hamper. He has a long, hot shower to wash the plastic smell from his skin and his hair. He uses a leave-in conditioner because he likes how glossy and thick it makes his coif look when he combs it back at the sides and leaves a swooping hill of hair on the top. Despite the shower, there's still a faint plasticky scent on his skin so he spritzes on a little cologne to mask it. He brushes his teeth and swishes some mouthwash around before getting dressed.

Clean undies, clean pants, clean undershirt, and clean shirt with a patch embroidered on the chest that reads "Jimenez." His reflection smiles and slings the tool belt back around his waist.

He feels good. He dances a quick bop, sliding and hopping back toward the kitchen.

Jimenez sweeps the change and paper from the kitchen counter into his palm and deposits them into his pocket. He glances in the mirror on the back of his apartment door.

I look good, he thinks. Maybe, instead of moping around the apartment, I'll treat myself to a movie tonight. His favorite actress has a new one out, and he can think of nothing better than popcorn and two hours with her. Maybe a cocktail before the movie. Maybe dancing afterward. Yes, tonight is definitely a night for dancing.

And besides, it would be a waste to look this good and not go out to show it off.

The elevator is still waiting up the hall with gaping doors when Jimenez leaves his apartment. He calls Marty on his cell phone as he makes his way back down the hall.

"Marty, the elevator's fixed up," he says.

"Great news." It sounds like Marty is eating soup. "I hope it wasn't too much a pain in the ass."

"No," Jimenez replies. "Wasn't too bad. Just a tripped fuse. Only had to throw a breaker."

"Can you take a look at the other one again?" Marty asks. "Maybe the same thing will get it running?"

"I'll take another look in the morning," Jimenez says.

"Great work, Jimmy. I don't know how much money that saved me." Marty slurps. "Take yourself out . . . Expense a meal, on me."

Jimenez uses the maintenance key to turn the elevator lock back to "Active" and sniffs the air as the doors slide closed. It's still a bit funky, but that will fade with time. He pulls the slip of paper from his pocket and hits the button for the twenty-fifth floor. Nothing happens, so he pokes at the button a few more times before the elevator shudders to life.

"Just need to stretch your legs before I take you dancing, hey?" Jimenez asks the elevator.

The lights flicker, and he is off, heading upward.

CHAPTER
THIRTY-TWO

In Which Garth Gets Scared, Gets Brave, and Then Gets Full-On Pretty

The package is wrapped in a tidy, symmetrical fourfold. Garth pinches the first two corners of the paper with opposite hands and lifts them, carefully unfolding the wrapping. Then he closes his eyes, reaches in, and scoops out the contents. He inhales the tactile experience, breathing deeply from the soft lace and cotton billowing gently between his fingers. Inside that bundle of fabric, he feels straps of smooth, glossy patent leather. The shoes — he feels their outline, slick leather through the fabric.

He exhales slowly, opens his eyes, and emits an involuntary, grateful squeak.

Carmine, he thinks. This is the best day ever. It was worth the wait, worth the long climb up the building. It's perfect, better than he could have pictured.

They made him the red dress. And it isn't some trampy crimson or a gaudy fuchsia . . . This is carmine. This is a beautiful, buttery, purple-tinted rust melting in his hands. On the phone they said they might be out of that color. Even if they had it available, Garth knew, it was so hard to tell the right color on the computer screen. He had learned that from the Palatinate blue dress he ordered a few months ago. The swatch on the screen had looked great, but the color had been too strong for his skin tone in real life.

But that's the past. This is now.

Garth holds pure joy in his hands, the perfect shade of red, folded and bound with a cross of beautiful burgundy ribbon. The seamstress is all about these extra touches. Harry, the guy at the store, had recommended her when he saw Garth's displeasure with the items on the racks. He told him about Floria, the seamstress the store used for custom orders. With a nod from Garth, Harry wrapped a measuring tape around Garth's various parts and took notes on his findings. Then, together, they placed a call to Floria.

Garth hoped so hard that they would have carmine in stock. It's costly to get these dresses made, being that he's a burly man. Now, to avoid the run-of-the-mill prêt-à-porter trashy cross-dresser look, he has Floria custom design his garments. For the price, he could look like a trashy cross-dresser ten times over, but his desire is not just about wearing the clothes. It's hard to not just look like a man in women's clothing. He has never wanted to be a woman, just a man wearing a beautiful gown. It's about feeling beautiful. There's a difference.

Because Floria is a specialist in this type of garment, and because she has such an amazing gift for creating wearable art, she's in strong demand. Garth can only

196

afford one gown every few months, but they are worth the wait and extra expense.

When the seamstress said they might not have that shade, Garth told her his second choice would be the laurel green. He would have been happy with that too because the pale gray-green was such an elegant shade and it would complement his eyes.

Harry nodded in agreement and said, "Good choice."

But here's the gown he dreamed of, liquid carmine draped across his fingers.

Maybe I'll order a laurel-green one in the next couple of months, he thinks.

Garth gently unfolds the delicate fabric. He pulls the shoes from the middle of the bundle and places them on the bed. He holds the evening gown, pinched between index finger and thumb. He knows he doesn't have the body type to properly handle a strapless number. As always, the craftsmanship is astounding. There are no puckered seams, no unintended ripples in the fabric. The neckline is a midtorso V with a fitted bodice. Affixed to one shoulder is a crepe drape that could be worn as a scarf or as a midsection wrap on those evenings he's feeling modest or self-conscious about his waistline. The sleeves are full length, not puffy but not restrictive either, perfect all the way to the wrist. It's not that Garth's afraid of his hairy arms; he just believes that the more that is hidden from the eye, the more there is to tantalize the mind, and the classier it is. It's the difference between an elegant gown like this and that trampy Palatinate-blue-and-yellow block-print bandage dress he first ordered.

Learned that lesson, Garth thinks to himself. Elegant is sexy. Trampy is for teenage girls and nightclub transvestites.

Without trying it on, Garth can see this gown will be fitted at the waist but the seams on either side of the midsection will draw the eye vertically for a slimming effect. It has an asymmetrical hemline, starting at the left knee and plunging to the right ankle.

Garth lays the dress flat on the bed and runs his fingertips over it to smooth the fabric flat. He turns his attention to the shoes. They are a mesmerizing black, a black so pure and smooth that he feels he could almost fall weightless into them. They have enclosed toes because Garth does not like the look of his toes. They are too workman and look like a bunch of hairy-knuckled clubs. The shoes are a strappy number, which will accentuate his ankles. Of all things, Garth feels he has beautiful ankles. He thinks there are too few manufacturers that make strappy numbers in men's size twelve, so he had Floria find a pair through her connections in the industry.

Nobody knows Garth's secret. He has held it close because it's hard to put into words. The drapes are always drawn across the windows, and the door is always locked, and at the end of each night, his gowns and shoes are always returned to their hiding place, hanging on hooks behind his clean work clothes. Garth knows what people would think of him. He reads the newspapers and hears the television preachers. He hears the guys talking at the construction site and always thinks, It isn't that simple. But it seems his needs are always summarized into bigoted sound bites and superficial judgments.

And so Garth hides and has felt a ravenous loneliness fester inside him for years. Nobody has ever met the real Garth, the one out of his overalls and hard hat. Sometimes he sinks so low, he cries for very little reason. There's one insurance commercial that gets him every time; the husband dies and doesn't even have coverage to pay for the funeral cost. Garth has always wallowed in his secrecy and has never once argued the innocence of what he needs, how the perversion most people see is only a mass affliction of past ideals.

Garth has only ever wanted to feel pretty. He doesn't want to be a woman nor does he care to impersonate one. He just wants to feel beautiful like one. Even as a kid, he didn't regret being born a boy nor did he regret later growing into a man. He has always been happy with his penis, just not always what it's attached to. He has suffered body-image issues, thinking that he could always be slimmer and taller and curved in different places. Over time, Garth has grown to accept his body hair and muscular arms. He is even fine with his thick facial hair and how he grows a five o'clock shadow by eleven in the morning whenever he shaves. He has never resented not being a woman and has never resented women because he is a man. No, he admires them for their grace. Their beauty and strength are so much subtler than his that, at times, his admiration turns to self-consciousness.

Garth bustles into the bathroom. He strips and trims. He showers and powders. He watches his blurry body jiggle in the steamy bathroom mirror as he brushes his teeth. The glum loneliness that he felt in the stairwell has begun to lift because this evening, he is going to do something to change it. No longer will he cry at that insurance commercial.

He's positively charged with the possibility of effecting this change.

Loneliness is a symptom of the cowardly and meek. Garth rallies and then spits a gob of toothpaste into the sink. His aim is off, and half of the minty spout hits the faucet with a flat splat.

But no more, he thinks. I will soon be revealed.

CHAPTER
THIRTY-THREE

In Which the Tripod Petunia Delilah Finally Reaches Apartment 805 and Realizes She Has No Plan B

The boy isn't that heavy, Petunia Delilah thinks and glances back at him. Good thing he's just a little guy.

She has him grasped by one ankle and drags him behind her. He slides and stops, keeping pace with Petunia Delilah's staggering gait. He lies on his back, his limp arms trail above his head, and his hair stands on end. A halo of fine strands floats in the air from the static buildup. The boy's other leg, the one not in Petunia Delilah's grasp, flops out to one side, bent at the knee and again at the waist. It's kept in check by the wall. The whole posture makes the boy look like a rag doll freeze-framed, falling from a great height.

Petunia Delilah grimaces and grits her teeth with her purpose. That and a weak contraction tweak her body for several seconds so she has to concentrate on letting it pass.

The leg between her legs twitches. Mere minutes ago, this was a cause for tears and panic. Now, her perception of this extra limb has changed. She doesn't stop to marvel how her thoughts have shifted so quickly and completely from utter fear of her predicament to drive for survival through her sheer force of will. They will all get through this. She will make it happen.

Alive and kicking, she thinks. That's a good sign. Keep it up, baby.

Kimmy's voice pops into her mind. "Giving a natural birth to your baby is a beautiful experience," it chirps. "Women have been doing it for hundreds of thousands of years without modern medicine. It's a wonderful milestone for your body, something you won't want to miss the full experience of because you're sedated and all whooped up on opioids. It's a blessing from nature. It's a marvel, the body unified by a single cause, working wholly in such a beautiful act. Your mind can overcome any discomfort with the right training and focus." Then she adds a perky "Thoughts become things."

"I'll punch you in the throat," Petunia Delilah murmurs to the hallway. "Next time I see you, Kimmy, that's what I'll do," she grumbles as she huffs and sweats the few remaining painful and exhausting steps to Apartment 804's door.

Thoughts become things.

A peculiar feeling crosses her mind, one urging her to leave the door and move on to the next one. The first thing she notices is the number four is missing from the door. In its absence, there are two screw holes and a darker patch of paint in the ghostly shape of a four. The doorjamb near the handle is gouged and splintered, like

202

someone forced it open at some point. There's a tarry black smear on the door handle and plenty of scratches in the paint around it.

A cough sounds from inside, and a chemical smell grows stronger as she approaches. It's a sharp, acidic smell that makes her wince. There's a grinding drone of some toneless, beat-heavy dance music.

She raises her arm to knock on the door, but another phlegmy cough from inside stays it in midair. She stands, arm raised and knuckles a few inches from the wood. There's something off about the place. The battered door, the missing number, the smell, the sickly hacking coming from inside, all foster a feeling that Apartment 804 is best left alone.

There's another racking cough from behind the door and a loud thump. It sounds closer than the previous ones. As if whoever is in there has moved closer to the door. A shadow forms in the light coming through the crack at the bottom of the door.

Petunia Delilah lets her arm drop. She averts her eyes from the spy hole and takes a small, shuffling step backward. She bumps into the kid on the floor and stops still.

"Come on, little unconscious kid," Petunia Delilah says quietly to the boy on the floor. "I don't think this is the one to help us."

She moves on, breathing heavily, the sound of it rasping in her ears.

One foot, the other foot, then back to the first one. Steps last for miles, and seconds take painful hours.

Apartment 805. It's not too far away. It has to be this next one, Petunia Delilah thinks, because I don't think I can make it to 806.

Thoughts become things.

The boy gets heavier with each step. He seems to gain weight, and the floor he slides across becomes tackier, holding him a little more persistently with every step she takes. Her legs burn with the effort, and her back seizes with pain. She can't think of a time when she felt more spent. Exhaustion begs her to lie down next to the boy and rest for a few minutes, but she knows she won't get up again if she complies. Her baby would die and maybe she would too.

Even so, Petunia Delilah feels like laughing. As she approaches Apartment 805, she hears the familiar strains of "Help Me, Rhonda" coming through the door. A course of elation works its way through her tired body. She leans beside the door and rests a hand on her knee, bending forward to relieve the pain tugging at her back.

Someone's home, she thinks giddily and looks at the boy for a moment. I can smell food cooking. Finally, someone who can help.

"I found us help, little unconscious kid," she tells him and knocks on the door. "Everything will be okay now. With a little luck, this person will have some fucking ice cream sandwiches for both of us when this is all over."

There's no answer.

The song plays on.

Petunia Delilah waits a moment, catching her breath. Maybe whoever's there didn't hear the knock over the sounds of the Beach Boys.

She pounds on the door again, with more force. It rattles in the frame.

"I need help," she tells the door. Her voice comes out cracked and strained. "Please, I need help. I'm having a baby and there's this kid who collapsed and he needs help too. Please open the door," she pleads. "Please."

Sweat trickles down the bridge of her nose, pools into a trembling drop, which then falls to the carpet. She knows she has no energy left to make it to the next apartment. It has to be this door or nothing. There is no plan B.

Petunia Delilah focuses on the dark, wet dot on the carpet for a moment and strains to hear anything apart from the Beach Boys, anything that might confirm someone is there on the other side of the door. She doesn't hear anything. It's possible someone left the music on, but it's unlikely that someone left something baking in the oven unattended.

Anger boils up in her. She knows someone is there. There has to be.

Why won't you help us? she thinks. Then she resolves: You are going to help us.

"I know someone is in there," she shouts and swings her fist against the door as hard as she can. It jumps against the frame. "I can hear your music and I can smell your fucking baking now help me."

Petunia Delilah hits the door again.

I'm coming through this door one way or another, she thinks.

"I can't" comes a reply, mousy and barely audible.

Petunia Delilah looks at the spy hole.

You're fucking kidding me, she thinks.

"What?" she snaps and then checks her aggression, calming it with a deep breath. "Could you please open the door? I need help. My name's Petunia Delilah and I'm having a baby and there's this passed-out kid I found down the hall."

"I can't." The voice is small behind the door. "I want to help you, but I really can't. I can't open the door. It's this . . . thing I have. It's hard to explain."

CHAPTER
THIRTY-FOUR

In Which Claire the Shut-In Comes to Terms with Losing Her Job at the PartyBox and Is Then Disrupted by an Urgent Pounding on Her Door

"That's just great," Claire says and clicks Gabby's email closed.

She empties the wineglass, slams the monitor of the laptop shut for good measure, and then drums her fingers on top of it.

One of the problems with being aggressively introverted is that the job market is quite limited. There aren't so many work-from-home jobs for a middle-aged woman with a college diploma in Theoretical Human Anatomy with a minor in Managerial Accounting for Non-Accountants. The last time she looked, this was it. The PartyBox. She was happy to sign on with Gabby and her burgeoning business, and now this: outsourced and unemployed.

Claire inhales the aromas floating around the apartment, once so comforting and now seemingly a bit less substantial. The quiche will be amazing and the night will be quiet, she thinks. She's looking forward to watching the news with a steaming slice and forgetting all about the PartyBox. Then, once the anchorman says good evening, she'll close the curtains as the sun goes down. She's looking forward to having a shower, putting on a clean housecoat, curling up under the tassel of her reading lamp, and putting a dent in the new copy of *To Kill a Mockingbird* that arrived in the mail the other day. She had disposed of her old copy because she was sure it was the cause of the musty smell her apartment had acquired after she read the last word. It's her fifth new copy because that smell seems to pervade her apartment every time she finishes it.

She can't wait to forget the strange phone call and the PartyBox and just read until she drifts off to sleep.

Tomorrow is for starting the job search, she thinks. Tomorrow is for replying to the email and getting the number for the placement company Gabby offered.

Tomorrow is for worry, but tonight, she resolves, is for tonight.

She turns on the oven light and checks on her creation again. Seventeen minutes left according to the stove timer, counting the time backward even though time has continued its unidirectional march forward. Claire guesses it's a matter of perspective. The top of the quiche is starting to brown, and tiny bubbles rise through the mixture slowly, getting caught in the newly gelatinous texture. She nods, dons a pair of yellow rubber gloves from a package, and does the dishes. Then she puts the mixing bowl and cutlery in the dishwasher, adds the detergent, dumps in a cup of white vinegar, and turns it on. She sprays down the counters again with a mild bleach solution followed by a disinfectant wipe pulled from a single sheet package. Then, another. Then a final wipe with the paper towel and it's good until the following morning.

Claire pulls one glove off, turning it inside out as it slides from her hand. She revels in the smooth feeling from the delicate frosting of powder that lines the inside. To her it's like the finest silk against her skin. Then she bundles the glove, the disinfectant wipes, and their packages in the other hand and pulls that glove off, inside out, making a satisfying, tidy, and entirely sanitary bundle of refuse. She drops the bolus into the garbage can and rubs her hands together.

Tomorrow is for worry, but tonight, she thinks, is for tonight.

She stands, the apartment quiet save for the occasional arrhythmic tick from the oven.

It's too quiet for a Friday afternoon, she thinks.

If she strains, she can hear the neighbor in the next apartment over. She thinks she recognizes the song playing but then becomes unsure when the beat takes an unexpected turn. The occasional horn bleats from outside, down on Roxy, but it only sounds once in a while.

She glances at the countertop radio and flicks it on. "Help Me, Rhonda" pours out of the speakers. Claire feels warmth start to spread through her again. She can't tell whether it's the wine — how much did I have anyway? — or the routine of a wonderful Friday night, the quiche and the music and the aromas filling her apartment.

She looks around, considers closing the blinds early, then decides against it. The sunlight is lovely. She dances. Her hips sway and her steps twirl her through the kitchen and into the living room. She raises her arms above her head and sways her body and spins it around, her legs and hips corkscrewing elegantly. She smiles and she sings, dancing her way through the warm smells of the quiche baking, and forgets all the day. She feels safe and at peace.

Tonight is for tonight.

There's an urgent pounding on the apartment door. Claire jumps at the noise and then freezes in midtwirl. She waits, staring at the door, her heart thrumming and her mind trying to convince her, logically, that she hadn't heard a thing.

The pounding sounds again.

What is it? Claire's heart skips into a panicked rhythm to match it. Is it the man from the front door coming to get me? Her body tenses. Her pulse rushes in her ears. Did he manage to get into the building?

"I need help." A woman's voice on the other side of the door. It's hoarse and strained and all too close. "Please, I need help. I'm having a baby and there's this kid who collapsed and he needs help too. Please open the door. Please."

Perhaps if I stay still and quiet they will go away, Claire thinks. She slowly lowers her arms and takes a creeping step in the direction of the door.

Cheerily, "Help me, Rhonda. Help, help me, Rhonda."

"I know someone is in there," the voice comes. There is a single bang from the door. It jumps against the frame. "I can hear your music and I can smell your fucking baking now help me."

Claire crosses her apartment on tiptoes, her arms held out defensively in front of her. Even the sound of her clothes moving seems too loud. Her hands are the first things to reach the door, her fingertips touching the cool paint. Claire leans in and sees a fish-eye forehead through the peephole. Claire jumps back a step. Another thump on the door unleashes a shock wave through the wood and into her palms.

"I can't," she says, wanting her voice to be strong, but it's weak and trembling. She steps up to the door again and peers through the peephole. A woman looks directly at her. They stare each other in the eye. Claire wants to shy away but doesn't. The woman looks a mess: shambolic hair, glistening forehead, and a bright-red shiny face. The woman also looks honest and kind, a face that would be transparent, unable to be devious in any way even if she was to try.

"What?" she says. Claire watches her lips move in keeping with her voice but more entrancing. Her face falls and her shoulders slump. "Could you please open the door? I need help. My name's Petunia Delilah and I'm having a baby and there's this passed-out kid I found down the hall."

"I can't," Claire says again. This time her voice finds a bit more strength. "I want to help you, but I really can't. I can't open the door. It's this . . . thing I have. It's hard to explain."

"You can't open the door? Lady —"

"My name is Claire." Claire watches the woman through the peephole. She stands for a moment and then places a hand against the door, right about where Claire holds her palm against the surface.

"Claire." Petunia Delilah's voice sounds weary and resigned. "Claire, can you please open the door? I don't know how much longer I can stay on my feet and I need to call for help. My baby's coming now and it's in trouble. My phone's dead — I can't get ahold of my boyfriend or my midwife or anyone. I'm all alone here."

"What about the kid? I can't see him," Claire says, then bites her bottom lip.

Through the keyhole, Claire sees that Petunia Delilah clearly knows she's being watched. She looks directly at the fish eye.

"He's here, just lying here on the carpet. Not doing much more than that and breathing." She looks down at her feet. "I don't know what's wrong with him, he just passed out. Please, Claire," Petunia Delilah says, "help."

"Okay, stay right there," Claire says as she pats the door with the palm of her hand. "I'll get my phone and call an ambulance. Don't move."

One step from the door, Claire freezes. Through the inch of wood she hears the most pained and animal noise she has ever heard. The woman on the other side, Petunia Delilah, groans and starts sobbing. It's a pitiable noise of pain and frustration. Claire responds on the same base level. Before rational thought can stop her, she unbolts the dead bolt, removes the chain from its track, and opens the door.

CHAPTER
THIRTY-FIVE

In Which Homeschooled Herman Suffers a Horrific Accident

And as the car drifted across the lane into oncoming traffic, the opening piano strain and Bonnie Tyler's smoky voice drifted through the speakers. From the back seat, Herman watched his mom shaking his dad's shoulder. Dad didn't respond. His head drooped forward, exposing the massif of vertebrae under the skin on the back of his neck. Herman could see Mom's mouth moving, but he couldn't hear the sounds coming out. She was screaming in Dad's ear. The veins in her neck and on her forehead stood out. Her face turned rosy; her cheeks flushed pink.

Dad didn't move.

Mom looked out the windshield. Their car had crossed fully into the oncoming lane. She grabbed the wheel and pulled it to the right. The car jerked back toward the centerline, toward the safe side of the road. It was a ridiculous line on the pavement, a ludicrous protection, those three inches of yellow paint demarcating the difference between safety and this.

And the chorus began to swell through the speakers.

As the front of the car crumpled with the impact, as the screeching of metal being folded and torn asunder battered Herman's eardrums, and even as the diamonds of safety glass sprayed across his body like hail, the radio played on. As Mom and Dad were thrown forward in their seats, only to come to an aorta-tearing jolt against the seat belt restraints, as his sister was tossed sideways into him, her head colliding with his in a shock of sepia sparks behind his eyelids, even through a second concussive whump and another shuddering jolt, through it all, Bonnie Tyler sang on.

The car whined and screamed in protest as it was bent and shattered. When the car spun sideways across the highway and the tires wailed against the speed and flinty asphalt, when gravity took a spin around the roof, leaving the debris of the crash suspended in opposition to its forces, and even when everything went silent except for a lone voice screaming somewhere outside, the song played on.

The car had come to rest on its side, and Herman hung sideways by his seat belt, suspended over his sister. The weight of his head bent his neck. His ear rested on his shoulder. He couldn't muster the energy to right himself. His arms dangled, one across his chest and the other splayed out in the space below him. The back of his hand rested against his sister's cheek, her hair tangled through his fingers, soft as feathers to the touch. Herman did not feel it though; his body was limp and he was gone. He had been for a while.

The radio played all seven minutes of the power ballad, and it took seven more for help to arrive.

But that length of time was nothing to Herman. He wouldn't come back for three more weeks. He didn't want to. When he did wake, he was in a hospital, and he was alone in a dark room. Every bit of him hurt as he tenderly moved his hands over his body. There were wires and tubes attached to him. There was beeping coming from somewhere in the dark. Through the window, he could see it was dark outside. There was a city of lights out there, just on the other side of the glass.

Later, the doctors said the reason he survived was because he seemed to be unconscious at the time of impact. His body was completely limp and was able to absorb the thrashing as the vehicle spun to its side and rolled over twice. They also told him he was a kid and his body would heal quickly. A few more weeks passed, and they released him into Grandpa's care, as per the directions in his parents' will. There was no other family on the continent.

Even later, Herman would revisit the scene. Going back to that moment was how he remembered what his mom, dad, and sister looked like. He reached across the invisible centerline of the seat, the one they had fought over for years, from his side to hers. He felt his sister's hair, her soft tangles woven between his fingers. When he looked down from where he was suspended by the seat belt, asphalt outside her window, she appeared to be sleeping. Occasionally, he would pop in to see it play out again, but he would always leave before the song ended. There was nothing to understand after that point in time. By then he would be gone, knowing where and when he could return should his parents' faces fade from memory or should his fingers forget the softness of his sister's hair.

He never told Grandpa he went back to the car crash, not even after he had settled into his room in the Seville on Roxy to work on his history lessons and language studies and trigonometry problems.

Herman stared at the page, his eyes dancing between the two dots that Grandpa had penciled in opposite corners. They were 13.9 inches apart, and no matter which way his eyes traced lines across the blank white page, they always wound up the same distance apart.

"I'll leave you to it," Grandpa said as he left Herman's room. "The distance between the two is variable. Those two dots can be the same dot, or they can be anywhere up to fourteen inches apart, like you think. Now tell me how that could be."

Herman chewed on his pencil eraser as he contemplated the puzzle. The kettle whistled from the kitchen, and then the newspaper rustled in the living room. The button of eraser came off in his mouth.

How can those two dots on the page actually be one dot? he pondered.

Or, alternately, he thought, how can one thing exist twice at the same time?

"Got it yet?" Grandpa called out from the living room.

"No," Herman mumbled loud enough for Grandpa. "It's impossible. You can't make the hypotenuse shorter," he said to himself. "It's an absolute."

"Herman," Grandpa's voice came, "the world being round was an impossibility. Now we live on a new continent. Human flight was impossible. Now we go into space. This is easy compared with those things. Think of that space between the dots as time, not distance. Time is a drug we're all addicted to. Sooner or later we have to kick the habit."

The newspaper rustled, and Grandpa went quiet.

Herman put his hands to opposite edges of the paper, pinning it flat to his desk. His brow furrowed in concentration. He scrawled out a few more calculations, his frustration mounting. They didn't work out, so he crossed them out. He circled the 13.9 at the end of his original calculation.

What did Grandpa mean? If distance is time, the only way to shorten it is to travel faster. But distance didn't travel at a speed, the combination of the two did, velocity did. They were tied together, but not the same, as Grandpa said.

With each passing minute, Herman felt his flustered brain become more agitated until he could no longer think. Had anger been in his nature, he would have crumpled the paper and thrown it in the trash. Instead, he swept his hand across the desk. The paper fell off the side and landed against the wall in a curl, and momentarily, the curve of the paper let the two dots touch before it straightened itself again.

"The two dots are the same," Herman said to himself. "They are no distance apart even though they're on opposite corners of the page."

He picked the page up and slowly curled the corners toward each other. All the while, the distance between the dots grew shorter and shorter until they touched. They were the same even though they were far apart. He let the page lie flat on the desk, excited to share his discovery with Grandpa.

He called out, "Grandpa, I know it. I know that they're the same dot."

There was no reply from the living room.

He contemplated the equations scrawled across the paper, some crossed out and others circled. The pencil strokes were clear and magnified; viewed from so close they were pockmarked, thick graphite lines striking out across the fibrous expanse of paper. The tip of the pencil was a waxy moon rock from this magnified perspective.

The quiet apartment was unsettling. Herman knew something was wrong. He could feel it. His body knew too. This silence often came before the blackness.

There was silence. The usual noises of the apartment were gone. The only sounds came from inside Herman, his heart beating a thump-thump to push his blood around. Herman breathing. His own voice in the silence of his apartment, sounding muffled in the flesh and bone of his head, calling out after a moment's ponderance.

"Grandpa," it said.

Herman stood, waiting.

There was no reply.

"Grandpa? Are you there?" he called out again.

Then, there is blackness and commotion and a persistent tugging at his leg. He hears voices, watery and far away.

"He's here, just lying here on the carpet. Not doing much more than that and breathing," a woman's voice says. "I don't know what's wrong with him, he just passed out. Please, Claire, help."

CHAPTER
THIRTY-SIX

In Which Things Below Are Rapidly Growing Larger from Ian's Perspective

Ian doesn't know it, but for a moment of time so short it is barely measurable, he passes the halfway point of his descent. Ian is starting to feel the physical stress of being airborne for so long. He gasps, his mouth gaping in an atmosphere too thin for him to process any oxygen. He can't get his gills to flare, no matter how hard he tries. The wind blasting by his body forces them to remain shut. The current is much too strong for the delicate mechanism to function.

For a moment, he wonders, Now . . . what was I doing? Then he realizes he's falling.

As he passes the thirteenth floor, he slips across a line drawn in the sky, out of the late-afternoon light and into the shadows cast by the surrounding buildings. It's a strong contrast to the light, and when the last glint sparks off his golden scales, he finds his mood is dampened. The once brilliant reflections off the glass and steel of the surrounding buildings become muted with a gloomy light. Everything that was once there and so clear is now a dimmed version of itself. All the details are diminished; the former clarity of the day grows muddy. The building alongside which he falls is less vibrant and the air itself seems to become more subdued. A deep sense of foreboding sprouts within him, as if he has passed around the dark side of the moon. He's alone in an alien environment, and the elation of his escape feels less certain now, more a chipped veneer covering something threatening and dangerous.

The thirteenth-floor apartment is pink, as a state of being as much as it is a color. The walls are painted pink, the furniture is pink, and the floor lamp has a gauzy Pepto piece of fabric draped over it. To Ian, it's a streak of late-sunset pink, the kind that shows itself moments after the sun drops below the horizon. The color is drawn into a vertical streak as he zips past.

Ian doesn't know it, but that apartment is rented by Raquel the bartender and Fontaine, her flight attendant roommate. They aren't home at the moment, but so many moments of their lives are still in there, between the walls, the ceiling, and the floor. Raquel and Fontaine split the rent, all the bills, and they get along famously. They've kissed each other a couple of times in a way friends typically don't: once when they were drunk at a New Year's Eve party and got a little carried away, and once at a party where a hot guy became creepy and Fontaine needed a way to flee his advances. Social lesbianism has always been a great escape. It simultaneously titillated the creepy guy and freed Fontaine from any obligations he perceived. Neither of

222

them identifies as queer, but both think the kisses were really nice. They have never told each other as much, however.

Ian can't see the future, but Fontaine is two years away from meeting the love of her life on a charter flight to Mexico. She has a twenty-four-hour layover, and he's booked into an all-inclusive resort for a week. She stays with him the whole time she's there, and they date often when he returns. At first their marriage is a dream, but by the end of the fifth year, both of them have become heavy drinkers. They attend couples' counseling groups and spend thousands of dollars on individual therapy. For some reason they're never quite sure of, they enable each other's worst tendencies. There are a few happy years and many hard ones.

Their marriage lasts eight years and four months. In the end, there're no kids to share, no dog to fight over, just a mortgage and a joint bank account to sort out when they separate. They don't talk after the split, and neither remarries. Fontaine quits drinking, but her ex-husband doesn't and prematurely loses most of his teeth.

Raquel keeps in touch with Fontaine. She's there for support, and they are even roommates again for a short while when Fontaine leaves her husband.

Raquel never gets married and she's okay with that. Now . . . what was I doing?

Ian's perspective changes along with the light. The ground is much closer and more portentous than it once was. It was so far away mere moments ago, way down there in the shadows, so innocuous that it was possible to ignore it without effort. But what was once a distant backdrop to his life has become a definite and dangerous player in his fate. The finality of his journey is approaching, and with it comes a foreboding that was not felt at the start. Initially, fresh with the excitement of adventure, he was blinded to the near certain outcome of his fall. Presently, the only control in his life is the constant pull gravity exerts. Were he capable of contemplating it, he might realize that this gravity is no different from the constant pull time wields against all things.

Ian enters one of the last cycles of his memory before he reaches the ground, one in which the realization of death lurks as he zips past an empty twelfth-floor apartment.

Ian doesn't know it, but the previous occupants of the twelfth-floor apartment moved out two days ago. They were well liked by their neighbors, a handsome newlywed couple with a lovely disposition. The few times they threw a party, they remembered to turn the music down at ten o'clock as stipulated in the building's rules. They would keep an eye on their neighbors' apartments when they went on vacation, collect the mail, feed the cat, and water the plants.

He was a salesman for new condos, and she was an engineer. Their sex was ordinary, but they had it often, quietly, and to the satisfaction of each. However, she was always mildly annoyed by his need to have a shower within minutes of them coming. She felt it implied that she was dirty or their sex was dirty, neither of which she believed to be true.

When they moved, they packed their dishes with newspaper between each bowl and plate. They labeled the boxes well and courteously packed their books in small boxes that weren't overly heavy for the movers. And then they moved out to their suburban house in a blissful new community called Burnt Timber Acres. Now, they have a yard and a fence and property taxes and furnace cleanings to schedule every couple of years.

Ian can't see the future for them, but there are two babies there, not so far away, one girl and one boy. Not everything is blissful, of course. There are several fights and some yelling. One of them leaves the other for a short while over money and trust issues, but they reconcile quickly and are evermore in love.

When he dies after forty-eight years of marriage, she grows lonely and follows him a year later. Both children speak at the funerals and give touching eulogies. The younger one deems himself a poet and reads a heart-wrenchingly awkward poem. Most mourners are brought to tears, even those who rarely cry. It's less for the poem's performance and more for its ill-executed potency.

And what Ian wouldn't do for the ability to generate tears. His eyes, burning from dryness, flit from the twelfth-floor apartment to the street below. A second ambulance pulls up to the curb. As with the first, the strobing lights remain on even as both doors open. The cars on the street continue their crawl by, a sluggish mechanical millipede. The bustle below seems so slow because of the speed of his descent. It seems to take an eternity for the ambulance doors to open, and by the time the paramedics emerge, Ian is staring sidelong and head down through the eleventh-floor window.

CHAPTER
THIRTY-SEVEN

In Which Our Heroine Katie Encounters the Evil Seductress Faye

There's no mistaking her pink nightshirt. This woman, paused in her descent half a flight of stairs away, is wearing Katie's nightshirt. It's wrinkled and stained and it's on some other woman, but it's definitely hers.

There's no mistaking where this woman got it from, and there's no mistaking why she is wearing it. It's simple to connect one thing to the other, especially since they're presented together right in front of her. It's abundantly clear now.

Katie left the nightshirt at Connor's a few days ago. She had gotten into the habit of leaving behind something on every visit. She wanted it to remind Connor of her. She had the romantic notion that he would smile when he saw the nightshirt. She even conjured beautiful visions of Connor snuggling up with it in bed, falling into a peaceful sleep with the soft cotton under his cheek and the lingering smell of her skin a subtle fragrance in his nose.

There's no mistaking what this woman is doing in the stairwell, just as there's now no mistaking the hesitation in Connor's voice that she heard before he buzzed her through the lobby door a few minutes ago. He told this other woman to take the stairs, assuming that she was coming up in the elevator. There's another woman in Connor's life whom Katie didn't know about, and this is her, in the flesh and a few stairs away.

Katie stands for a moment, dumbfounded by these cascading revelations. They happen so quickly that she reels with each one; each layer reasoned out falls into place upon the previous one to build a picture of that which she did not know mere seconds ago. That old world she was in is gone. This is a new one in which this other woman exists.

And now, reason is done, revelation has been had, and reaction can reign.

Katie thinks to punch this other woman and even thinks specifically where she would punch her, right in the snatch. Katie thinks to scream at this woman wearing her nightshirt, becoming a raving and ranting banshee, waving her arms and backing this other woman against a wall and accusing her of sabotaging her love. Then again, maybe this woman doesn't even know of her existence. Is it her fault that she's the other woman, or is it Connor's? Before her mind even frames the question, she turns all her hurt and rage toward Connor, somewhere up there, thirteen floors above their heads, still thinking she is ignorant to his harem.

This other woman stares at Katie, who can do nothing under her gaze but choke back a sob of confusion, brush past her, and run up the stairs. Once she's out of sight, Katie's vision is a jarring and twisting one of the stairwell leading her upward toward him. It's his fault more than it's hers, she reasons through the blurring rush of emotion. It's Connor who had the ability to say no, not to pursue, not to hurt. And he had chosen to do it all.

Or is it my fault? Katie wonders. Is it something I did or didn't do? What need does Connor have that I'm not fulfilling? Am I expecting too much of him too soon?

They have only known each other for three months, she reasons, actually, less than three months by only a few days. Still, things have been so good between them. They have never strained to talk to each other and have never been uncomfortable in each other's company. Katie had pictured them together a year from now. She saw them beyond that too, going to a movie or having a morning coffee and reading the paper together. She hadn't yet pictured them married or with kids or old together, but surely, that was only a matter of time too.

The sign reading "Floor 21" bounces by.

Exhaustion sets into Katie's body. She's drained, but she panics that she can't get to him soon enough, to stand in front of him and make him explain himself. She begins to doubt what she saw five floors below.

Had she been too quick to judge, or had she seen what she suspected of him instead of the truth? Maybe it wasn't her nightshirt. Maybe it's all a coincidence and that woman shops at the same store she does and bought the same nightshirt she has. Maybe it's all a mistake and Connor will be there waiting for her, none the wiser about the woman in the stairwell, just like he doesn't know the elevator's broken.

He would be confused by the raving maniac she has become. He would smile at her and explain that he didn't know what she was talking about. He would calm her fears and she would believe him and then everything would go back to normal.

That has to be the truth, Katie thinks. Please let it be the truth. It's all an unfortunate coincidence and he's waiting for me and he'll take me into his arms and, after a few moments, he will tell me that he loves me.

He will say, "Katie, I have never known anyone like you, and even though we have only been together for three months, less a few days, I know you're the one for me. All the things I thought were so important until now don't matter anymore and I'm scared because of that. You've changed everything for me, so completely and so definitely. Even though I'm terrified by how consuming my feelings for you are, I'm also excited by the thought of spending the rest of my life with you."

And she wouldn't say a word because she wouldn't have to. She would just bury her face in his chest, and his chin would rest on the top of her head. There would be something between them that was so strong and complete that it wouldn't have to be spoken; it could just be felt there, between their bodies. It would be so much stronger than any words she could say.

Everything can still work out. There's no way it can't this time. Even though she had stood in front of the other woman sneaking down the stairwell, and even though Connor had been caught, she so strongly doesn't want it to be true that she feels herself willing to be lied to just to make everything she's thinking about go away.

Even though she wanted it, the door handle to the twenty-seventh-floor hallway comes too quickly into her hand. She pushes through the door even though she wants to stay amid her delusions in the stairwell forever because she figures not knowing at all is so much better than realizing the truth. It hurts so much less than the confirmation of her suspicions.

As Katie rushes down the hallway toward Connor's door, she wishes she had never taken the stairwell. She wishes that she'd never seen that woman and that everything was as simple as it had been a minute ago. She wishes Jimenez hadn't been there in the elevator, telling her it was broken. She wishes she had never walked past the catcalls of the construction site a few blocks up Roxy, and she wishes she had called Connor on the phone instead of arriving unannounced. It would have been so much easier if she had never said yes to going to coffee with Connor and so much simpler if she had never taken Anthropology 305, "The Crossroads of Scientific Magic and Cultural Realism," if she had never gone to college, if she had never left the house.

It all would have been so much easier but, she realizes as she reaches for the doorknob to Connor's apartment, not necessarily better.

If he tells me it isn't true, I'm going to believe him, Katie thinks.

The apartment door is unlocked, so she doesn't knock. She just enters.

He's there, sitting on the edge of the bed, wearing nothing but his sweatpants. His head is held bowed in his hands, as if it's too heavy to hold up without help. His elbows are planted on his knees as if he isn't strong enough to support its weight with the weak mechanics of his arms. He looks up at her, cheeks wet and tears streaming from his eyes. A glistening pearl of snot snails its way from his nostril to his lip.

"I'm sorry," he says. His voice cracks, raw with emotion. "I've made a terrible mistake."

CHAPTER
THIRTY-EIGHT

In Which the Villain Connor Radley Admits He Made a Terrible Mistake and Then Inadvertently Makes Another

"I'm sorry," Connor says. "I've made a terrible mistake."

Katie stands at the door. She doesn't move. She doesn't say a word.

Connor looks at her, his eyes begging hers, misinterpreting her fury for confusion. And as quickly and pointedly as he sought her gaze, he averts his. His guilt will not let him look at her. He hangs his head again, staring at the dark spots on his gray sweatpants, where his tears make constellations in the fabric.

He draws a ragged breath before continuing.

"I've only realized now what I should have seen months ago." He wants to say more, but his body clenches as he chokes off a sob. The sound comes out as a weak hiccup. He waits for the wave of emotion to pass.

"Let me explain," Connor stammers. He sucks in a wet sniff and runs the back of his arm across his face in an attempt to clean up his leakings. Then he falls silent, sitting on the bed with his head hung.

Katie crosses the room to the kitchen and leans against the counter. She looks out at Ian on the balcony. His bowl is a dewy drop in the larger scene, his body an even smaller golden pixel in the picture. A stack of paper is piled on top of his bowl and weighted there with the coffee mug she bought Connor. She lets her gaze be led slowly around the apartment by all the things she left behind, connecting the reminders of their time together, her residual presence in his place. There's a beauty magazine draped open on the arm of the couch where she didn't leave it. She doubts Connor had been leafing through it for makeup tips. There are her slippers in the corner. She tries to remember if that's where she left them. While Katie continues her appraisal of the room, Connor sits, meek and whimpering.

Her eyes finally fall on him and the puddle of misery that is his face. She feels overwhelming anger now more than anything.

"Go on," she says in a measured voice.

"There was this woman —"

"Was?"

"Yes, was, just until now but definitely was. When you called up . . . she was here."

"I know. The elevators are broken, and I had to take the stairs to get up here." Katie fights to keep the emotion she feels from creeping into her voice. She doesn't want to be the hysterical one even if she deserves to be. "You gave her my nightshirt." She crosses her arms and doesn't know how much longer she can stave off her tears.

"There's something in me that needed her then. I needed her here and I need you too. Now, I know I need you more and I was so blind to that before. I guess I just got caught up in the excitement of someone new —"

"New? We've only been seeing each other for three months," Katie says. She can't stop herself. She starts to cry. "Less a few days."

"I know, but even that's still so new I didn't know I felt this way about you until now. I didn't know I could feel so seriously about someone. About you." Connor's lip trembles. "Faye —"

"Her name is Faye?"

Connor nods. "Faye's a leftover of my old life and she'll never happen again. I promise. All I need is you. It's just that I've never had someone like you in my life. I've never had someone that I missed when she was gone and I never had someone who I've been this open with. I'm telling you about Faye because I did this wrong, I know it, and I want to make it right, start again clean. I can't be without you and I don't know what to do about that." Connor raises a hand from his knee and holds it out to her. "I haven't felt this before." He looks at her, his puffy eyes rimmed in red and jeweled with tears. One breaches his eyelid and traces a smooth line down his cheek. It pools into a trembling drop on his chin before becoming another dark spot on his sweatpants. "I've never felt love before and I didn't know what it was. I didn't know what I was doing. Now I do. Katie, I love you."

And there are the words Katie has been waiting for. They are the reason she's here, though this is a circumstance completely different from the one she envisioned so many times.

She believes him. He does love her. She can see it in his face and see it in the tension coursing through his body. That manic anxiety can only be love. Those words, they were the simplest thing, the only thing she wanted from him, those three words.

Now, they're entirely less simple.

She feels like laughing. She feels like crying. She doesn't care that she will look crazy if she does both at the same time.

"No," Katie says. The word comes out as a percussive bark though she hadn't meant it to. She takes a deep breath before continuing. "No. You do not get to say those words. Not now. Not to me."

"Katie." Connor stands and takes a step toward her. "I know you're mad —"

"You're wrong." She's crying uncontrollably. She can't hold it back anymore. "I'm not mad. I'm hurt. You hurt me."

Connor crosses the room to her. She swats Connor's outstretched hand away. Then she takes a swing at him. He steps back to dodge her fist.

She's screaming at him now. She becomes that hysterical person she had been fighting not to become. "What kind of twisted fuck says all those words together, all those ones you just said? They're all backward and fucked up. I love you, so I fucked Faye? That doesn't make any sense. You don't make any sense. I feel sorry for you for being so fucked up. I feel sorry for me for being so blind to you. Do you know how badly I wanted you to tell me that you love me? No." She laughs through her tears. "An emotionally retarded sociopath like you couldn't possibly know, and I pity you for it. I pity you."

Connor reaches out for Katie again. She swats his hand, but he persists. And she hits him and punches him, and he brings his arms around her to embrace her. Katie punches him as hard as she can. She knows she's hurting him, but after a short time, she can no longer swing at him because he is holding her too close to his bare chest.

She gives up. She's suddenly very tired, and there's no punch she can throw that can hurt him as much as he hurt her. So, she stands in the warmth of him, her body pressed against his naked skin, both of them shaking with sobs they no longer care to control.

Connor says her name again and again. "Katie, Katie, Katie. I know I fucked up. I know I hurt you. You're right. I'm a moron. I'm an asshole. I'm horrible. Katie, Katie, Katie, let me make it up to you. I can make it up to you for the rest of my life if that's what it takes. I'm ready to do that. Every day of forever. You can hate me and make my life a hell and make me suffer every hour until I die and that's okay with me, as long as I'm with you until then. It will be the purpose of my every waking breath to try to make this up to you. I know I have no right to ask anything from you, not after what I did, but can you do this for me? Can you please hate me for the rest of my life?"

Katie can't help but gulp out a laugh at the absurdity of it, him asking her to make his life a living hell until he dies, just so they could be together.

Connor continues, "Katie, Katie, Katie. Hate me the rest of your life because I love you so much."

A breeze blows over them through the patio door and brings them the quiet hiss of traffic from the street below. After a few minutes, Katie's crying subsides. Connor's body stops trembling too.

"Connor?"

"Yes."

"Let go of me."

He does and steps back.

Katie continues, "I'm getting my stuff and I'm going. I can't see you right now, but if everything you're saying is true, then maybe I'll see you around sometime. Maybe it'll be good then because it definitely isn't now. I look forward to the day I can forget this. If I forget it with you, then I look forward to the day I can forgive you. But how can I ever trust you again? If all you're telling me is another lie, which I think it is . . . then I hope you rot in hell."

A moment passes.

"Okay," Connor whispers. "I'll see you around sometime."

"Help me get my stuff together?" Katie asks.

"Okay."

Connor grabs a plastic bag from under the kitchen sink and puts two boxes of herbal tea into it. Katie

238

picks up her magazine from the couch and tucks it under her arm. She gets her slippers from the corner of the room, goes to the bathroom but can't find her toothbrush. She meets Connor in the middle of the room and loads her belongings into the bag.

"I'll grab the mug," Katie says. "You take care of Ian."

"I will," Connor says. "And here —" He scoops a pair of lacy panties from where they had been peeking out from under the pillow on his bed. "Don't forget these."

Katie looks at the panties bunched up in his hand for a moment. Then she cocks her head at Connor and smiles.

"You can hang on to those," she says.

Connor's face breaks into a naughty smile. "Really?" He bunches them up in both hands and brings the rosette of lace up to his face.

"Yes," she says. "Keep them. They aren't mine."

CHAPTER
THIRTY-NINE

In Which the Evil Seductress Faye Judges a Cloacal Kiss to Be an Insufficient Source of Pleasure

As the slapping sound of footsteps recedes above her, Faye shakes her head at the memory of the weird girl who seemed to be so close to a random violent emotional outburst. She thinks she can hear crying echoing back down to her, but it's hard to tell in this sound-altering space.

Faye takes one last glance behind her before continuing downward and resuming her thoughts about how many ways Connor will pay for making her take the stairs. She won't let him forget.

Faye passes a sign on the wall that tells her she has ten floors to go, ten floors of daydreaming of all the ways she will exact her toll on him. So far, all them involve piles of clothes on the floor. Some of them involve ropes and others handcuffs. One of them involves the cork from a wine bottle, a rubber band, and a wooden spoon. A few of them involve her trying to wrap her head around the idea that she could do to him what he said Deb likes having done to her. Surely

240

that would be an interesting form of punishment, though she's not sure she could really follow through with it and ever look at herself in the mirror again.

The idea of Deb doesn't bother Faye as much as the idea of Connor clearing her out of his apartment for the girlfriend. The other girls in Connor's life are not a problem for her. The problem is that this one holds something more over him than she does. Not that that's a big deal either, but it means that Connor will, at some time in the near future, realize that his feelings for his girlfriend override his feelings for her and she is the one who will lose out. While the existence of her and Deb in Connor's life may be unfair to the girlfriend, the girlfriend is just as unfair to them. And Connor is at the center of all of them, the common factor and therefore the problem.

I mean, she thinks as she releases her hold on the railing and sniffs the palm of her hand, are we meant to be together forever? What are we, penguins?

Her hand smells like metal, like the handrail she had been intermittently guiding herself down the stairs with. It smells of the thousands of hands that have touched it in the past. And she decides that, while penguins are cute, she is not one and it's just not in her nature to be mated to a single partner until she dies, no matter how nice a pebble he presents her with.

She thinks back to the biology field school she attended in Australia two years ago. It was an easy way to earn some extra course credits, and she got to tour the surfing beaches of the country for a few months after class was done. One day, a group of students rode a rickety old bus from the university to some beach outside of Melbourne to try to count penguins. The difficulty of the task seemed to be lost on the mustachioed, middle-aged professor who had dedicated his whole life to studying the little creatures. They're all colored the same, and they became a dazzling blur of black and white as the huge waddle made its way onto the beach. It made counting them a near impossibility, which left Faye's mind wandering from how many hundreds there were milling about the beach in front of her to what they tasted like. She wondered why nobody ate penguins because there are a lot of them and surely they would be pretty easy to round up. She thought back to the class and there was never a mention of anyone eating them. Not even the Aborigines. Surely, someone had tried one at some point in time.

As she passes the eighth floor, she sniffs her hand again and wonders if the smell is getting stronger. She resolves to not use the handrail anymore, deeming it unsanitary and particularly malodorous.

Then she wonders if it's because penguins are cute. She ponders a moment and decides that can't be the reason. Baby cows are cute, and people eat them all the time. There's lamb too. Perhaps someone did try a penguin once, and it wasn't very tasty, so it became a taboo.

Faye is pleasantly surprised by the "Floor 4" sign bolted to the wall as she rounds the next flight of stairs. As she carries on, she remembers a documentary she saw that said penguins are one of a few species that mate for life. Truly mate for life, not just serially monogamize the hell out of one another. And she thinks of being tied to Connor for decades until one of them dies and decides that it's not for her. She's only interested in the physicality of him. If she could be truthful, if she could forget her mother's expectations and just be real, he holds little more to intrigue her than that.

Faye knows she would make a bad penguin because, as Connor-penguin grew old, she would be looking for a way out, perhaps a convenient ice floe to leave him on . . . or a well-timed orca attack. Besides, as a penguin, Connor would lack the point of his being. He wouldn't have a dick, as penguins don't, and she imagines the intimacy of their brief cloacal kisses would get pretty tiresome pretty quickly.

No, Faye reasons, cloacal kisses are an insufficient source of pleasure, and that's just not in her. Now, Connor's girlfriend, from all Connor has said about her, she would be a good penguin. Faye doesn't understand the draw though. Connor's just a dick.

I mean *it*'s just a dick, she thinks, nothing to get overly excited about. Half the human population has one, and it's not like it ever saved a nun from a burning building or anything. And, she reasons, just because you order from the tap doesn't mean you need to buy the whole keg.

Faye passes the "Floor 2" sign affixed to the stairwell wall. Her legs tremble because, after the vigorous bouts of fucking she shared with Connor, there really wasn't twenty-seven floors' worth of descent left in her muscles. Regardless, she is almost there. With one floor left to the lobby, she swears that's the last time she will ever take the stairs. Anywhere.

Next time, if he wants to hide me from his girlfriend, Faye thinks, he can carry me down the fucking stairs . . . and he can take out his own garbage.

Faye stops as she steps through the stairwell door into the lobby. A silent and uncommon commotion unfolds outside of the building that gives her cause to pause and contemplate.

CHAPTER
FORTY

In Which Jimenez Heroically Acts on the Final Service Request

By the twentieth floor, the elevator's trembling has ceased and the compartment is running smoothly. The rattling of the fixtures has quieted, and the elevator lights no longer flicker. Jimenez feels good, looks good, smells good, and is of elevated spirits. His mind is made up to go out on the town tonight, and even if he has to do it alone, he will do it alone amid a crowd of people. Nearly dying fixing an elevator has instilled in him a desire to live and a need to do it daringly.

His brow furrows when he raises his eyes and watches the numbers ticking by above the doors. He leans back against the handrail and crosses his feet at the ankles, proud of the work he did to get this machine moving again.

What was once broken is now fixed, Jimenez thinks. From the safety of hindsight, he chuckles at his misadventures prompting the elevator into motion.

And so it all begins again, he thinks.

There's a song stuck in Jimenez's head, an old song and a happy song that he hums toward catharsis. It's a good tune that was originally a folk song but was later used in a scene from an old black-and-white song-and-dance movie he saw many times as a kid. That's the association he makes with the tune whenever it plays, little Jimenez watching a fuzzy image on a black-and-white television at his *abuelita*'s house. At the time, he understood only a few English words, but he fell in love with the characters and the vibrant motion of the show. He liked all the old song-and-dance movies; he didn't need to know English to understand them.

Jimenez hums a baritone "Chiapanecas" and thinks of the beautiful Lupe Vélez in her role as the stunning and vivacious Carmelita Fuentes in *The Girl from Mexico*. He loved her vivacity, that same energy that earned her the nicknames "Spitfire" and "Hot Pepper."

In the scene from the movie that runs behind Jimenez's humming, Señorita Vélez spins on the polished tile of the hall, dancing, sole to sole, with her reflection on the floor. It's as if there are two of her whirling in opposite gravities, dancing on either side of a pane of glass, and if one of them were to misstep, the other would stumble and fall.

Señorita Vélez wears an elegant gown. Her sequins flash in the spotlights and are only outshone by her smile. That gown — Jimenez shakes his head to the memory. Tiered ruffles run around her body from her waist to her ankles. The lace bindings flare like fabric on fire as she spins circles and kicks her feet past one another. The dress lifts from the floor, exposing her perfect ankles, the marvels of divine engineering they are. The strongest collection of the most delicate bones,

246

alone pointless, but arranged perfectly and working together, they support the beauty of her movements.

Jimenez sighs. She was the pairing of subtle strength with grace.

The elevator chimes and jolts to a stop, announcing its arrival at the twenty-fifth floor. The doors slide open, revealing that the elevator car and the floor are badly misaligned. Jimenez ducks and hops the foot down onto the carpet in the hallway. Still whistling, he glances at the misalignment from the outside as he walks down the hall. An unappealing mass of mechanical bits hangs in the thin, dark gap underneath the elevator. They are the things no one ever sees and don't even deign to think exist. Those things that make the machine work, they're exposed now for anyone caring to look.

The ugliness that keeps everything moving, it can stay exposed for now, Jimenez thinks. I'll deal with it tomorrow. After fixing this sink, I'm going to find an old-time movie playing in some small theater. I'm going to get popcorn and watch whatever show is playing. All the better if there's singing and dancing, even more so if the film is in black-and-white. All the more to lift the soul. And after the movie, I'll go dancing.

Jimenez pulls the crumpled service request from his pocket and double-checks his destination. Apartment 2507. At the end of the hall, on the left. He knocks on the door, whistles, and rocks from heel to toe and back again as he waits for an answer. He thrusts his hands into his pockets, causing the tools hanging from his belt to jingle.

The next-door neighbor pops out of her apartment and locks the door behind herself.

Jimenez nods to her.

She nods back and smiles before making her way up the hall to the elevator.

Jimenez knocks on Apartment 2507 again and watches the neighbor clamber the foot up into the elevator. She stubs her toe on the step and almost falls forward into the compartment. She recovers though and disappears inside. Then the doors slide closed.

Jimenez knocks on the apartment door again, louder and longer this time. A few more moments and Jimenez pulls his key loop from his belt, fingers several keys around the ring until he finds the one for this apartment. He knocks once more and then unlocks the door. If anyone were home, surely they would have answered by now.

Normally, residents have the right to their privacy. It would be considered an unlawful intrusion for Jimenez to enter any apartment, and he had always respected that. The only occasion when he is allowed to enter uninvited is when there is an emergency threatening other residents or when there's a request for service. It is in the building's bylaws that, on those occasions, the superintendent can enter an apartment in the following forty-eight-hour period to perform the repair.

Jimenez calls into the apartment, "Hello, it's the superintendent here to fix up the leaking sink."

There is no answer.

Jimenez whistles the last few bars of his song as he enters the apartment and shuts the door behind him.

He slips off the heels of his shoes with the toes of his opposite foot and leaves them on the doormat. He wanders the short hall, past the kitchen, and into the living room. The bedroom door to his left is closed. He thinks he hears a whisper of movement behind it, so he calls his greeting again.

"Hello? It's the super here to fix up the leaking sink."

When there's still no response, he figures he is alone. There's no way a resident couldn't have heard him. Jimenez turns his attention back to the view and lets out a low, appreciative whistle. There's nothing blocking the sunlight here like there is in his apartment. The view sprawls to the horizon, and Jimenez marvels at the density of the city. So many people living piled up from the ground, stacked on each other, moving all around each other.

He checks his watch and spins back to the kitchen. It's a tidy apartment, which pleases him. There are a few crumbs on the counter near the toaster and a full drinking glass with a lipstick smear catching the faucet's drip, but nothing more is out of place. Jimenez contemplates the drip and then takes out a wrench and unscrews the spout. The rubber washer looks good, not cracked, just caked with calcium carbonate buildup from the hard water. Jimenez rubs the washer between his thumb and forefinger. It's gritty and crusted with minerals. He finds some vinegar under the sink, dumps the water from the glass, and fills it a finger deep with vinegar before dropping the washer in it. The buildup begins to fizz.

Next, he plugs the basin and runs it full of water. Then he pulls the plug. As the basin drains, he slides the garbage can out from under the sink and hunkers his head and shoulders into the cabinet. There's no leak and no puddle under the sink. He runs his fingers from slip nut over p-trap to the elbow and can't feel any moisture. He frowns as he rubs his dry fingers across this thumb.

It's dark under the sink though, so he grabs his flashlight from his belt. He clicks it on and nothing happens. Of course, the batteries are dead.

Jimenez mutters, "*Tonto,*" to himself. He puts the flashlight on the floor beside him and turns his attention back to the plumbing.

Jimenez jumps when a voice comes from behind. He bangs his head on the sink, which retorts with a hollow, metallic resonating ping.

"*Gracias por arreglar el lavamanos,*" the voice says.

"*No hay de qué,*" he says, rubbing the back of his head while extracting himself from under the sink.

He sits back on the floor and turns to see who thanked him.

CHAPTER
FORTY-ONE

In Which Garth Steels His Nerve and Performs the Most Courageous Act of His Life

Garth zips up the gown. The smooth buzz of the zipper travels up his back. He turns his back to the mirror and looks over his shoulder to check out Floria's handiwork. The steam from his shower has receded to a muted frosting at the upper corners of the mirror and a sporadic powder of moisture across the surface. It evens the edges and frames him with an antique Gaussian smoothness.

Garth admires the gown and thinks of what a gift Floria is in his life. She has made him seem subtle and strong, just like he wants. The dress is uncanny, and Garth can't help but slide open palms over his carmine second skin. He runs a blow-dryer through his hair and applies a little styling paste to maintain a roguishly styled mess. He pulls a comb through his beard and applies his razor to some errant hairs that have sprouted up on his cheeks. A little spray of deodorant under his armpits and a drop of cologne to his collarbones, then to makeup.

Garth has found deep neutral tones complement his skin and thick bristles. He can't abide the garish war paint he sees in fashion magazines and music videos. Makeup is to enhance beauty, not to be beauty. Nearly Nude lipstick, a bit of foundation to even out the skin tone, a subtle blast of earth tones above the eyes to enhance the contrast, to add a bit of mystery. Something to thicken his eyelashes is the last thing needed. A final appraisal in the mirror and Garth knows this is how it's supposed to be done. He's beautiful. He flips the light dark, retreats to the bedroom, and shuts the door behind him.

He sits on the bed, his heart pounding in a way it hasn't since he kissed his high school crush at the spring dance. They had dimmed the lights in the gymnasium. Savage Garden's "Truly Madly Deeply" played in the dark. It had been a quick kiss, she leaned in to him, wanting, and he put his lips to hers. It had to be a quick kiss because there were three chaperones circling the gym, monitoring for such things. The illicit act, the anticipation of the touch, the uncertainty of that night, floods back into Garth's veins.

He laughs at himself for feeling like that kid again but, at the same time, is relieved that he can still feel such things. To him, it proves that life still has surprises and challenges left that can make his heart pound and set his stomach aflutter. He hopes he never gets old enough to lose these occasional moments of adolescent giddiness.

There's a knock at the apartment door.

Garth's thoughts and pulse freeze.

He's here, Garth thinks. He's at the door, knocking to see if anyone's home.

Garth had fully planned to answer the door. He had wanted to be brave, but now that the moment has arrived, he bites his knuckles and wants nothing but to disappear, to crawl under the bed and hide and hope to be magically transported somewhere else.

There's another knock, this time louder.

Garth regains his courage, steeling it by reaching into his nightstand drawer and pulling out a delicate silver necklace. He decides he won't answer the door. He has second thoughts whether revealing himself like this is the right thing for him to do. He needs every second left to think and fortify his nerves. The necklace clasp is fiddly, such a delicate contraption for such beefy and trembling fingers. On the fumbling third attempt, the loop slides through the clasp and then is secured.

"Hello," comes a call, so close, separated only by an inch of bedroom door. "It's the superintendent here to fix up the leaking sink."

He's a good man, Garth thinks. He works so hard to keep this place operating. He fights the battle daily, unnoticed and unappreciated, a struggle every waking hour just to keep things the same. He sees the dirty underbelly of the building, wrestles with its shorting electrical wiring, its overflowing toilets, and its plugged sinks. He sees the ugly underside so the residents didn't have to, and he still manages to give everyone a passing smile.

And he's whistling some song. The last few faint bars filter through the bedroom door, something familiar yet unknown to Garth.

He's a good man and I'm going to tell him so, Garth decides as the song ends and a single, low whistle comes from the other side of the door. I'll tell him so, but not without the proper footwear.

Garth snatches a shoe from the bed beside him. In his haste, the straps become entangled, and while he has a good grip on the one shoe, the other swings with it, dangling precariously before falling to the floor. It lands on the carpet with a muffled thud. Garth stops breathing. He freezes, all muscles contracting in fear and his mind scolding his clumsiness.

How could he not hear that? Even through the door it must have been audible.

Sure enough, the super calls out again.

"Hello? It's the super here to fix up the leaking sink."

Now is the time, Garth thinks. He stands, shoe still in hand, and strides the three steps toward the bedroom door. He reaches for the handle and then stops with his hand on the doorknob. Clanking and banging sounds come from the kitchen. Jimenez has moved on to the task at hand.

Garth realizes he's holding his breath. He slowly lets it out. His hand falls from the doorknob, slowly too, as if deflating with the exhalation.

Garth returns to sit on the bed. He leans forward and slips his foot into the shoe he had been holding. It fits beautifully, and as he buckles the strap into place, he can't help but embrace the shoe in both hands for a second. There is power here. Everything fits and everything feels perfect. There's no danger here, no shame, he realizes. He retrieves the other shoe from where it had fallen and dons it like a piece of armor.

There's nothing here but me, he thinks. This is me.

He stands again and puffs up his chest a bit. He smooths the fabric by running flat hands from chest to knees. He fastens the crepe drape as a scarf. He will not dampen the impact of the gown by using it as a midriff sash, even though Floria designed the gown so it could be used as such. He takes one manly stride toward the door, then another, his pace building speed and his mind building confidence with each step. The two-inch heels are easy to maneuver in, easy to swagger in, much more manageable than the ostentatious four-inchers he had ordered the first time.

Subtlety always wins out.

I'm as tough as that woman that Danny pointed out at the construction site, Garth thinks. The one who walked past on the other side of the chain-link fence. The chain-link fence wasn't there to protect her from me and Danny; it was the opposite. Or Faye, the one from the stairwell who had been so strong and seemingly lost in love. Garth pitied her boyfriend. He was no match for her. Most men didn't know what to do with that beauty, that innate righteousness. That which is flowing now through me.

Garth flings the bedroom door open and crosses the short distance to the kitchen. He is the most stunning man ever to put on a dress, and he's going to thank the man who performs the thankless tasks that keep this

255

building humming along every day. He's going to acknowledge him and demand to be acknowledged in return.

He hears Jimenez mumbling to himself.

As Garth rounds the corner of the cabinetry, he sees Jimenez sitting cross-legged with his head under the sink. It is both cliché and a truth that Garth's eyes are drawn first to the crack, exposed through the gap where his shirt has lifted and his pants have dropped. And, like a burly, hairy man in a dress has to accept, Garth thinks it is wonderfully endearing and uniquely human to simply be how one has to be.

And this is how it will be, he thinks, right now.

"*Gracias por arreglar el lavamanos,*" Garth says, his voice rolling smooth and deep.

Jimenez jumps and bangs his head on the underside of the sink. He backs out and sits on the linoleum, his flashlight on the floor under one knee. A wrench in one hand and the other rubbing the back of his head.

"*No hay de qué,*" Jimenez says, then looks up at Garth.

CHAPTER
FORTY-TWO

In Which Petunia Delilah Reminisces About How She and Danny Fell in Love During the Zombie Apocalypse

Petunia Delilah drags the boy into the apartment by his leg. He's dead weight, a limp and gangly burden of boy who thankfully doesn't weigh too much. She lets go when he's past the doorjamb, then takes two more steps and leans against the wall. She can't help but let out a squeal as a contraction ripples through her body, and when it has passed, she slides down the wall to the linoleum. That position is uncomfortable, so she jiggles and shifts until she lies flat on her back. The floor is cool against her skin; the feeling through her sweat-soaked nightgown is a relief because she feels like every inch of her flesh is on fire.

Claire tries to close the door, but it jams halfway when it bumps against the side of the boy's head. He mumbles and his eyes roll under his eyelids. She uses the toe of her fuzzy slipper to ease his head out of the way and quickly closes the door.

Claire raises trembling fingers and locks the dead bolt before sliding the chain back into place.

Petunia Delilah crooks her neck and watches the woman look down at the boy crammed, his limbs loose like a marionette's, in the corner near her closet. He's breathing slowly, and his features are pacified by unconsciousness. She envies him his peace in light of the confusion and panic she feels. She wishes she could be unconscious through this. Then Claire spins to look at her lying on her floor, beside the island.

"What can I do?" Claire asks. Her face is sheer terror, and her words are fast and quavering with apprehension. "What can I do to help?"

"Call Kimmy," Petunia Delilah says. "My midwife."

Claire hops over the boy and dashes to the kitchen. She takes the long way around to ensure she maintains the maximum distance from Petunia Delilah. She snatches the headset from beside the computer and puts it on. Petunia Delilah recites the numbers, and she types them into the calling program.

Over the whoosh of blood pulsing in her ears, Petunia Delilah hears Claire ask for Kimmy. She says a few other things too, but Petunia Delilah can't concentrate. A sharp, piercing pain strikes her stiff, and a ringing blots all other sounds from her ears. She lets out a guttural wail and, as it fades, is aware of Claire by her side, not touching her but holding her hands near her shoulder and her forehead as if she really means to.

"Kimmy isn't home," Claire says. "Mel said she went to the market and won't be back for an hour or so. Mel said Kimmy doesn't have a cell phone. She says Kimmy thinks that they cause brain cancer. Who doesn't have a cell phone? Especially in this day and —"

"Call my boyfriend," Petunia Delilah gasps through clenched teeth. "Call Danny."

She's sweating profusely. She feels it cascading down her face and tastes the salt on her lips. She needs to hear Danny, needs to hear his voice say that it will all work out. She needs him with her, holding her hand and rubbing her back. Then, once this is all over, when there's a beautiful little baby in her arms, she needs him to get her a fucking ice cream sandwich.

"Call him now." She grunts out the numbers, and Claire leaves her side to dial them into the computer.

"Here," Claire says after a few seconds of touching her finger to the earpiece. She puts the headset on Petunia Delilah. "It's ringing."

Petunia Delilah needs Danny's voice. She needs his love, and she needs him here. She needs to hear those words that make her fall in love with him every time he talks. He always has almost the right thing to say. She thinks it so sweet, his talent for getting so close to saying the right thing all the time.

The phone rings.

Petunia Delilah loves it when he says those almost romantic things. Like after their first date: He had taken her to a movie and was so embarrassed when he realized he had forgotten his wallet and she had to pay for the tickets. He was even more embarrassed when she had to pay for his popcorn and soda at the concession as well. After watching that movie, the one in which the undead overran the world, he said, "Baby, if it were just you and me to survive the zombie apocalypse and we were trapped in a sporting goods store and they were breaking down the door and busting through the windows to eat us alive and we had a gun with just one bullet left, I would use that last bullet on you."

It was so sweet. She knew they belonged together.

The phone rings.

And that's just how he is, all the time. He would save her from suffering the ravenous horde of undead and die by gruesome disemboweling in her stead. With his last breaths, he would rather watch creatures eat his own entrails than let her suffer for a second. But in that particular case, Petunia Delilah had reasoned, the sporting goods store would probably have more ammunition at the hunting counter that they could use, so it was an unnecessary act of chivalry.

But that's just how he is, passionate to the point of being illogical. That is how his love works, and it belongs to her. Petunia Delilah didn't want to ruin the moment by pointing out there would probably be lots of ammo around.

The phone rings.

And Danny always has something almost romantic to whisper in her ear or tell her when they snuggle in bed. Like, "Baby, of all the women I've had in this bed, you're the most beautiful. Ever," he told her. "Of all of them."

He'd say things like, "I like how you are so soft and squishy all over, way nicer than those skinny girls," and,

"That new haircut is so hot, it makes you look ten years younger. It makes me want to do you right now."

Petunia Delilah is only twenty-six, but she didn't think it an odd thing for him to say. She knew what he meant to say but didn't seem capable. He would say all these things with a smile, his eyebrows raised and his head nodding as if he were giving her a gift and he was so excited to see her open it.

There's a burst of noise on the other end of the line. Danny shouts, "Hello?"

"Danny, the baby's coming," Petunia Delilah says.

"What?" Danny's voice is drowned out by loud music and noise from a crowded space. "Who's this?"

"Danny, the baby's coming," Petunia Delilah shouts into the mouthpiece.

"What? No." Danny's voice rises with excitement. "Yes. Holy shit. I'm having a baby," he shouts. There were some drunken cheers in response. "I'm having a baby." More cheers, this time from a larger group of people.

"Danny," Petunia Delilah says into the receiver. "Danny," she says louder when there is no response.

"Yeah, baby? The guys are really excited too." He laughs. "They say I have to buy them a round."

"Danny, you aren't having a baby. I am. Right now. On a floor in some lady's apartment. Apartment 805."

"Holy shit. Yeah. Okay. I'm on my way right now," Danny says. "I just ordered another beer, but I'll chug it. And I'll get my burger to go. I'll be there in a few minutes." He hangs up.

The boy lets out a moan from where he lies. He wriggles a bit, and his eyes flutter open. He doesn't move for a few moments but then slowly rolls onto his side. His body convulses with a retch, but nothing comes out of his mouth. Slowly, he pushes himself to a seated position, gags once more, and starts huffing deep breaths into his lungs. After a few moments, he looks around with bleary, uncomprehending eyes.

Petunia Delilah clenches again and lets out a harsh growl.

"We need help," Claire says to her. "Real help. Now."

Claire makes to snatch the headset from Petunia Delilah but stops short when she sees it tangled in her sweaty hair. She glances at how close the mouthpiece is to Petunia Delilah's mouth and a look of revulsion spreads across her face. Claire runs back to the kitchen and picks up the receiver from her personal phone.

"I'm calling 911," she says.

CHAPTER
FORTY-THREE

In Which Claire the Shut-In Works Hard to Deliver Petunia Delilah's Baby

Claire punches 911 on the phone. She watches Petunia Delilah writhe through another contraction on the floor. The leg projecting from between her legs wriggles a bit, and the two humps of the baby's bum protrude from her vagina. The boy near the door kneels with his hands on his thighs and his elbows locked. His head hangs low toward his lap, and Claire thinks how she absolutely couldn't stand it if he threw up on her floor.

"911," a man's voice comes through the receiver. "Where's your emergency?"

"8111 Roxy Drive," Claire says. "It's the Seville on Roxy. Apartment 805."

"Okay." There's a moment filled with the sound of typing. "What's the nature of your emergency?"

"We need an ambulance. There's a woman giving birth on my floor," Claire says.

"Okay, please stay on the line with me," the man says. "An ambulance is being dispatched." The sound of more typing comes through the line. "Their ETA is four and a half minutes."

Petunia Delilah screams. The veins on her neck stand out, and her skin flushes a sweaty purple as she pushes. The baby's hips appear between her legs. One leg is still folded up inside her, and the other lies on the floor. The boy in the doorway jumps at the noise and then again at the scene in front of him. He quickly looks away and brings his forehead to rest against the door, his eyes clamped tightly, the skin wrinkled at the corners with tension.

"I don't know if we can wait that long," Claire says. "It's already coming out. There's a leg and a butt hanging out."

"A leg and a butt?" the operator asks.

"Yes. A leg and a butt."

"You're right. This woman needs your help now. What's your name?"

"Claire."

"Okay, Claire. She's having a footling breech birth and she can't wait. I'm going to walk you through this. Can you see the umbilical cord? Has it prolapsed? It will be a blue-gray-colored cable looping out of the mother."

Claire crosses the kitchen and examines Petunia Delilah sweating and straining on the linoleum.

"I don't see it," she says.

"Good, you'll need some clean towels and gloves. Do you have those?"

Claire takes an instinctive, momentary offense at the question. Of course, her towels are clean. Any implication otherwise is an insult. Then, she reasons, no offense is implied by the question. This man on the phone doesn't know her.

"I have those things," she says.

"Okay, get them and lay them out under the mother. Wear gloves if you have them. Otherwise, wash your hands thoroughly for thirty seconds."

Petunia Delilah shrieks, filling the apartment with the animal noise.

Claire panics, barking at the operator, "I know how to wash my fucking hands and there's no way I'm touching that."

"Excuse me?"

Claire takes a deep breath to calm herself.

"I'm not touching that woman or her baby," she says, her voice quavering on the brink of crying.

"Claire, you have to. You have to help them."

"I can't," Claire snaps and sobs. "I just can't. It's a long story."

"Is there anyone else there with you?" the operator asks.

"There's this boy here. He doesn't look well either." Claire replies, her voice cracking with hysteria. "All I did was open my door. I was making quiche —"

"Claire, I need you to focus," the operator says. "Give the boy the towels and gloves and get him positioned to help with the baby. He needs to be able to manipulate it. I'll help. I'll talk you through it, but I can't do it all. I need you. That woman needs you. The baby needs you right now."

Claire sucks in another deep breath. The smell of quiche calms her. She pushes the air from her lungs. She nods to the phone.

"Okay," she says. "I'm okay."

Then she runs down the hall to the linen closet and pulls a stack of towels from the shelf. She returns to the kitchen and places the towels near Petunia Delilah. She jumps back when Petunia Delilah's body clenches and she releases a hoarse bellow.

Someone in the next apartment over thumps on the wall a few times.

"You." Claire points at the boy. "What's your name?"

"H-Herman." Herman takes his forehead from the door and looks at Claire.

"Herman," Claire says. "Come here and help. You're the hands here. I'm going to tell you what to do, and you're going to do it. This woman and her baby need us." She opens a cabinet and pulls out a box. She dangles two lemon-yellow rubber gloves in his direction. "Put these on."

Herman looks from the gloves to Petunia Delilah lying, knees akimbo, on the floor and then back to Claire. He looks hesitant, pale and trapped. His eyes plead with her not to make him do this.

"Now," Claire commands. "Put some towels under her. You're going to take care of her through this."

Herman hesitates and then crawls over, snatches the gloves from Claire, and pulls them on. He arranges a towel under Petunia Delilah's buttocks and positions himself between her knees. His eyes don't know where to settle. He glances from the baby's bum and leg

266

protruding from Petunia Delilah, to her knees, to the wall, to Claire, and finally he settles on Petunia Delilah's face. That face spasms and screams suddenly. Herman scoots away in terror, his legs scrabbling, pushing himself backward until he winds up pressed against the door.

"The baby's hips are out," Claire says into the mouthpiece. "Only one leg though. The other is all folded up inside."

"That's okay," the operator says. "It will come. Claire, I need some information from the mother."

Claire listens and then asks Petunia Delilah, "Is this your first baby?"

Petunia Delilah pants that it is, and Claire relays the information.

"Are you full term?"

Petunia Delilah screams that she is supposed to be due in five days. Herman has moved back into position and is tentatively rubbing Petunia Delilah's knee in a soothing manner.

Claire tells the operator this and then asks, "How long have you been in labor?"

"I don't know. Five minutes?" Petunia Delilah screams. "Not fucking long. Holy fucking shit, it burns!"

Herman looks at Claire. The terrified expression on his face begs her for either direction or dismissal.

"I heard that," the operator says evenly into Claire's ear. "We can do this. There's a lot working in our favor here. The cord is okay. The baby's full term. Its hips are out, and they are going to dilate her as effectively as the head would. Both are the same diameter. Which way are the baby's toes pointing?"

Claire peers at the baby's leg and grimaces at the mess on her floor. "To the ceiling."

"They need to be rotated to point to the floor. The baby's bum needs to point to the ceiling. Now, the baby needs as much support as possible. Full hands on the baby, never just fingers. Rotate it gently but firmly."

Claire relays the instructions to Herman. She watches the boy cup the baby between his palms and slowly twist it in one direction. When the hips are perpendicular to the floor, the other leg pops out of Petunia Delilah. With it comes a loop of umbilical cord. Herman flinches but does not let go. He continues the slow motion until the feet are pointing to the floor. When he's done, he straightens both of its legs and sits back on his heels. He looks at Claire with less fear and more interest than before.

"The other leg came out," Claire exclaims. "It's a little girl. You're having a little girl." She laughs and moves closer to Petunia Delilah.

Petunia Delilah laughs and smiles. Her face glistens.

"Some umbilical cord came out too," Claire tells the operator.

"Okay," he replies, his words coming quickly to Claire's ear. "That's not good. The paramedics are still two minutes away. That's too far. The umbilical cord needs to be untangled from the baby, and we have to get the baby out quickly. We have to do this fast. The cord is likely constricted, which will deplete the flow of oxygen. The longer this takes, the greater the chance

268

the baby will suffer brain damage. Now, Claire, this is what we have to do."

CHAPTER
FORTY-FOUR

In Which Homeschooled Herman Holds a Life in His Hands and Sees a Life in His Mind

Every time he touches the baby, Herman feels his grip on consciousness fade. He fights hard to stay there in the room, to not go anywhere else. He feels the baby through the rubber gloves, warm and wet cupped in his hands. The tile is cool and slick under his knees. The towel under Petunia Delilah's hips is soaked with viscous pink fluid.

The baby's two legs are freed and her torso slips out of Petunia Delilah to the shoulders with little effort. Still, no arms are visible, so he reasons that they must be held up above her head.

"There're no arms," Herman says to Claire. He looks to her for direction and asks, "How do I get the arms out of her?"

Claire relays this through the phone and then tells him, "Gently turn the baby from one side and then to the other. You should be able to see them, and when you do, you can gently pull them out."

Herman takes a deep, grounding breath and holds it. Then, cupping the tiny torso between his palms, he

270

twists it to one side. The crook of an elbow pops out. Herman hooks a finger there and uses a gentle tug to help free the arm. Then he repeats the motion, twisting the baby slowly to the other side. As he does, Petunia Delilah screams through another contraction, which pushes the other arm out unaided.

The neighbor bangs on the wall again, more forcefully now.

Herman lets his breath out and smiles at the result of his work.

"I've got them," he says excitedly. "They're both out now." Herman turns the baby chest-down again and then looks to Claire for more instructions.

Claire peers at them from the other side of the island, craning her neck to better see what's going on. She gives him a thumbs-up.

"Arms are out," she says into the receiver. "Now what?" She listens and nods at the response.

"This is the hardest part," she tells Herman. "Baby's got a big head, so we all have to work together to get it out. Petunia Delilah, are you ready?"

"Get this fucking thing out of me," she growls through clenched teeth.

Claire turns her attention back to Herman. "Can you reach up in there a bit? From underneath? Put the baby's body on your forearm and reach under. Feel for the baby's chin — don't block her mouth though. Put your fingers on either side of it." Claire holds her hand to her mouth, her fingers splayed into a V shape in demonstration.

Herman nods, so completely fascinated now he doesn't even feel scared. He drapes the baby on his forearm and pushes his fingers into Petunia Delilah. There isn't any room there, so he has to work against the resistance until he feels the baby's jawline. He can't figure out where the mouth is due to the pressure exerted by the compressed tube of flesh. He makes a guess and decides that will have to suffice.

"Okay," he says. "Her head's wedged up in there pretty tight though. Now what?"

Claire listens to the phone and then says, "Now put your other arm along the baby's spine. Wrap your index finger around one shoulder and your ring finger around the other. Run your middle finger straight up the back of her neck for support."

Herman does as he's instructed. The baby lies limp, pinned between his forearms.

"She's not breathing," he says in a panic.

"It's okay," Claire says. "She will. She has to come out first."

Herman nods, and Claire continues.

"Petunia Delilah, in a moment, you're going to give a big push. Herman, when she does, keep the baby sandwiched between your arms and lift upward, the baby's whole body flat like a plank and in one motion. You have to support her neck while you do it. You got it?"

Herman finds he can't speak, so he just nods. There's a life in his hands. He feels his mind focus like it never has before. Any threat of blacking out is gone. He isn't going anywhere but here, and he isn't doing anything but bringing this little baby into the room.

When Petunia Delilah pushes, she growls from deep in her chest. Her eyes close with the exertion, and her lips curl back from her teeth. Herman's spindly arms strain to keep the baby flat, like a board held between his forearms. He starts to lift the body and for a moment nothing happens.

"Push," Claire yells at them.

The neighbor pounds, rattling the pictures on the wall.

Petunia Delilah lets out one last, agonized scream.

With a smooth motion, the baby's free. The umbilical cord snakes out, attaching her from her belly button to her mother's insides. Herman falls back onto his bum, his feet flat on the floor and his knees touching Petunia Delilah's. Petunia Delilah lets out a groan and pants. Her body goes limp. Herman looks at the baby in his arms. She's covered with a wet wax that smears onto his arms and shirt. Herman grabs a tea towel from the pile on the floor and wraps it around the little girl.

"She's still not breathing," he says to Claire.

Claire relays the message to the phone and then tells him, "Wait a sec. Rub her body. See if she starts on her own."

Time is slow. It's not a surprise to Herman because he has experienced the sensation many times before. He keeps calm and looks down on the little girl's face, waiting for it to break to life. He rubs her body with the towel and holds his breath, willing her to start breathing.

"Check her mouth," Claire says.

With a thumb on her chin, Herman gently pries the baby's mouth open.

Petunia Delilah moans, rolls her head to the side, and asks with an anxious voice, "What's happening? How's my baby?"

"Her mouth is full of stuff," Herman tells Claire.

"It's full of stuff," Claire tells the phone and listens. Then she relays to Herman, "You're going to have to suck it out. Just a very gentle suck."

"What's happening to my baby?" Petunia Delilah's manic voice fills the apartment.

"I have to what?" Herman asks Claire and then looks at the glistening baby with her mouth full of gelatinous goop.

"Your lips go over the baby's mouth and then gently suck the stuff out."

Herman steels his nerves for a moment and thinks how he doesn't really have a choice. He leans forward and encircles the baby's mouth with his lips. He sucks gently, as if the baby is a straw. A dollop of jelly slips into his mouth, which causes Herman to gag at the sensation. He turns his head and spits the glob on the floor.

"Don't spit on the floor," Claire yells. "On the towel, keep it all on the towel. Christ —"

And then the baby starts to gurgle and cry. All of her limbs start to gyrate as she sputters and wails to life.

274

Herman spits again, this time onto the towel. He wipes the back of his arm across his lips. Herman realizes he's sitting between Petunia Delilah's legs and quickly grows uncomfortable with the familiarity of her exposure, the intimacy of their touching knees. He rearranges himself into a kneeling position and, with the baby girl cradled carefully, uses a free hand to take the remaining towel from the floor and cover Petunia Delilah. Herman then shuffles on his knees to her side.

The baby girl, swaddled in the towel and cradled in his arms, gurgles and yawns. Her eyes are so big that Herman finds himself lost in them. He can see her. How can she be so tiny yet hold so much? She's frail but strong with the potential she has. Herman can see her growing up, learning to walk and learning the words to express her thoughts, playing on the street with friends. She picks dandelions for her mother and paints paintings with her fingers that will be stuck on the fridge by letter-shaped magnets. At the playground, she will push her best friend off the teeter-totter and learn what regret is. She will both make mistakes and learn to live right.

"She's so little," Herman whispers.

Petunia Delilah reaches out to him and rests her hand on his forearm.

Herman sees the little girl going to school and studying and making friends. She grows up and goes to college. She plays guitar and writes bad, rhyming ballads. She cheats on a university test and feels awful about it so never does it again. She does things both good and bad. She falls in love with a boy and becomes a social worker. Later, they have babies together. She lives to see her children grow and have babies of their own, and she cares for her grandchildren so fully and happily. And when she dies, she is remembered as a mother and a grandmother, and she lasts so long in the memory of the people who loved her that her lifespan is tripled.

Herman watches it all.

And here she is, just beginning, nothing more than a tiny thing in his arms and nothing less than a brand-new life.

Then Herman remembers Grandpa, his arm draped down the side of his easy chair and the pile of newspaper on the floor. He's still there in their apartment.

"You probably want to hold your daughter," Herman says. He can't take his eyes from the everything he holds in his hands. She's all those things he saw and none of them. That's the root of wonder he felt. He can't plot her course and won't know it all. These things are unknown to anyone.

"I do," Petunia Delilah says. "But whenever you're ready." She sounds so grateful.

Herman takes one last, deep look and then hands the little girl to Petunia Delilah.

Petunia Delilah's happiness is infectious. Her eyes lock on her daughter, and Herman can't help but smile along with her. Herman and Petunia Delilah sit side by side. In the quiet that follows the birth, they hear Claire talking. She's still on the phone, thanking the emergency operator.

276

"You know my name," Claire says. "I don't know yours."

Claire listens to the phone for a moment.

"Jason?" she asks. "Pig? It's you?"

CHAPTER
FORTY-FIVE

In Which Ian's Plummetous Descent Continues Past the Eighth Floor

By the eleventh floor, Ian is physically exhausted, desperate for breath, and mentally drained. It has been a tense few seconds for our little golden explorer since he vaulted from the comforts of home. There have been stresses and revelations and terrors to last a lifetime, and his fall is not yet at its conclusion. Since the halfway mark of his journey, the tedium of travel has deepened within him. There's no longer the thrill of starting the journey. The dream of the possibilities that the adventure holds has waned. What remains is the anticipation of the destination and the impatience for just arriving and being done with the whole escapade. The trip has grown tiresome, and Ian longs for a rest.

He takes a momentary assessment of his body. The fine webs of his fins are plastered to his sides. Even his dorsal fin, usually flaunted erect and proud, is lying flat from the wind shear. His lungs are wanting for breath but not yet desperate enough for his brain to lose consciousness. A dryness has crept into his scales and into the jelly-filled discs of his eyes. His throat is parched, and his tail riffles uncomfortably in the wind with such vigor that he worries the delicate membrane may begin to tear. There's a heady sensation in his stomach and a nauseating sensation in his head.

And then there's the feeling of falling, the wind buffeting his sides and baffling his lateral line. The act of plummeting is often likened to being weightless, which is a gross misrepresentation as weightiness is entirely the problem. To be weightless would be a welcomed absolution from the incessant pull of gravity. Ian knows the difference between the two, for living a life in water is more akin to weightlessness than falling.

The eleventh floor slips by, a flash past the eye, and then it's an unsteady memory. The tenth is gone in the span of time it takes him to realize the previous floor has passed. So much else is gone.

Ian doesn't remember the cramped aquarium at the pet store where Katie pointed at him and traced the meandering path of his swim with her finger, picking him out of the crowd of a hundred other identical goldfish at the shop. He doesn't remember the sign taped on the tank, scrawled with clumsy felt marker lines that read, "Feeder Goldfish: 99 cents." Nor does he remember the tiny plastic bag or the odd sensation of that bubble of water jostling around as Katie carried him up Roxy toward Connor's apartment.

Ian doesn't remember the lazy afternoons and evenings in his bowl on the balcony, watching the city as dazzling reflections of brilliant sunlight turned into the twinkling of office lights in the dark. Ian doesn't remember sleeping late into the morning, inside the pink castle, and Ian doesn't remember the easy company of Troy the snail, who never complained or demanded or crabbed about anything. An entire lifetime has been forgotten and exchanged for the immediacy of the plummet.

Ian doesn't remember how he got here, outside the ninth-floor window with that fat, naked guy sitting on the couch, watching television and eating chips right out of the bag. That fat, naked guy, absorbed by flickering images and calories, doesn't see Ian flash by the window. Even if he did, he may have mistaken him for bird poop or something of the sort. He's oblivious to the two ambulances parked at the base of the building. He's vigorously scratching under his balls, that pair of nubbly walnuts in a saggy flesh sack draped casually over the back of his hand as he roots around beneath them. He licks chip salt from the fingers of the other. His eyes are locked on the television set.

And, thankfully, the naked guy is gone as quickly as he appeared.

Naked fat guy nut-scratcher's private offense is no more in Ian's sight, though Ian does not judge him. Ian has seen many a thing when people thought they weren't being watched. All goldfish are privy to a secret world where how one acts in private is at odds with one's conduct under scrutiny. Most people don't recognize the unblinking eye of their pet fish, but Ian's owner did. That is why Ian was on the balcony of the twenty-seventh-floor apartment in the first place.

Connor had been partaking in a nasty bit of the nasty with a busty brunette when he had noticed Ian staring at them. Connor had lost his erection almost immediately, and the woman he was pinning smirked. Then Ian was on the balcony. Ian was not aroused or judgmental in any way. He had simply been attracted to the motion of her tits swinging back and forth, just the movement, nothing more. It was the same way his eye was locked on Connor's dangling member as he took the bowl out to the old card table on the balcony. The motion attracted the eye, not the subject. To Ian, human copulation was a mere novelty, and having no external reproductive organs of his own, he was not one to offer opinions on Connor's member. Indeed, their activities didn't even register as a logical act in the fish's mind.

Naked fat guy nut-scratcher is not alone in the world even though he is alone in his apartment, observed fleetingly and then left to root around under his balls.

The eighth-floor window offers a sight beyond that of the ninth floor. In the shadows of the surrounding buildings, even in the late-afternoon light, this apartment shines like a beacon. Every light is on, and every surface gleams. The glow blasts through the windows to fight back the late-afternoon shadows.

Inside lies a woman on her back on the floor; her legs are bent at the knees, and her knees are spread akimbo. Another woman stands in the kitchen, stooping to look in the stove. Her head, cocked to one side, pinches a phone between her shoulder and her ear. The apartment door is open to the hall, and two men in blue uniforms bustle in, one shoving past the other. One kneels beside the woman on the floor, placing a hand on her shoulder and looking into her eyes. He talks constantly, and the woman on the floor nods. The other paramedic steps over them and places a large toolbox on the island in the kitchen.

The woman at the stove stands up and glances over her shoulder at the bustle. She says something into the receiver and smiles in a shy, cutesy sort of way, as if flirting. The movement and the lights are dazzling to Ian's goldfish brain and so much more engaging than the view into the ninth-floor window. He is almost sad when he passes by the scene.

The seventh floor is black, the windows dark. The air becomes cooler as Ian approaches the concrete . . . the concrete below that has grown so close. It's spotty with people mingling around the ambulances. The few dawdlers look at the building, not upward. He can see a few of the larger cracks in the pavement, their dark and jagged lightning strikes across the sidewalk's surface.

Ian can also see the dark splotches of spat-out and trod-upon gum, their shapes similar to what he imagines a splattered fish making.

CHAPTER
FORTY-SIX

In Which Our Heroine Katie Assaults the Crockery and Defends Her Heart

"What?" Connor says, lowering the bunched panties from his face and exhaling the breath he had drawn through them. He looks at the wad of purple fabric in his hand.

"Those aren't mine," Katie says again.

She shakes her head, and Connor doesn't raise his eyes from the handful of wadded-up material. She wonders how anyone could be so clueless but doesn't pursue the thought too far considering she was duped by him. She doesn't want to contemplate how clueless she has been to be fooled by the foolish.

"Faye's panties?" Katie asks.

Connor furrows his brow at them. He holds them like a lavender-colored bouquet, the fabric folds setting the light in deep contrast.

Katie can tell he isn't sure whose they are. It's a moment of honesty in his face, and to his credit, he doesn't try to hide it.

"There're others?"

"Maybe they're Deb's," Connor mumbles to his chest.

"Maybe?" Katie slumps, exhausted by him.

He looks up at her. His eyes are streaming tears again, and she can tell he exhausts himself as well. There's a blunt look into which she reads, I'm so tired of myself, I'm so sick with what I've done to you, and I love you, I really do.

Katie winds her arm back and then punches him in the shoulder as hard as she can. It makes a flat smacking sound, and a shock of pain races through her fist, radiating up her arm and spreading into her shoulder.

Connor's body jolts back with the impact, and he grunts. Instinctively, he raises his hand to his shoulder.

It hurt them both.

"I can't —" Connor stutters, rubbing his shoulder. "I don't —"

"Shut it," Katie says. "You're done talking."

She grabs the plastic bag full of her things, spins on her heel, and storms toward the balcony door. Connor blinks once at the panties and then follows her.

"Katie, wait," Connor calls. "You can't — They're just an artifact. Leftovers from the past. It will never happen again."

Katie steps one foot over the doorsill and onto the balcony. She spins to face him, raising a finger in his direction. Connor freezes at the threat of her and then takes a step backward so he's just out of striking distance. Just when he thinks she isn't going to say anything, she does.

284

"I can't believe I was even considering forgiving you." She shakes her head, tears welling up in her eyes again. "I can't believe I was so stupid. I mean, look at you. You're so fucking gorgeous. You aren't built to do anything but what you're doing. Why I thought I could be the one for you . . . why I thought there could be just one for you . . . I should have my fucking head examined." She pauses and takes a step toward him. He takes a step back. "No, on second thought, it's not me, it's you. You're the one who needs his fucking head examined. I can't believe it. You're such a fucking . . ." Katie trembles, her eyes wild, searching for the right word. "You're such a fucking butt."

And then she's laughing. That wasn't the word she was looking for, but it was the one that came out of her mouth, and once it had escaped, she realized it was completely ridiculous. It's just that she couldn't reach a word that was strong or hurtful enough to call him, and she wants so badly to hurt him like he did her. She can't help but laugh because she knows the perfect word will come to her when she gets home and she will have to shout it at her empty apartment instead of his face.

Connor stands, still clutching his shoulder, a few steps away from her. He's confused by this hysterical woman laughing and bawling at the same time. Then he laughs too. And for a few seconds they laugh together until Katie stops cold and raises her finger at him again.

"You don't get to laugh," she says. "Not at me."

Connor stops. He flexes at the knees, leaning back and dropping his arms to his side in frustration. "Katie, please don't go. Let's talk about this."

Katie is already out on the balcony. It feels good to be under the sky, out of the oppressive confines of the tiny studio apartment. There's sickness between those walls. She instantly feels a weight lifted from her. The late afternoon sun warms her skin, and she breathes in a sweet, gentle breeze. The city stretches far beyond her, thousands of glass windows looking into concrete rooms from the outside. Thousands of people doing thousands of things out there, all at once. For a moment, her problems seem a lot smaller than they had a second ago.

She reaches for the coffee mug, but Connor grabs her elbow before she has a good grip on it. It falls from the stack of papers on Ian's bowl and shatters against the cement. Dozens of shards skitter across the balcony, and there is a powdered, comet-shaped smear where the mug made contact with the concrete.

The first pages of Connor's thesis start to silently peel off in the breeze. Page by page, Connor's arguments curl back and unfold out into the void, over the safety of the balcony railing, shuffling and flipping through their descent.

Connor spins Katie around, his hand still firmly latched to her elbow.

"I can't be without you," he begs. "I know that now."

"I knew I couldn't be with you as soon as I saw that girl in the nightshirt," Katie said. "And even so, you almost talked me into it again."

"I'm slow. I need to be taught this stuff."

"Most people know their feelings. It's not something you learn, it's something you know. That's why it's a feeling and not a thought."

"Please, I'll do anything. Just tell me what I have to do and I'll do it."

Katie looks at Connor's hand grasping her elbow, his skin on her skin, him touching her, controlling her. Then she looks at Connor, who withdraws as if she were a searing heat.

Unblinking in his gaze, Katie asks, "You'll do anything?"

"Please. Yes, I'll do anything," Connor pleads. "Just give me another chance."

Katie glances over the balcony railing at the cement twenty-seven floors below. The people walking down there are so small. She watches the flickering sunlight reflecting off the hundreds of sheets of paper cascading and twisting through the breeze below. There are two ambulances parked in front of the building. A small crowd has gathered around the entrance.

"There is one thing you can do," she says and brings her eyes back to hold his. "There's one thing you can do to get me back."

Connor mouths the word "Anything." His face contorts with emotion, his eyes begging her and his eyebrows arched in the hope he can make it all better. His hands are held in front of him, wrists together as if bound by invisible handcuffs.

Katie jerks her chin in the direction of his hands. Connor looks down confusedly and realizes he still holds the wadded-up panties. She can't stand the sight of them just like she can't stand the sight of him. He throws them over the edge of the balcony and then holds out his empty hands, palms up, to show her.

Katie nods and then continues, "Here's what you can do. You can figure out how to travel back in time. Go back three months. When you're there, convince your former dog-self that the current, reformed Connor is the man he should be. And then, when I show up at your office with questions about the exam, ask the former naive me out for a coffee. Ask her on a date and to dinner and to go to a movie and to join you in your bed. Treat her well, every day, like she's the only woman for you, ever. Tell her early that you love her and mean it. It's all she wants to hear. You'll make her so happy. Treat the former naive me like a fucking queen for the rest of her life because you've wrecked this me, the one that's here right now."

"That's impossible," Connor murmurs.

Katie shrugs. "That's the only chance you have. Until then, take care of Ian and get out of my way."

Katie storms past Connor and into the apartment.

CHAPTER
FORTY-SEVEN

In Which the Villain Connor Radley Discovers the Impossibility and Certainty of True Love

Connor watches the final pages of his thesis unfold into the void. He doesn't even care that the pages, covered with scrawling ink, are the only copy of his supervisor's comments. He'll never recover them, and it doesn't matter to him now.

Connor follows Katie back into the apartment. The air inside still smells musty and stale. Everything seems so dark compared with the bright sunlight out on the balcony. Connor's also struck by what a pathetic hovel his apartment seems: the scatter of dirty dishes on the counter and clothes strewn across the floor, the rumpled sheets on the bed and stains on the carpet.

Katie heads for the apartment door. Connor rushes past her, putting himself between her and the door just as she reaches for the handle. Connor turns his back to the door and his face to Katie. He flinches, scared she will push right through him, but she doesn't; she stops inches from him.

She's stopped, he thinks, she's listening. That means I still have a chance.

"Nothing's changed, not since you said I could keep trying," he says. "Those panties weren't yours. Okay, I get it. But they are no one's now. I don't really know whose they are. I get that too. But you said it yourself, I was a former dog-self . . . *former*. That's the thing that's changed, and it'll be my only purpose from now on, to prove that to you. Even if it takes until we are old and gray and dying, you've given me purpose."

"Stop talking, Connor."

"No, Katie." He puts his hand on her shoulder, and her muscles tense under his palm. "Please, just hear me out. There was a Faye and there was a Deb — I can't change that. But there aren't anymore. Not after this minute. There isn't anyone else but you. I admit it, I made a horrible mistake, but I see that now and I'm different. I know you don't trust me and you think I'm an asshole. I can see why, because I broke your trust and I *am* an asshole. But knowing that now, I can be so much better, so much more faithful."

Katie sighs, shrugs Connor's hand off her shoulder, and pushes him into the corner behind the door. She opens the door just enough to get through and steps out into the hallway. Connor follows her up the hall toward the elevator.

"You still don't get it," she growls at him without looking back. "You can't be 'more faithful.' It's an absolute, not a scale. You are faithful, or you're not. Once you're not, you can never be again."

"I can learn," he said. "I want to do whatever it takes."

Katie stops at the elevator and jabs the button a few times. Then she remembers it isn't working. She looks at Connor, dejected and beautiful beside her.

"You don't get it. Love is a choice, one you have to make every day. It isn't magic, but it is magical." She pauses. "I can't stand the sight of you."

"I'm going to make it better. I have to," he says. "I love you."

"I don't want to ever see you again."

She turns and storms back down the hallway to the stairwell door. Connor doesn't follow her this time. He watches her go through the door and stays watching until the door hisses shut behind her. The latch catching sounds like a gunshot in the quiet of the hall. A few seconds later, the elevator dings and the door slides open. It's empty and waiting. Connor thinks to go and call to Katie that the elevator has come. Connor thinks maybe he should take it down to the lobby and beg her some more, make her see he has changed, but then the doors slide closed again and he thinks better of it.

Defeated, Connor turns back to his apartment. Once inside he gently closes the door and rests his forehead against it for a moment, the paint cool and smooth under his skin. Then he goes into the kitchen and picks up the cordless phone. He speed-dials the first number, and a woman answers after the first ring.

"Hello?"

"Faye?"

"No. It's Deb. Who's this?"

"Oh, sorry. Deb, it's Connor. We can't see each other anymore."

"Oh," the voice says. "Who's Faye?"

"No one." Connor hangs up the phone even though Deb is starting to say something else.

He speed-dials the second number. The phone rings a few times before it's answered.

"Hey, Connor."

"Faye. We can't see each other anymore."

"I kind of figured this would happen," Faye says. "I'm just leaving the building, and it's raining paper out here. It's beautiful."

"Faye, I love Katie. She knows about you now and she hates me."

"Oh. That's a tough spot to be in," Faye says. "I'm okay with it. I hope she gives you a second chance. You're not all that bad. Don't delete my number, okay?"

"I'm sorry. I have to."

"You never know when you'll need it." She giggles. "Hey, Connor?"

"Yeah."

"If you find my panties, could you let me know? I think I left them —"

The earpiece goes quiet save for some background traffic noise.

"Hello?" Connor says.

"Yeah, sorry. Don't worry about it. I just found my panties," she says. "Keep my number, okay? Just in case."

"I won't. Bye, Faye."

"Bye, Connor."

Connor hangs up, and before he can speed-dial the next number, his eyes are drawn to the balcony. He drops the phone, which bounces off the counter and clatters to silence in the sink. He sprints to the balcony and squints in the sunlight.

The thesis is gone, sure, but worse, the fishbowl is empty; just the snail is left.

Ian is gone.

Connor leans over the balcony railing and scans the scene below. Far below, the last few pieces of paper settle to the sidewalk. From his vantage his thesis looks like tiny squares of confetti spread across Roxy. Every time a car passes or the breeze blows, the pages move into a new configuration. He doesn't see Ian anywhere, but after a certain distance, his tiny orange body would be indiscernible from everything else.

Connor takes a step back from the railing and cringes at a sharp stab of pain from his foot. He hops backward a step and lets himself fall heavily onto his lawn chair. He crosses his ankle over his knee and sees a splinter of his coffee mug protruding from his foot. A thin bead of blood wells from one side of the wound and trickles a line across the ball of his foot. With trembling fingers, he pulls a long shard of ceramic from the sheath it has made in his skin. He drops the shard to the balcony and presses the wound with his thumb to quell the bleeding.

Connor looks out on the city while he sits, waiting for the flow of blood to stop. He doesn't know what to do. He has never felt so alone. Katie has left him. Faye and Deb are gone. Even Ian has fled. Thinking of all those apartments out there, the homes of every person he can see and all that he can't, he contemplates the idea of finding Katie in all of it and then feels the hollowness of losing her.

Why did it have to be Katie?

Surely there isn't just one true love, one person and one person alone in the whole wide world that he's meant to be with. Surely that kind of love has to be an impossibility. But then again, maybe the certainty of it is what makes it love. There is only Katie and he found her and fell in love with her.

But why did it have to be Katie?

And Faye?

And Deb?

CHAPTER
FORTY-EIGHT

In Which the Evil Seductress Faye Receives a Call from Guy #2 and Experiences Panties from Heaven

Faye pauses in the doorframe of the stairwell and contemplates the scene unfolding on the sidewalk in front of the building.

Across the highly polished tile, beyond the silk plant forest, and on the other side of the lobby door, there is a mass of movement and lights. All noises are blocked by the doors, but the visual cacophony on the opposite side of the glass takes her eyes a moment to sort through. The lobby flashes in the white and red lights, coming in from where they spin atop an ambulance that has parked on the sidewalk. A smattering of people linger in front of the building, milling about, talking through moving mouths, though no sounds come to Faye's ears. Traffic is at a crawl on Roxy, a slow-moving ticker backdrop to everything going on, and from above, hundreds of sheets of paper are twisting, falling down on the scene like leaves from a tree.

Then a low, faraway siren reports through the lobby's silence. As she passes the elevator on her way to the front door, Faye figures the siren is growing louder. By the time she reaches the lobby door, a second ambulance is jolting slowly from side to side as it mounts the curb and pulls onto the sidewalk behind the first. The siren goes quiet, but the lights atop still twirl frantically.

Faye stops with her hand on the door handle and watches two paramedics scramble out of the second ambulance. The people on the sidewalk part and watch them from a safe distance, pointing and chatting to one another. The paramedics open the back doors and pull out a gurney. One of them loads a blue duffel bag onto it. They slam the doors closed again.

Faye lets her hand fall from the door handle, unscrews the lid from her water bottle, and takes a gulp. A trickle of water runs down her chin from the corner of her mouth. She wipes it with the back of her hand, all the while watching the paramedics make a quick check of their equipment. One of them talks into his radio and nods.

For a moment, she wonders if this is the result of Connor getting caught by his girlfriend. It's a quick thought. Maybe Connor missed something when he was cleaning up his mess of an apartment and she noticed. Maybe he missed hiding a tube of lipstick that wasn't hers and she finally put two and two together and this was the outcome, two ambulances at the front door. It's an amusing thought, but Faye knows, even if Connor confesses his infidelities, it will probably just result in a bunch of yelling and crying. Maybe there will be some stuff thrown around his apartment, but an ambulance would be an unlikely necessity.

This is way too quick a response anyway.

The paramedics rush to the lobby door, scowls of concentration on their faces. Faye pushes the door open and holds it for them as they race past. They offer her a quick nod of thanks but are too focused on their task for much else. She watches them pull up to the elevator and press the button, their hustle forced to a halt by the wait.

Faye steps out into the street noises, the people wondering aloud; the cars passing by are all overwhelmingly loud from the sidewalk when compared with the peace inside the lobby. Sheets of paper still fall from the sky. They swoop gracefully from side to side, teetering on the breeze as they float with a near weightless grace to the ground. Faye looks up and sees the top of the cloud of paper. The highest sheets of paper are still several stories up, rocking back and forth with clear skies above. She holds out her arms to either side and smiles at the exquisite peculiarity of it. There's an odd beauty in the two silent ambulances, a group of strangers, and hundreds of pages twisting all around them in the flashing lights.

Faye takes another swig from her water bottle as sheets of paper drift across the sidewalk in a wave with the breeze. Just as she's about to screw the lid on and wander off down the street, her cell phone vibrates. She pulls it from her front pocket.

The call display shows "Guy #2." She thinks for a moment about which one that is and commits herself to clarifying her contact list, perhaps putting in a few real names to these mnemonic pseudonyms she always punches in when people give her their number. Really, it should have been done after that embarrassing "Daddy" mix-up last week, when it really was her father calling and not that older guy she met at the Laundromat. Had she known, she would have answered the call more appropriately.

She remembers "Guy #2" is Connor.

Faye brings the phone to her ear and says, "Hey, Connor."

"Faye. We can't see each other anymore." His voice is subdued.

It's what she was expecting really. As she reasoned in her hike down the stairs, the difference in Connor's behavior toward her and the girlfriend told her this was coming. She knew Connor was close to realizing his stupidity. She could see it in the vague recognition on his face when she left him, and his actions spoke to something his brain hadn't realized yet. He loves his girlfriend, and these infidelities were a gross mistake.

"I kind of figured this would happen," Faye says. "I'm just leaving the building, and it's raining paper out here. It's beautiful." She spins around once again to take in the entire scene. The last few pages are just settling. A few people look up to see if they can find the source of it, their hands curved over their brows to shield against the bright sky.

"Faye," Connor says, "I love Katie. She knows about you now and she hates me."

"Oh. That's a tough spot to be in," Faye says.

She does feel for the guy, and she thinks how, someday, when she's ready, she would like someone to feel that way about her. Not anytime soon, she thinks, but someday, she'd like someone to love her and break up with all his other girlfriends for her.

"I'm okay with it," Faye says. She knows she'll find other Connors in her life, but at the same time, she would like to keep this one on her list. He's such a great toy. "I hope she gives you a second chance. You're not all that bad. Don't delete my number, okay?"

"I'm sorry. I have to," Connor says.

He sounds disappointed, she thinks, or is it ashamed?

"You never know when you'll need it," she teases. "Hey, Connor?"

"Yeah."

"If you find my panties, could you let me know? I think I left them —"

Faye jumps back a step when some dark mass narrowly misses her head and lands on the sidewalk in front of her. She looks up to see if any other surprises are falling from the sky before taking a step closer. It's a crumpled pile of purple fabric. She bends over and picks it up: her panties.

"Hello?" Connor's voice comes through the phone.

"Yeah, sorry. Don't worry about it. I just found my panties," she says. "Keep my number, okay? Just in case."

"I won't," he says. "Bye, Faye."

"Bye, Connor," she says.

Faye puts her phone in her pocket and screws the lid on her water bottle. She looks up at the building again, contemplating how her panties became part of the paper rain, and then shrugs.

As she turns, she's nearly bowled over by a dumpy little man in filthy clothes. He brushes by her, his hard hat falling to the pavement with a clatter as he twists to avoid knocking her over. Its inertia carries it down the sidewalk, but he doesn't stop.

"Watch it, fucker," Faye calls after him.

The man fumbles with his keys, and she thinks he says something like "Sorry, girlfriend's fuck bubble popping" as he bolts into the lobby and the door closes behind him. She can't be sure though because she recognizes all the words but not the order they arrived in.

Faye stuffs her panties in her back pocket, leaving them hanging out a bit, like a little purple flag for anyone who is paying attention. Then, with her water bottle swinging from one hand, she starts off along Roxy.

A few blocks up, she nods and winks at the security guard in front of a construction site. She thinks he's cute. He smiles back and introduces himself as Ahmed when she stops to ask him the time.

CHAPTER
FORTY-NINE

In Which Jimenez Finds That, Like Choosing to Live with a Leaky Sink, Loneliness Is a Choice

Jimenez sits cross-legged on the kitchen floor. He rests the wrench in his lap and contemplates the man in the dress standing in front of him. It's a stunning outfit, he has to admit. It fits his bulk beautifully. However, it does take Jimenez a little time to reconcile the finery with the manliness underneath. When he does, he decides this is a fine-looking man in a fine-looking gown. And, to top it off, the shoes are perfect. Jimenez wouldn't have thought a strappy number like that would fit the man's girth, but then he has never really had cause to contemplate how a woman's clothes might fit a man, let alone the best way to accessorize such a look. But now that he sees it all together, it works.

"My name's Jimenez," he says, "and there's nothing wrong that I can see under the sink." He gestures with a light wave to the open cabinet.

"My name's Garth," the man in the dress says, "and I'm sure it was leaky."

"Nope," Jimenez says. "Just the faucet was a bit leaky."

Garth doesn't say anything else, so Jimenez considers Garth for a moment longer. He's ruggedly attractive with an amazing set of ankles, and Jimenez can't take his eyes from the dress.

"Is it carmine?" Jimenez asks, gesturing at the dress. "The color?"

Garth blushes and nods. "It is, thank you," he says and touches the dress.

Jimenez nods, takes the wrench from his lap, and huffs as he clambers to his feet. He bends to scoop the flashlight from the floor and then holsters it in his belt. He hikes the tool belt up from where it slipped from his hips.

"I used your glass and a bit of vinegar," he says, retrieving it from the counter. "I hope you don't mind."

"Not at all."

"It was just some calcium buildup on the washer. It happens here over time." Jimenez fishes the rubber loop out of the vinegar and rubs it between his fingers. The last few crusty flakes of calcium come off. Then the rubber is smooth and slick. "It's because of the hard water."

"Fascinating," Garth says and leans on the counter. He watches with interest.

"Yep," Jimenez says. "It's a simple fix, easier than the plumber's. And doesn't cost as much."

Jimenez busies himself reassembling the faucet, and Garth watches intently. Once Jimenez is done, the faucet is quiet. Not a drop breaches the seal.

"See," Jimenez says. "All better."

He holsters the wrench.

"I wanted to thank you," Garth says.

"*De nada*," Jimenez replies. "It's nothing really."

"Not just for that, but I've noticed how hard you work around here. To keep things running in the building. It must be a lot of work, all the upkeep."

"Just don't try the elevator," Jimenez says and smiles to himself. He's flattered though. It's the first time a resident has thanked him, or even seemed to notice him for that matter. Marty has on occasion, but it's partly his obligation as an employer, Jimenez thinks. At Christmas, Marty always gets him something extra, like a gift certificate for a restaurant or tickets to a movie.

Jimenez looks at Garth again. He seems a bit uncomfortable and stands awkwardly, one arm on the counter and the other flat on his hip, like he doesn't really know how to present himself. Jimenez thinks it's endearing — obviously Garth's out of his element at the moment. His blush has stayed, his ears are red, and his cheeks still carry a uniform flush that disappears under his beard. That blush is probably also fed by the silence that descends between them as Jimenez looks him over.

"Your dress is pretty," Jimenez says. "It looks really good on you."

"Thank you," Garth says with a quick, choking laugh. His voice cracks with emotion. "Thank you so much."

"You get it at a store?"

"No, I had it specially made," Garth replies. He looks down at it. "I ordered it. I've got a few of them."

"Oh," Jimenez says and then after a brief pause, "I'm really not sure what to say here now."

"That's okay. I don't either," Garth says. "It's nice to talk though."

"It is."

"Would you like a drink of something?" Garth asks. "Can you stay and talk a bit more, or do you have other things to do?"

"I don't have anywhere else to be," Jimenez says. "A glass of water would be good."

"Water, I can do," Garth says. "How about we move to the living room and chat for a little while? It's more comfortable there."

"That would be nice."

Garth and Jimenez sidle awkwardly past one another. Jimenez goes into the living room and contemplates the couch and the armchair. There's a coffee table in between the two. He decides on the couch. He unhooks his tool belt and rests it on the floor beside him as he listens to the cupboard door thudding closed, followed by the tap running. Jimenez smiles at the copy of Dee-Dee Drake's *Love's Secret Sniper* resting on the coffee table.

Shortly, Garth appears from around the corner, a glass in each hand. He stops when he sees Jimenez on the couch. He seems to make the same appraisal of the seating, the formality of the chair or the intimacy of the couch. He opts for the couch as well, the farthest edge of it.

"Thank you," Jimenez says, receiving the glass. "I'm really thirsty."

They both sit and drink their glasses empty, both in a bid to buy time to think of something to say.

Jimenez finishes first and takes a deep breath. "That's good."

"Thanks," Garth says.

Jimenez leans forward and puts the glass on the coffee table.

"You like the book?" he asks, picking it up and flipping it over in his hand.

"I just started it," Garth says. "So far it's pretty good."

"Dee-Dee Drake is one of my favorite authors," Jimenez says. He scans the back cover before returning it to the coffee table. He glances outside, his eyes as uncertain as his feelings. He is intrigued by Garth but is uncomfortable outside his realm of experience. "It's a lovely view. I like it better than mine. I'm down on the third floor. I look at the alley. And the Dumpster."

"It's why I took the place," Garth says, admiring the view over Jimenez's shoulder. He leans back into the couch and crosses one knee over the other. He rests his arm along the length of the backrest. "I like how it reminds me that there is a whole city full of people out there. So when I'm alone, I don't really feel alone."

Jimenez examines Garth for a moment.

"I know what you mean," he says. "Sometimes I forget that too. I don't really know anyone here."

"You know me now," Garth says.

"I do. Not well yet, but I think you're nice." There's another silence, and Jimenez uses the time to work through the words he wants to say in his head.

"I have to ask you," he says and puts his hand on Garth's. "Don't be mad at me asking."

Garth laughs, his heart pounding, sparked by the simple touch. "I can't promise that without knowing the question, but I can promise that I'll do my best not to get mad."

"Why do you dress in a gown? It's beautiful, but I don't understand. Do you want to be a woman?"

Garth laughs again, and Jimenez smiles, uncertain and a bit embarrassed by his question.

"Whew," Garth says. "I thought you would ask a hard question." He pauses. "As a kid, I used to love the old song-and-dance movies. Debbie Reynolds. Irene Castle. Rita Hayworth. Lupe Vélez. There's nothing I could think of that was more beautiful in the world than those ladies. Then, as I grew up, I started seeing that in women everywhere. All of them so graceful and strong. I don't want to be a woman — I'm happy as I am. I really admire that beauty though. I guess that's why I do it."

Jimenez watches Garth while he talks. With each word, he grows more calm and confident. He understands what Garth is saying and sees it in him.

Jimenez thinks, It's a shame that the idea of beauty has all become so sexualized and twisted about. That subtle, graceful strength rarely exists anymore, and in its place the booty-shaking, skin-exposing perversion has become the base currency of admiration.

Garth continues, "I can't be that beauty, but I can admire it." Garth looks Jimenez in the eye. "Tell me, is there nothing that's a part of you that you wish you could act on?"

Jimenez lets out a long sigh and contemplates the view. He speaks just when Garth is sure he wouldn't.

"I love Lupe Vélez too," Jimenez says. "I dance. I dance to those old movies, but I only do it in my apartment. Not out in front of anybody." He motions with sweeping hands down the length of his body. "I'm no Fred Astaire, but I do love to move."

"Would you dance for me?"

"No, I couldn't."

Now it's Jimenez who becomes flushed. He has never danced for anyone before, only in an empty apartment or in a dark and crowded room. His pulse races, and his first instinct is to excuse himself and retreat to his apartment.

"Sure you can," Garth says. "You've seen me. Now show me you."

Jimenez looks out the window at the city again. He knows people are out there, but he can't see them. He doesn't know any of them. That is the difference.

"There's no music."

"I heard you whistling when you came in. You could whistle a song to dance to."

Jimenez knows, if he flees, nothing will change; his microwave dinners and his lonely apartment over the Dumpster are all that await him. He won't get to know Garth. Garth will just become any person behind any window in any building out there, and if Jimenez perishes in an elevator fire, there will still be no one to write his obituary.

Without a word, Jimenez stands. He pulls the coffee table closer to the couch to make more room. Garth helps him move it, and then he slides to the center of the couch.

Jimenez walks around the table and positions himself in the center of the living room.

CHAPTER
FIFTY

In Which the Glimmer of True Love Is Revealed to Garth and Happiness Spreads in His Belly Like a Gulp of Hot Cocoa

Garth is giddy with the anticipation of Jimenez dancing for him. Excitement burbles in him, and it takes a conscious effort to remain composed.

It's obvious Jimenez is nervous by the way he flutters his fingers at his sides and intermittently wipes his palms on his pants. He fusses a bit more about the room, moving things out of the way, sliding the floor lamp back to the wall. He paces the periphery of the room once, as if measuring the space, and, finding it adequate, arrives back in the center of the floor. All the while, he mumbles to himself, murmurations of which Garth catches only snippets.

"This'll look silly . . . There's not enough room . . . What am I doing?" And the like.

Finally, Jimenez stops pacing and shaking out his arms. The rug has been rolled up along the wall, exposing the old honey-colored parquet floor beneath it. The coffee table is tucked up so close to the couch that Garth has to sit sidelong to the room because there's barely enough space to put his legs and remain in a dignified position.

Jimenez takes a deep breath and exhales it quickly. His shoulders rise to his ears and fall again, and then he's completely still.

The chair's tucked in the corner, and the lamp has been moved as well. At one point, Garth angled the lamp to spotlight Jimenez and the room, and at first, Jimenez gave him a pleading look but then resigned himself to the spotlight. Garth couldn't help but giggle at the time, at the theatrics of preparing the room, but now here he stands, the man who is about the dance for him, and he's so in awe of his bravery. It's an uncomfortable exposure to let oneself be true in the presence of another.

In sharing this scene, Garth feels infinitely more at ease in his gown and shoes than he first had, partially reclined with one knee crossed over the other and his leg sandwiched in the sliver of space between the couch and the coffee table. Garth wonders if that's the point and if Jimenez knew it was, subjecting himself to potential embarrassment in recognition of Garth's exposure. Garth hopes it is, that the big man is dancing as a chivalrous act to make him feel at ease.

"I don't think there's any more furniture to move." Garth chuckles.

"I'll put it all back," Jimenez says apologetically.

"It's okay," Garth says. "Don't worry about it."

"I just don't want to break anything. I'm not that good."

310

"You're fine," Garth says.

And what a picture he makes, Jimenez, handsome and poised and alone in what was once a small apartment but is now a spotlit stage in front of an audience of one. The waning afternoon lights the city behind him, blurring it into a stage-set backdrop, as if the glass weren't there and it were just a painted scene on canvas. As if Jimenez were about to dance along the edge of a cliff overlooking the buildings. An impression of the city is reflected in the hardwood under Jimenez's socks, as a rippled texture where the polish had settled between the patterned hardwood slats. The lamp spotlight casts a sharp contrast, highlighting only one side of everything and, in the backlight of the city, leaving the rest in deep shadow.

When there's nothing left to fidget over, Jimenez stands still in the middle of the room. His socked feet, one big toe peeking through a small hole in the fabric, are staggered one in front of the other. His heels are set slightly inward, and his toes are slightly splayed. His knees are loose, crooked at such an obtuse angle that it's barely noticeable, ready for the movement to come. He runs a hand through his hair, pushing it back from his forehead, and he shakes out his thick arms. He pushes his sleeves up over his elbows, exposing his meaty, hairy forearms. He is a hefty man with lamppost legs, but Garth can tell there's something graceful there, just by the way he stands.

"I feel so stupid," Jimenez says.

Garth smiles and gestures to his own body with wrists bent and fingers unfurling toward his gown.

"But maybe I'm not as brave as you," Jimenez says.

Garth feels a blush rise again at the compliment. He hopes that it can't be seen from where Jimenez stands, but then he wonders what it matters after the last ten minutes they have shared. Surely a blush is the least of his insecurities. Jimenez has been so willing to look past the incongruities of their encounter and see something worthwhile and good. Now he's going to return the favor. There's no reason this kettle-bellied man can't dance like the old movie actors he admires.

"Just dance." Garth smiles.

"There's no music." Jimenez fidgets with his pant leg.

"Whistle a tune to dance to."

"Won't work."

"Dancing doesn't need music," Garth reasons. "It can be its own thing."

"It's easier with it," Jimenez says.

Garth sighs, flashes Jimenez a strained smile, and then extracts himself from the couch. He shimmies his way around the coffee table and then smooths his gown with two sweeping palms from his hips to his knees. He goes to his bedroom and grabs his alarm clock radio from the nightstand before returning to the living room and plugging it in. The display flashes a row of red eights. Garth flips the switch from "Alarm" to "FM," adjusts the tuning knob a smidgen to clarify the sound, and then turns up the volume. A thin song comes through the speakers.

"There," Garth says, returning to sit on the couch. "Anything else?"

He has to smile at Jimenez's expression. There's nothing else. Garth recognizes the song, "Military Madness," but not the cheesy Graham Nash version; it's the Woods remake. It's a jaunty, midtempo, lo-fi number with a drumbeat fit for some neo-hippie fantasy, skipping across a grassy hill covered in wildflowers.

And without further delay, Jimenez begins to dance, slowly for the first few steps but then coming up to double-time the music. Two steps to the one side, a heel up and toe-to-ground shuffle with his leading foot. Two steps back to the start and a quick rock-step back.

A jive, Garth recognizes. A solo jive.

Jimenez's hips drive the movement, and his ankles are springs to compensate for their push. Two steps, two steps, and then a rock back onto his heel. Then arms to one side, legs kicking out to the other. Then arms stiff on both sides and legs moving a flurry for a while. A little Charleston thrown in. Then a smooth transition to a twist, his arms held out, elbows tucked to waist, palms down but fingers daintily arcing toward the ceiling. His hips pivot, but his body stays still. The whole thing unrehearsed, nearly perfect, and completely wonderful, to see him move and the happiness that the movement brings him. When Garth sees the expression on Jimenez's face, he also notices that Jimenez has been watching him the whole time.

Jimenez's cheeks become flushed with the effort. For as unexpectedly agile as he is, he's still a big man, and the exertion brings a sheen of sweat to his brow. Yet he doesn't stop moving, working the whole floor from windowsill to kitchen counter. He doesn't stop smiling at Garth. Garth smiles back and they hold each other's eyes for a few moments.

Then the song ends and Jimenez stops.

Garth claps, and Jimenez smiles and dips his chin in acknowledgment.

On the radio, the DJ babbles a quick weather forecast and then introduces Deerhunter's "Basement Scene" as the next song in the "commercial-free rock-and-roller coaster." The new song begins, and Jimenez holds out his hand to Garth.

"Dance this song with me?" he asks.

Garth shakes his head. "You're too good a dancer for me."

"That's not the point," Jimenez insists. "Come dance with me. I'll teach you." His invitation arm is outstretched and unwavering.

Garth stands and begins to shimmy his way around the coffee table again. His attention is drawn to the window, to a quick movement, a shadow that flashes through his peripheral vision. But when he looks, there's nothing but the expanse of buildings. Nothing outside, and here, here's Jimenez waiting to take his hand and join him in a dance to the music coming through the alarm clock radio's tinny speakers.

And that's what Garth does, dances with Jimenez. They share a slow sway to the billowing lyrics and the occasional psychedelic interjection. During the sauntering dance on the parquet with his head on Jimenez's sweat-dampened shoulder, his gaze focuses on nothing in the fuzzy middle distance out the window. With the smell of Jimenez's cologne in his nostrils, Garth feels happiness spreading in his belly like a gulp of hot cocoa.

CHAPTER
FIFTY-ONE

In Which Petunia Delilah Gets a Fucking Ice Cream Sandwich

Her body has never been so truly spent, and her mind has never been so completely calm. Petunia Delilah floats in that spot for a minute, the one where there is no world outside her consciousness. Her eyes are closed, and her brain basks in the deep-red light filtering through the delicate skin of her eyelids.

The apartment air is warm and comfortable and smells homey, like the quiche baking in the oven. The linoleum she lies on is cool and soothing on her back. The constant stresses, both physical and mental, have passed.

Her baby is alive. She can hear her daughter fussing in the boy's care. Her arms long to hold her, but she waits for a moment.

She is alive. She can see it through her eyelids, her blood feeding her body. She feels the air going in and out of her lungs. A bead of sweat tickles its last lines across her skin, seeking the lowest places it can find before it will rest, evaporate, and then disappear into the air.

Claire's talking to the emergency operator, the thread of their conversation rambling away, over there near the oven, where she checks to see how her quiche survived the whole ordeal.

Petunia Delilah opens her eyes. She can't keep herself from smiling. The boy kneels beside her, and he cradles her daughter in his arms.

"She's so little," he whispers, the wonder transparent in his voice. He's an odd sight, Petunia Delilah thinks, merely a baby himself, with her daughter in his arms and his eyes transfixed on her. She thinks he might cry; his face betrays that even though the wells of his eyes remain dry. She wonders if he has a little brother or sister. She hopes so because she can tell he would be a great big brother.

A tea towel is wrapped around her baby. There are others, stained and crumpled on the floor beside the boy. He must have wiped her daughter clean before swaddling her. He's the reason she is here, safe and gurgling in his arms. He has delivered her. He brought her from peril to safety, and Petunia Delilah feels a love for the boy swell in her.

She lays her hand on his forearm.

"You probably want to hold your daughter," the boy says in response to her touch, his eyes never leaving the little girl in his hands.

"I do," Petunia Delilah says. "But whenever you're ready."

The boy glances at her. Petunia Delilah remembers Claire calling him Herman.

"Herman," she says, "how old are you?"

Herman shuffles closer and offers her her daughter. Once the baby has been transferred into her mother's arms safely, he replies.

"I'm eleven," he says. "And a half. I'm actually closer to twelve."

Petunia Delilah nods. Her daughter peeks out from a hood of tea towel. Embroidered on the waffled fabric is a sprig of lavender flowers, purple and curving around a brown teapot. A few curls of blue-gray stitching denote steam coming from the spout.

"Herman, you were the first person in the world to meet my daughter. Her name is Lavender," Petunia Delilah tells him. She hadn't discussed the name with Danny, but Danny isn't here, and she can't stand to let her daughter live nameless for a second longer. They had discussed names but couldn't narrow it down beyond some two hundred choices. To Petunia Delilah, "Lavender" is fitting to both the baby and the situation. Danny will just have to agree.

Herman smiles. He leans forward and inches a finger back and forth on Lavender's cheek.

"And," Petunia Delilah continues, "you probably saved her life. And mine too. Thank you, Herman, for being the bravest guy I've ever met." Petunia Delilah starts to cry from a mix of exhaustion and relief. It's over, they had all fought so hard, and now everyone is safe.

Thoughts become things.

"You're our family now," Petunia Delilah says in a few choking sobs. "You're Lavender's brother and my hero. If you ever need anything, if I can ever do anything for you . . ."

Herman sits back on his heels. His hands rest in his lap, his fingers interlaced, fidgeting. The corners of his mouth twitch downward. His eyes are fixed on his fingers.

"I have to go now," he says. "There's something else I have to do."

Herman gets Claire's attention and asks her to have another ambulance sent to his grandpa's apartment. He tells her the buzzer number.

Claire waves her hand and nods, pointing that she's talking on the phone.

With that, Herman stands and walks out the door.

Before Petunia Delilah can say anything, he's out of sight. Moments later, a short way down the hall, she hears the stairwell door's hydraulic arm hiss and the latch click shut.

Petunia Delilah will find Herman again. She wants to be his friend and to know him. She wants Lavender to know him as she grows up. Herman is going to be a part of their lives for as long as they all last. She will make sure of it.

Then she's left listening to one side of Claire's conversation but doesn't hear any of the words; they're just background noise. She watches Lavender and is struck: Kimmy was right all along. Women have been doing this for hundreds of thousands of years without modern medicine. Petunia Delilah is sure it isn't always such a shit show, and she's also sure that, most of the time, things work out. And when they don't, you salve your scars and pick up the pieces and do the best you can.

"Hey," Petunia Delilah calls to Claire.

Claire bolts upright. She holds her hand over the mouthpiece of the phone and looks at Petunia Delilah expectantly.

"You wouldn't happen to have an ice cream sandwich, would you?"

A puzzled look crosses Claire's face. Then she nods and says, "I do."

She opens the freezer, pulls one out, and crosses the room to hand it to Petunia Delilah. Then she goes back to the phone and continues her conversation.

Petunia Delilah doesn't know whether to savor or savage the ice cream sandwich. She rests Lavender on her belly, tucked against the crook of her elbow, and runs the package between her fingers while she contemplates how to consume it. The plastic wrapper is velvety and cool. The sandwich contained inside is firm but has the slightest give to it under a gentle squeeze. It isn't frozen solid, and Petunia Delilah likes it that way. The cookie parts will be slightly gooey on the outside. It will leave chocolate gunk on her fingers, which is perfect. She opens the package with her teeth and gazes upon the wonder inside.

Two paramedics arrive at the door. The burly men in blue uniforms announce themselves. One is trailing a gurney loaded with equipment.

Claire sweeps a hand in Petunia Delilah's direction, as if they would miss her lying on the floor in front of the door, as if to say, "Clean that up, there." She keeps talking on the phone.

Petunia Delilah starts devouring the ice cream sandwich before they can find reason to stop her.

With practiced ease, the paramedics set about examining her and Lavender. They check blood pressures and listen to hearts beat and ask questions about family histories and medications and if there's pain and where on her body it is. Petunia Delilah answers through mouthfuls of ice cream sandwich. She licks the wrapper and accidentally drops it to the floor when they load her onto the gurney.

With a wave to Claire, she's wheeled down the hall to the elevator. One of the paramedics presses the button, and the two of them talk quietly about getting a pizza later, ". . . or did you want a gyro?" The sounds of the elevator descending from above grow louder through the doors.

"Gyros," the one says and checks his watch.

The other nods. "Good call. We'll grab them after we drop these lovely ladies off."

The elevator dings, the button light goes out, and the doors slide open. There is a foot-high step between the elevator and the floor, but with minimal jostling, they maneuver the gurney into the compartment.

Petunia Delilah looks at her reflection. There is ice cream sandwich gunk in the corners of her mouth and on her fingertips. Lavender rests peacefully, her lips working but her eyes closed. Petunia Delilah wonders for a moment if her baby can dream yet. Everything is all right. She's a mom. She smiles.

One of the paramedics holds the gurney in place, and the other presses the lobby button. Both of them stand with their backs to Petunia Delilah, staring at the number above the door. The doors slide closed, and the elevator starts its descent.

"Smells smoky in here," says one paramedic.

"Yep," the other says, shaking his head in disapproval. "Smokers."

"No, that's not cigarette smoke," the first says. "I used to smoke and that's not it. This smells more plasticky."

"You used to smoke?" the other asks.

"I did."

"I didn't know that about you."

"Well, it's true. I used to."

"That will kill you, you know."

"Well, I don't do it anymore, do I?"

They fall silent and watch the number six become a number five in the little display above the door.

"I worry about you sometimes," the one says. "You're a risk taker."

There's a metallic grinding from outside the elevator compartment. It echoes up and down the elevator shaft. The compartment shudders to a halt somewhere around the fourth floor.

The paramedic jabs at the button, but the elevator doesn't move.

CHAPTER
FIFTY-TWO

In Which Claire the Shut-In Gets a Job and a Date and Possibly a Life on the Outside

"My name's Jason," the emergency operator says.

"Jason? Pig?" Claire says. "It's you?"

"Yes," he replies and then adds, "but please, these calls are recorded. You can call me Jason."

"Okay," Claire says. "Jason, do you know who I am?"

"I do. I recognize your voice." Then he says more quietly, "Sometimes I call on my coffee breaks."

"I know you do," Claire says.

"I always hope to get you. I like you."

There's some bustling by the door, and the baby starts to fuss. One of the paramedics talks into the radio clipped to his shoulder. Claire can't make out what he says. He stands by the door, chin crooked to shoulder and a thumb hooked heroically through his belt loop. The other paramedic inflates a blood pressure cuff around Petunia Delilah's arm. He pinches her wrist, his finger pressed against the nook below her thumb as he counts her pulse.

Petunia Delilah's eyes are on her baby. Her mouth moves, jaws side to side and lips together as she savors her ice cream sandwich. Her eyebrows are raised slightly, and her forehead is smooth. The baby wriggles in her arms. It gurgles and she smiles.

Claire glances around the room. That weird little kid who came in with her is nowhere to be seen. Unless he's passed out somewhere. She looks around the corner of the island to see if he's lying on the floor, but he isn't. No one seems to notice he's gone, and no one pays attention to her or her conversation.

Claire realizes she needs someone to talk to. She has needed someone for quite a while but has been working hard at ignoring the fact. Normally, she would call her mother and unload a few little burdens from the week, just enough so Mom feels included but not so much to worry her. Claire finds herself disinclined to burden her with the larger complications as she ages.

Mom doesn't need my problems, Claire thinks, but I've kept them all and now . . . maybe Jason.

Claire ponders for a moment whether this will be too awkward or not and then decides. "It's been a hard day, Jason. I think I may need someone to talk to."

"I'm sorry to hear that," Jason says. "Would you like to tell me about it?"

"I don't know. It's just, things haven't been overly normal for the last little while even though I work hard to believe they are. When I said it's been a hard day, what I mean is, it's been a hard few years," Claire says. "I seem to have built a routine to my life to add a normalcy that isn't there. I didn't notice it before, but I guess that was the point. I do this routine so I won't have to think about doing anything or trying anything different. I see it now. I want to change it. Now, I don't know what to do about it."

Jason is silent.

"Are you there?" she asks.

"I'm here. I'm listening."

Claire appreciates his silence. A lot of the guys she dated always tried to fix everything. She would confide in them, and in a sentence, they would offer a solution. Then they would dismiss the issue as a problem that now had a solution should she only choose to correct it. They always turned it back on her, fixed her and moved on. She doesn't want Jason to solve all of her problems. She just wants him to listen to her, acknowledge what she says, and, at a stretch, maybe understand that things aren't perfect. She appreciates his silence.

"A woman gave birth on my floor today." Claire sighs. "I felt two things. The first was terror that she was in my apartment. The second was pride that my floor was clean enough to give birth on. I haven't left my apartment for years, and no one has been in here either, and now I'm staring at three strangers — no, four now with the baby, four strangers in my apartment. And I'm most worried that there's a splashy blast of afterbirth on the linoleum and that the paramedics' shoes are dirty." Claire's voice cracks. "I know I should have felt fear for the woman and her baby. The fact that I have to think about how I should feel scares me. Doesn't it just happen for everyone else?

"I should have opened the door with no question, yet I asked questions. I should have gone out to get my own groceries this week. I should go to a bookstore and touch the spines of every book on the shelf without worrying who touched them before and whether or not they washed their hands. I shouldn't want to tell the paramedics to take their shoes off at the door. I should kiss someone. I haven't been touched in years, by anyone. I should go visit my mom. I should —"

"Claire," Jason says, "it's okay. Everyone's okay, but I think you may need to talk to someone about it. Tell me everything now, yes, but you have to tell someone else too. Maybe a professional. Someone who can help you."

"I just never thought I needed help," Claire says.

"I know," Jason says. "But you do."

They listen to each other breathing for a moment.

"I lost my job today too. They're outsourcing the PartyBox to Manila, and we all got laid off," she says. "It's been a hard day."

"Claire," Jason says, "we're hiring, here at the call center. There're two positions available on the switchboard. What system does the PartyBox use?"

"Linksys 9000."

"That's the same one we use," Jason says excitedly. "You should apply. I can put in a good word for you."

"Surely I don't have the education."

"You have call experience. That's the big one. You're good under pressure, I can vouch for that. Ideally, they like some related postsecondary education like criminology or nursing or something, but they do most of the training on the job."

"I have a diploma in Theoretical Human Anatomy with a minor in Managerial Accounting for Non-Accountants," Claire says.

"Perfect," Jason says. "Email me your résumé and I'll turn it in to HR. If you get an interview, you'll have to come here to the call center though."

"I know."

"Can you do that?"

"Maybe."

Claire watches the paramedics secure Petunia Delilah and her baby onto the gurney. They cover her with a blanket, and one of the paramedics looks at Claire and gives a quick wave. She waves back as they wheel out of the apartment. The other paramedic pops his head back through the door and mouths a "Thank you." Then he's gone, closing the door gently behind him.

"What else, Claire?"

Claire's emotions wane for the moment. She thinks it odd to unload her thoughts on her past client and grows a bit uncomfortable.

"Nothing, Jason. Thanks for listening."

"Claire, I hope this isn't too out of line, but I'd like to get to know you better. If I won't be able to call you anymore, I don't know what I'm going to do. And I wouldn't forgive myself if I didn't ask," Jason says. "Can we grab a coffee or something sometime?"

"Well . . ." Claire pauses. She closes her eyes. Her hand shakes. The receiver quivers in front of her mouth, and she draws a deep breath. "When do you get off of work?"

"My shift ends in fifteen minutes."

"Do you like quiche?" Claire asks.

"I do," Jason says.

"Would you like to come over to my place for some quiche?" Claire asks and then rushes to say, "I know it's short notice. If you can't, if you've already got plans, that's okay, I get it, we can chat some other day or something," she says and then adds, "if you want."

"I would love to join you for quiche," Jason says. "But I should go home and change out of my uniform first."

"No," Claire says. "That's all right. You don't have to." She glances at the stove clock ticking backward. "The quiche will be done in four minutes. Then it has to sit for ten minutes before it's ready."

"It'll probably be closer to forty-five minutes or so before I can get there," Jason says. "I can't leave early. If I could, I would, but we're pretty short staffed."

"No, that's okay. It's good warm or cold," Claire says.

She looks around her apartment. Petunia Delilah's afterbirth has stained the foyer with goo. There's a sodden pile of linens. The paramedics didn't take off their shoes, and while they looked relatively clean, they did come in from outside. Nothing is as it was, not even from five minutes ago, and Claire wonders if she'll ever feel the complacent comfort she once did. Then she realizes that she shouldn't ever feel that again.

328

Her voice wavers when she says, "That's perfect, Jason. I have to clean up a bit around the place anyhow. You know the address?"

"Yes. It's in the system here." Jason laughs. "I can stop and get a bottle of wine, if you like."

"That would be nice . . . Pig," Claire says and smiles.

CHAPTER
FIFTY-THREE

In Which One of an Infinity of Homeschooled Hermans Bids Farewell to His Grandpa

The elevator chimes down the hall as Herman leaves Apartment 805. It's a quiet and faraway noise in his mind.

What was once broken is fixed, Herman thinks, remembering his earlier misadventures in the elevator. And so it begins all over again.

The elevator door slides open, and two paramedics bustle out into the hallway. The first stumbles because of the misalignment of the floors. He points and warns the other. Navy-blue pants whisper with movement, and the ripples of their pressed blue shirts make the fabric look liquid. One talks in a radio attached to his shoulder, and the other drags a gurney burdened with equipment in his wake. Both of their heads swivel, trying to get their bearings in their new surroundings. Both sport intense looks of determination in their eyes. They spot him.

"Hey, kid," one calls. "Where's Apartment 805?"

Without looking back, Herman points over his shoulder to the door he just left. Then, he opens the door to the stairwell and passes through.

The stairwell lights are dim and yellow, casting the space in a hue like an antique photo. The air smells ancient too, trapped in the column that falls below and rises above him, like it has been stuck in there since the building was built. Herman has seven floors to go up and he isn't in a hurry. His apartment will be there just as it has been in the past and as it always will be in the future. He takes his steps, measured and one by one. There's no need to run, like he had earlier. Herman isn't sure he can run anymore even if he should want to. His legs are leaden and his body exhausted from his journey. He uses the handrail as leverage to help out his tired legs.

"Think of that space between the dots as time," Grandpa said, "not distance."

I don't have far to go, just a short time to go, Herman thinks.

It seems an eternity ago, running up these steps from the lobby where he had woken in the elevator. He really doesn't know if that just happened and he's still in the stairs, ascending from where he had lain on the tile floor. Everything that has occurred is jumbled up and out of place in his mind. He remembers standing up in the elevator with his reflections fading a million times into the deep infinity all around him, his image bouncing forever, back and forth between mirrors.

Which one of them is me? Herman wonders.

Then he knows the answer: all of them are.

The paper has folded to touch Herman to Herman, and they are one and the same. And as they track his movements, mimicking him as he leaves the elevator, they all step out of different elevators into different lobbies. An infinity of Hermans go their separate ways once they are out of his sight and he is out of theirs.

There's a jumble of noises a few flights of stairs above him. The clamor grows louder as it comes his way. As he passes the sign bolted to the stairwell that reads "Floor 11," he's shoved to the side by an explosion of crying woman. He bounces against the wall and stays there as it seems to be the only solid thing around.

The woman rushes past him, blubbering hysterically, neglecting to acknowledge his presence, oblivious of him to the point that Herman wonders if he's even there. He leans against the wall and watches her stumble around the landing below and then out of sight. He continues upward, the sounds of her crying fading by the time he reaches the sign that reads "Floor 14," and by the time he pushes the bar to release the lock to shoulder through the door by the sign that reads "Floor 15," he can no longer hear her at all.

The stairwell door's hydraulic arm hisses itself toward closed while Herman stands in the hallway that leads to Grandpa's apartment. He spends a moment there, contemplating how perspective shrinks the hallway the farther it gets away from him. Grandpa's apartment door is three down from the stairwell and much smaller than those closer to him.

When the stairwell door clicks shut and when the only notable sound is the hallway's blower unit exhaling, Herman walks toward the apartment. He doesn't bother pulling his key from the shoelace looped around his neck. The door is still unlocked. He knows this because he has never felt as grounded as he does now, so rooted in this place and this time. He opens the door and walks into the apartment. The light from outside has faded since he left, so he flips the kitchen switch as he walks past it to the living room. There's still some light coming in from outside, but it's weak and shadowed by the surrounding buildings.

Herman stands in the silence of the living room. It's an actual quiet, a real silence, not the false one that comes when he's about to lose consciousness. The room seems expansive as it stretches before him, Grandpa's chair in one corner and Herman standing in the doorway in the opposite corner.

Herman's arms weigh heavily, exhausted and dragging his shoulders to curve with their unwieldiness.

With all that has happened, he feels small and out of control. Life's taking him in its own direction, at its own speed, and for its own purposes. It's an anchor for him, and though he wishes to flee, he knows he can't. Not this time. There's no guide and no force of will, or if these things exist, they're an out-of-date map and a weak whisper of a force. Herman resigns himself to be this one of an infinity of Hermans and observes the scene before him. The distance between him and Grandpa's recliner seems grand even though it isn't.

Herman thinks, If I could go back, if I could make this outcome different, I would. I know how to resuscitate someone. I've studied how to. I know where his medication is. I know how to give it to him. I could have brought him back to life. This is my fault.

Herman watches Grandpa's inert body. Grandpa's inert body doesn't return the honor. While his eyes are open, they don't see anything. The biology is gone, the blood has expired, and he is over. Grandpa is no longer there. The thing that used to be him wears a blue knit cardigan and has his favorite crocheted blanket draped across his lap. But he's gone, and Herman knows that resuscitation and medication can't stop what has to happen. It's nobody's fault but time's. Grandpa leans to the side and slumps forward a bit from the chair back. One arm hangs over the armrest. The teacup on the side table doesn't send steam into the air anymore. It has long since cooled. A section of the newspaper is draped across his knee, and the rest has slid to a cone-shaped pile on the floor.

And, like at the birth of Lavender, Herman sees his grandpa as an infant in the dark night of the farm where he was born. Grandpa told him so much about the farm Herman knows it as his own. He sees Grandpa as a kid standing on the gravel road to the house, surrounded by tawny fields of late-summer wheat. His knobby arms fire rocks at the wood posts, but his aim is off, taking the rocks wide of their mark a lot of the time. Grandpa's skinny neck, seemingly too fragile to support the weight of the head it's forced to support, still manages to move through its seemingly impossible tasks with delicacy.

Herman feels the elation Grandpa felt when he met Grandma at the community's little wooden church. They are teenagers and married at nineteen. Together they see the coming of electricity, the wonder of the telephone, the magic of the automobile, and the impossibility of space flight. There was so much more. Herman sees them smile at each other with the birth of their daughter. He imagines everything in between then and now, and like the dots Grandpa put on the page, that beginning and this ending are the same thing when the corners of the page are folded to touch. And so it all starts again.

"Bye, Grandpa," Herman says, and the room only responds with silence.

Herman is shocked from his reverie by a golden streak passing from top to bottom, just outside the window. His eyes track the movement, but his brain isn't quick enough to make sense of the image. On instinct, Herman sprints across the living room toward the window. By the first step, the golden flash is gone from sight, below the bottom edge of the window. Herman rushes past the recliner. By the time he reaches the window and presses himself flat against it to look down, all he can see is a milling crowd on the sidewalk below and two ambulances parked at the curb.

That one would be for Grandpa, Herman thinks. The paramedics are somewhere in the building right now, coming up to this lonely apartment.

The golden streak is gone.

CHAPTER
FIFTY-FOUR

In Which Ian Begins and Concludes His Perilous Plunge

And this is where it all begins, here at the end with the goldfish in his bowl. The snail is here too, sucking algae off the glass.

Ian swims his fishbowl from one end to the other, gyrating around the circumference in clockwise circles. He slices through the water, cleaves it to either side of his body, and momentarily imagines himself a predatory fish, perhaps a shark or a barracuda.

Ian swims past Troy.

Troy munches on algae.

Ian looks out at the city, a wavering and aqueous vision of buildings in front of buildings behind other buildings in the bright afternoon light. The sun has started setting on the lower stories. The ninth floor slips into a premature twilight.

Then Ian gets a little confused and finds himself swimming counterclockwise for a while where he had once been doing so clockwise. He ponders how this came to be. Surely, one would notice a complete bodily reversal, Ian thinks, if I was even swimming in the other direction to start with. He cannot remember, and then he forgets that it was confusing.

Now, he thinks, what was I doing?

In the center of the bowl, regardless of the direction he swims, is the plastic castle. It is nestled in a geology of pink and blue pebbles. The castle's drawbridge is down, the portcullis is open, and the barbican is broad and sturdy. There are four bastions with arrow loops. There are even tiny bartizans and corbels and embrasures. The detail is impressive. The pink bricks etched in the battlements are tinted with a frosting of purple along the edges to give it extra depth and a shade of realism. It's the most realistic neon-pink castle Ian has ever seen, and he counts himself lucky to call it his home. It beats a sunken galleon or bubbling treasure chest, even though those would be more fitting in his nautical-themed world.

Kitschy tchotchkes, Ian thinks.

He swims past Troy the snail.

Now, he thinks, what was I doing?

It's that incessant munching that could drive a fish crazy, really. The subtle, gravelly noise of Troy's crop grinding away at his harvest day and night makes it hard to concentrate. The frequency travels through the water, textures it with a noise he can feel in his flesh.

Ian pecks at Troy.

Troy doesn't notice and keeps munching.

It's everywhere, that sound — dry, like pulling apart a cotton ball, like two stones rubbing together.

Ian pecks at Troy some more and, after some effort, dislodges him from the glass. All becomes quiet as Troy drifts like a leaf, swinging back and forth in gentle arcs, down through the water, seesawing until he lands at the bottom of the fishbowl. The silence is absolute but not permanent. It's only a matter of time before Troy slips back up the glass and starts again.

Ian circles the bowl.

He doesn't remember when the yelling started. He's discovering all the new areas of his fishbowl all over again when it comes to his attention though. He doesn't remember what is said, but he can feel it. The meaning of the words is lost on him, but he feels tension in the frequency of their sounds; it climbs and the oscillation tightens. Vibrations set to the wavelength of anxiety and conflict course through the water. They agitate Ian for a moment.

He sees ripples of movement through the water, things on the other side of the glass, big things. Through the sliding patio door, two aqueous bodies flash by the opening, first in one direction and then in the other. Then they are through the door and standing on the balcony. Their bodies are close, leaning into one another and gesticulating furiously. Ian watches and then grows tired of the long seconds of drama viewed through this watery filter. He turns his tail on the balcony door, turns his back on the couple.

Before him stretches the city, beautiful and so big. There's so much more to it than this little corner of the balcony. So much more to see than this gallon of water, so many possibilities and opportunities outside of his little bubble. Ian yearns to see it all, to be immersed in it, to be more than a tiny fixture in the middle of it but looking upon it from the outside.

Ian's startled from his train of thought when the vibrations become much stronger. He spins on the spot. One of the figures, a quivering blur of light and color, moves swiftly and close. Ian's scared, but there is nowhere to flee to in a gallon of water. There's the crack as the coffee cup breaks against the balcony. Ian watches the paper, page by page, unfold in the breeze, and suddenly, the bowl becomes brighter. The thesis that blocked the mouth of his bowl is gone; the exit is revealed. It takes Ian some time to realize the bowl is no longer covered — how long he doesn't know because he has no concept of time. When he does notice though, he grasps the opportunity.

He circles the bowl once to gain momentum, and then, with a flick of his tail and short wriggle of effort, he propels himself upward. Ian breaks the surface of the water and is free. He easily clears the rim of the bowl and, rather unexpectedly, watches the balcony railing pass by underneath. There wasn't a plan beyond leaving the bowl, but had there been one, it wouldn't have involved the surprise of being twenty-seven floors above the concrete. It's an odd sensation, a full-body shiver and shock. It's not that Ian has a plan, just a strong instinct for freedom. That is how Ian finds himself passing through the fluttering strata of thesis pages, gaining speed.

It takes a goldfish less than four seconds to fall the distance between the twenty-seventh floor and the sidewalk below. A flash. It's the span of time it takes to unlock the front door of your house. The time it takes to read a sentence or two. For Ian, it's a lifetime of wonder.

At first there's this new world that he has entered into. Everything is foreign to his mind, the beauty of being cast out amid the fluttering thesis pages, the feeling of, for the first time, being free of the constraints of any bowl or aquarium or plastic bag. There was a world beyond the rim this whole time. And up until this moment, he only saw it as a quivering backdrop to his life. Now here it is, crystal clear and interactive.

Like a skydiver without a parachute, like a sunburned cosmonaut rocketing back to earth from orbit, Ian is dragged toward the ground. The initial elation fades, and his uncontrolled descent is realized. The only certainties are the direction he travels and the velocity mounting with each passing second. The lack of control is at once exhilarating and terrifying. It's hard to maintain any trust in this, this being pushed from the sky to the earth. There's also no turning back, no returning. The only surety in the journey is that the end is there, below, and that is it. The only certainty is the downward direction and the inevitability that he will be face-to-face with the concrete sidewalk in a moment.

The fall passes with ever increasing speed and confusion. As it matures, it happens with less control where it seems there should be more. Ian watches the end approach, the hard concrete below growing bigger and quickly dominating the entirety of his field of vision. Ian watches it approach, not with a fatalist's resignation but with a pragmatist's acceptance.

Ian sees the Roxy's door opening, Faye stepping out of the building, taking a swig of water from her wide-neck sport bottle. Faye is on her phone and doesn't notice Ian slip into the water bottle with a plop. He hits his head on the bottom of the container, causing stars to float in his vision and a headache that will last the day, but luckily there isn't much brain to damage.

Ian takes several deep breaths. The water passes by his gills.

Faye screws the lid onto her bottle, unaware of her stowaway.

With the lid secure, Ian is plunged into an absolute darkness.

Now, he thinks, what was I doing?

CHAPTER
FIFTY-FIVE

In Which We Conclude Our Journey and Say Farewell to the Fine Residents of the Seville on Roxy

This has been a glimpse into the box. And time marches on and lives are shoved along in tiny, second-long increments. The box fills up with infinitely thin layers of experience. With each halting movement of the clock's hand, one falls atop the previous. These layers are so fine and the experiences so fleeting that it will never become full. The layers just lie one atop the other, compiling over time, becoming something bigger but never becoming something that will be complete or finished. The remnants of experience float and twist like sheaves of cellophane in the breezes caused by the custodians walking past and in the breaths of their living and dying.

Less than thirty minutes have passed since Katie stepped out of the pharmacy two blocks up the road from the Seville on Roxy. In that time, Danny and Garth ogled her and then, shortly after, parted ways. Danny went for a beer, and Petunia Delilah's baby decided it wanted in on the world and went through a rather difficult passage to get here. Herman woke up and passed out a few times, which is in keeping with Herman's life on the more stressful days. In that fifteenth-floor apartment, a life ended peacefully. Grandpa had a full and happy time there, but the organics of him grew tired and stopped moving. Everything else about Grandpa just carried on without his body, transforming into a different kind of life, one lived in memory.

It's been less than thirty minutes since Jimenez left his little yellow office near the boiler room in the basement of the Seville. He faced malfunctioning equipment, darkness, immolation, and leaky plumbing and survived all these with grace. He'll do it again tomorrow because someone has to keep the building running smoothly.

Garth returned to the Seville on Roxy from the Baineston on Roxy, stared down the heart of loneliness in the stairwell, found comfort in his new outfit, and then found a burgeoning happiness of acceptance as the sun set. Jimenez too found someone to fill the void in his life and now his one-bedroom, rent-subsidized apartment above the Dumpster seems a little less empty, knowing Garth is in the building.

It took Ian the goldfish just under four seconds to complete his fall from fishbowl to water bottle. In that time, we witnessed the magic of love at first sight, and we felt the pain of a love dying. In just under four seconds we experienced the heady thrill of lust and the sadness of life leaving a family. There was self-realization and self-doubt and a new life entering the world and the gratification of an elevator being fixed. There was the threat of a fire and a secret quiche recipe shared from generations ago. There was so much more. It may take a lifetime for an individual to live, but it takes just under four seconds for the occupants of the Seville to live a collective life. We've seen a few moments here, and there are many more, in the building, in the city. And they'll do it again and again, as long as time exists.

There has been a cross-dresser and an agoraphobic and a telltale pink nightshirt. There has been a plummeting goldfish, a mother fighting for her baby's life, and a poor little fellow who is entirely ill equipped for life yet soldiers bravely on. The bonds of loyalty have been tested and passed, and the same bonds have been tested and failed.

In that time, the goldfish cast into seemingly hopeless peril found salvation in the unlikeliest of places. A miracle or a coincidence? Most likely both one and the same because they aren't exclusive; they can exist side by side, a miraculous coincidence.

In that time, life took its course, all the players doing what they could but none in control. Not really. It's said that everything happens for a reason, but it's never said that reason is always a good one. That reason is choice, chance, fate, or not.

Right now, at the Seville on Roxy, the story is starting all over again. Not the exact same story but entirely new adventures.

Perhaps Claire the shut-in has opened her window as a first step in reintroducing herself to the outside world. She has to prepare for her date with Pig after all. Then she'll have to see about leaving her apartment for her job interview, but . . . one step at a time.

Perhaps Jimenez and Garth share a cigarette on the balcony, wearing matching housecoats cinched at the waist with a belt, the tops of their round and furry bellies exposed to the evening. Maybe they're talking about whether to move in together, but more likely, they're not at that point yet and just want to see where their experiment takes them.

Perhaps Petunia Delilah and Danny are planning to have another child. Perhaps it's too soon to consider that. However, it is likely that Herman will wind up living with them, being that he has nowhere else to go. All he has to do is ask Petunia Delilah, and he will in time. She'll say yes. Of course, Petunia Delilah and the paramedics have to get out of that troublesome elevator first.

Perhaps the villain Connor Radley, having realized his harmful ways, will treat the next girl right and love her like she deserves. Perhaps not. Even so, it's too late to mend the ills he wrought on Katie.

Katie will fall in love again, there's no doubt. She just does that. It's her superpower. Next time, however, she will do so more cautiously. It's a loss to the world that Katie will temper her feelings with reason because what is love but a thoughtless and reckless abandon of reason in favor of emotion. Her next love will treat her well. He'll talk with her at romantic dinners, hold her purse while she tries on a new coat, and smile often in her presence. Her next love will last, but not forever.

Everything happens for a reason. Sometimes that reason is a choice that was made, sometimes that reason is serendipity, and sometimes it is divine. It doesn't matter; life cascades on in response. Everything happens for a reason, but most often, that reason is blurry without the benefit of hindsight.

Most times, these things just happen. There's no control, not really. A person can choose his blend of coffee or her breakfast cereal, but they can't choose not to eat or drink. They can choose their partner or religion, the make of their car, but they can't choose to love, to believe in something, or to live forever.

Sometimes you have to just let it happen.

Perhaps Ian will have other adventures. That's if Faye realizes she has a stowaway in her water bottle before she drinks him. It's really out of Ian's hands now though. Ian took his plunge and wound up in a water bottle, and that's where he has to stay for the moment.

There's something nice about knowing Ian is out there in the world, at this moment, trapped in Faye's water bottle but without a worry in his aching mind. Ian's not worried for two reasons. Firstly, fish don't have the capacity to worry. Secondly, Ian knows that a goldfish can only do so much, and in the end, the rest is up to life and life takes care of him in one way or another. If that way is well or poorly, no bother; he'll only revel in its glow or suffer its neglect for a short time.

Only the Seville on Roxy can ever know all that has taken place and all that will take place between its four walls, beneath its roof and above its parking garage. The building stands, shackled at its heel to its shadow in the fading light, the only witness to the fact that no single person lives their own life; we all live each other's together. It's a mute sentinel that observes this fact and everything else. It gets a fresh coat of paint and a sprucing up every few decades. It leaks occasionally, here and there, but then is repaired. It crumbles a bit on the corner and has its boiler replaced and its plumbing upgraded.

At one point the neighborhood will become bad, but then it will become good again. There will be futuristic insulation and a futuristic security system installed in the Seville on Roxy. There will even be a time when the building is abandoned and then reoccupied years later.

But for now, it sits there, two blocks from the Baineston on Roxy, a building that is scheduled for completion next spring. One hundred and eighty luxury suites are now selling. According to the sticker with the curled edges, forty percent of them have already sold.

Acknowledgments

Fishbowl would have missed the water bottle without the love and help of a group of great people.

First and always, my husband, Nenad Maksimovic, for his unwavering support of my rambling dreams of writing books. Sometimes I think you have more faith in me than I do, and I'm wholly grateful for that.

Thanks to my agent, Jill Marr, with the Sandra Dijkstra Agency. You're an amazing soul. I knew that from the moment we first met. Thank you for your hard work, support, input, and direction. Thanks to Silissa Kenney and the crew at St. Martin's Press. Your insight, energy, and enthusiasm for this project have been second to none. You have exceeded the reputation of your press, which is not an easy feat.

Once again, I thank the ever-growing, ever-changing, and ever-wonderful people in the critique group I attend. Elena Aitken (for the inspiration of your commitment to the writing life), Nancy Hayes (for your pursuit of exactly the right words in exactly the right order), Leanne Shirtliffe (for your unrelenting support, kind heart, and kind words), Sam Burke (for being the English teacher I wanted to have teach me), and Trish

Lloye (for your demands for storied movement and meaningful action) have all offered wonderful input and keen eyes for style, structure, content, and editing. Also, a tip of the hat to Amanda Dow (for reading every word).

The adventures of Ian the goldfish were originally documented in a short story entitled "Sunburnt Cosmonaut," which was published by the fantastic folks at the *Potomac Review* (issue 52, winter 2013). I've had the pleasure of working with them on a couple of occasions, and it truly is a wonderful journal that promotes some amazing writers.

And, as always, thanks to you, the reader, for allowing me to hijack your imagination. Without that, this book would be a lowly and inert artifact. Writing a story is only half the work . . . Thank you for carrying the weight of making it come to life, proving that no single person lives his or her own life; we live each other's together.

My Inspiration

By Bradley Somer

Fishbowl began with an arresting image. I was in a vacant penthouse in the downtown core, preparing it to go on the market. There were only a few things left behind: a toaster on the scratched countertop, a doormat at the front door and an empty fishbowl sitting out on the balcony. I didn't think too much of it at first, but as I worked it dawned me that the simple scene contained an entire story: there's an empty fishbowl sitting on the balcony of a high-rise apartment overlooking tens of other buildings in the failing afternoon light.

I always consider three main qualities in weighing whether an idea can become a novel that's engaging for me to write, and hopefully engaging for a reader as well. That image was the first feature, a scene that inherently draws questions out of a person. There are the obvious ones like, where did the fish go? How did it wind up out on the balcony surrounded by high rises in the first place? And then there are the more subtle questions that follow, like: Who bought the fish and brought it home? Why? Who lived in this now vacant apartment? Where did they go and why did they take everything but their toaster, doormat, and fishbowl? What's that weird noise and where is it coming from? The next apartment over or the apartment below? It sounds like a baby crying. Why's the baby crying? Who's talking in the hallway? They sound a little upset.

The next thing I look for is a point. When you can tell absolutely any story you can imagine, what's the point of telling one particular story over another? Because I believe a novel is a dialogue, that a reader is just as invested in the story as the author of it, I always think about what I want to convey to a reader. The apartment I was in was vacant because the previous owner passed away. That knowledge creates a unique species of quiet in a place, only here being broken by the crying baby and whoever was bickering in the hallway. It struck me that I was in a building in which everybody shared walls and it wasn't a huge leap to see that all the residents of the building were influencing each other's lives, even in the minute way a baby crying on the other side of a wall can. And there was the point; there's no way to live your own life, we are all living each other's together.

The final quality I look for is a vehicle to carry the weight of the story. In this case, the setting, the building becomes integral to the structure of the story. It dictates how every character interacts; it influences every storyline and, when extrapolated through time, the building lives a life itself. The mechanism is the building and all that was needed was a catalyst, which became Ian the goldfish's job, to tie everybody's story together. Over the course of the story's arc, and even more specifically, in Ian's four-second plummet from the 27th floor, all the major life events take place. His fall becomes a life itself, one where gravity plays the role of time. The idea was that a life could be turned on its side and everything that happens in a linear life will happen in a blink for a collective life. And it happens again and again. That's why each of the book's plotlines touches on a life event: birth, death, falling in love, falling out of love, getting a job, losing a job. That's what Ian ties together and the Seville on Roxy embodies, when we all live each other's lives together, a lifetime's worth of experiences happens in every blink of the eye.

Other titles published by Ulverscroft:

THE PAST

Tessa Hadley

Three adult sisters and their brother meet up at their grandparents' old cottage during one long, hot summer. The house is in need of expensive renovation, and the siblings must decide whether to commit the funds or sell up. But under the idyllic surface, tensions are growing. Alice has brought with her Kasim, the twenty-year-old son of her ex-boyfriend — who makes plans to seduce the quiet Molly, Roland's sixteen-year-old daughter. Meanwhile, Fran's young children uncover an ugly secret in a ruined cottage in the woods. Passion erupts where it's least expected, blasting the self-possession of Harriet, the eldest sister. And Roland has come with his new (third) wife, whom his sisters don't like. A way of life — bourgeois, literate, ritualised, Anglican — winds down to its inevitable end: both a loss and a release . . .

THE SUMMER OF SECRETS

Sarah Jasmon

The summer the Dovers move in next door, sixteen-year-old Helen's lonely world is at once a more thrilling place. She is infatuated with the bohemian family, especially the petulant and charming daughter Victoria. As the long, hot days stretch out in front of them, Helen and Victoria grow inseparable. But when a stranger appears, Helen begins to question whether the secretive Dover family are really what they seem. It's the kind of summer when anything seems possible — and then something goes terribly wrong . . .

GOD HELP THE CHILD

Toni Morrison

What You Do To Children Matters. And They Might Never Forget. Sweetness wants to love her child, Bride, but she struggles to do so as a mother should. Bride, now glamorous, grown-up, ebony-black and panther-like, wants to love her man, Booker, but she finds herself betrayed by a moment in her past, a moment born of a desperate burn for the love of her mother. Booker cannot fathom Bride's depths, with his own lovelorn past bending him out of shape. Can they find a way through the damage wrought on their blameless childhood souls, to light and happiness, free from pain?

SUMMER ON THE RIVER

Marcia Willett

As summertime beckons, Evie's family gathers once more at the beautiful old riverside house they all adore. But when Evie discovers a secret that threatens their future, a shadow falls over them all: this summer by the river could be their last together . . . For Charlie, a visit home to see his step-mother Evie is an escape from his unhappy marriage in London — until a chance encounter changes everything. In the space of a moment he meets a woman by the river and falls in love, and his two worlds collide. As Evie and Charlie struggle to keep their secrets safe, they long for the summer to never end. Can the happiness of one summer last for ever?

THE SCHOOL GATE SURVIVAL GUIDE

Kerry Fisher

Maia Etxeleku is a cleaner for ladies who lunch. With mop and bucket in tow, she spends her days dashing from house to house cleaning up after them, as they rush from one exhausting Pilates class to the next. But an unusual inheritance catapults her and her children into the very exclusive world of Stirling Hall School — a place where no child can survive without organic apricots and no woman goes a week without a manicure. As Maia and her children, Bronte and Harley, try to settle into their new life, she is inadvertently drawn to the one man who can help her family fit in. But is his interest in her purely professional? And will it win her any favours at the school gate?

THE ALTOGETHER UNEXPECTED DISAPPEARANCE OF ATTICUS CRAFTSMAN

Mamen Sanchez

Atticus Craftsman never travels without a supply of Earl Grey and a favourite book. So when he is sent to shut down a failing literary magazine in Madrid, he packs both. A short Spanish jaunt later, he'll be back in Kent, cup of tea and smoked salmon sandwich in hand. But the five ladies who run the magazine have other ideas. They'll do anything to keep their cosy office together — even if it involves hoodwinking Atticus with flashing eyes, the ghosts of literature past, and a winding journey into the heart of Andalucia. With not the most efficient of detectives in hot pursuit, it's only a matter of time before Atticus Craftsman either falls in love, disappears completely, or — worst of all — runs out of Earl Grey.